IT ALL CAME OUT IN THE WASH

by

Christopher Pearson

It All Came Out in the Wash

ISBN: 9781804674987
Perfect Bound

First published in 2023 by bookvault Publishing,
Peterborough, United Kingdom

An Environmentally friendly book printed and bound in
England by bookvault, powered by
printondemand-worldwide

To Helen

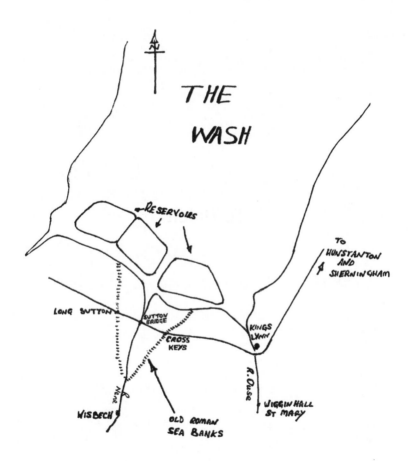

"Then, journeying towards the north, in the river which is called Wellestrem, by an unexpected accident King John lost all his wagons, carts, and sumpter horses with the treasures, precious vessels, and all the other things which he loved with so much care; for the ground was opened in the midst of the waves, and bottomless whirlpools, which swallowed them all up, with the men and the horses, so that not one foot escaped to announce the disaster to the king. The king nevertheless, having barely escaped with his army, passed the following night at an abbey which is called Swineshead, where, as it was thought, there befell him so great grief of mind on account of the things swallowed up by the waves that he was seized with sharp fevers and began to be grievously sick."

Roger of Wendover,
Flores Historiarum (Rolls Series 84), ii, 195, 196.

Chapter 1

Recovering consciousness after you have lost it violently can never be a pleasant sensation; at least that is what I am advised by people more experienced than I. As a piece of information given clinically after the event, I found it reassuring, but at the time it did not help: apart from the obvious fact that I received it too late to be of practical use, I had more urgent things to think of. All my faculties, as they returned, were immediately pressed into service to work out where I was, why I was there, which parts of my body were functioning properly, which were not, and whether indeed there were any parts so totally incapacitated that I was as yet unaware of their previous existence, and therefore of their present absence.

To begin with: where was I?

My eyes told me I was indoors, and my other senses that I was horizontal, on my back, on something soft. The shape of the room, its curved ceiling and the small window set in the thin wall, made me realise I was in a caravan. I do not often enter caravans, still less lie down in them, still less pass out in one; therefore I had plenty of food for thought, and gradually I remembered...

It had started two days earlier with the news that Dick had died.

He was my brother, still in his mid-twenties and therefore much too young to die, that is, to die naturally. But he did not die naturally. They had fished him out of the sea one morning, out of that indentation in the coastline called The Wash, familiar to me only as an outline traced with clumsy care at elementary school.

Dick was not a full brother, only a half-brother, but even that half was the only blood relation I had known since my mother died when he was born. Once she was dead, Dick's own father - my stepfather - had taken no further interest, so Dick had hit the

1

foster trail. In fact, of course, we both hit it at the same time, but it had been worse for him: after all, I had had two or three years of my own home life with my mother after my father had died, but Dick had not even had that.

By the time Dick died his father had long ago disappeared into oblivion, so I was Dick's next of kin, his only kin, which is why they sent for me. Bureaucracy likes to have its t's crossed and its i's dotted, and for that purpose it needs someone to pin down: a relative who will sign the forms, arrange the funeral and in Dick's case, just take the responsibility of certifying that it really was Dick. In a sense, too, it is something I am used to doing, certifying that a statement is correct. Usually it is an account, but it might just as well have been the identity of a body. It is the correctness which matters, I had told myself, not the thing which is correct.

But when I came to do it, I found it was not like that at all. A body is different; the dead body of your own brother even more different.

And another thing: it was when I came to identifying Dick that I started to appreciate that The Wash exists as something more than just a feature on a map. As I walked from my car to the mortuary in King's Lynn I was beginning to realise that the town and the landscape round it are very different from other places I have been to in England. And when I saw Dick lying there with his eyes closed, grey, inert and dead, it came home to me that since he had last walked and talked and let out his nervous, cautious, laugh, he had spent twelve hours in The Wash, twelve hours as a speck in those shallow waters bordered by the fertile flatness of the fenlands,

The inquest did not last long. The coroner seemed more interested in getting it over so that he could go home to lunch than in questioning the information which was served up to him. He was soon through the evidence of Dick's identity, of how he had been picked out of the sea by two fisherman who had set out from King's Lynn as soon as the mist rose one morning, and of how he had died from drowning. You might have thought that there would have been a search for him before he was found, but no, apparently nobody had even noticed that he was missing during the twelve hours since he had set out lug-worming.

Lug-worming? For the first time the coroner seemed to prick up his ears and indicate that he was something more than a kind of legal slot machine. When these non-legal words clicked into the slot he reacted as if the machine had rejected them – as if he were human.

"Lug-worming?" He looked enquiringly at the policeman who had been laboriously explaining things to him.

"Looking for lugworms, sir."

For a moment the coroner appeared to consider whether to take offence at the simplicity of this explanation, but he must have decided against it. Instead he sat still higher on his perch, still looking at the policeman and waiting for him to go on.

"I've looked for lugworms, too, but I wasn't drowned. What happened?"

"As I said, he went out lug-worming - seems he'd just taken to fishing so he hadn't enough experience of it. It was low tide, and the best lugworms is right out at low water, a mile from the shore. And when he was out there, digging up the worms, the mist came down on 'im. It came down sudden, and it came down thick. So 'e lost 'is bearings, didn't know which way to go to get back to the land." The policeman shrugged his shoulders to indicate what had happened after that. "Of course if he'd been experienced," he went on, "it wouldn't 'ave happened. He'd have took a compass with 'im or he'd have dragged 'is spade be'ind 'im to leave a trail; or stood with 'is feet pointing towards the land when he was digging." The policeman paused again, and then he seemed to brighten. "Or he wouldn't have gone in the first place, seein' it was the kind of evening the mist might come down." Finally he said lamely, "'e was caught by the tide."

I think it was at that moment that my thoughts went off on their own. I was dimly aware that the proceedings were continuing, but I had already played my part in them, so there was no occasion to bring my attention back.

Poor Dick - what a way to die!

If the mud and sand extended a mile from high-water mark, as the policeman had said, there must have been a vast expanse of near flatness. I could picture him, at one moment digging for lugworms with his immense concentration, at the next shrouded in sea mist and quite lost, with the sea lapping round his ankles; no indication to show him which way to go; his own footmarks wiped out by the incoming tide, and the ground shelving so gently over its mile of foreshore as to make it impossible to judge which way was uphill, which way down; which way was safety, which way death.

Dick was nobody's fool and that must have made it worse. I could feel for him, and I shuddered; I could feel that awful moment when he must have realised that short of a miracle he was as good as dead, with the water rising, impenetrable mist all round, no stars visible, and pervading everything, the knowledge that it was all due to his own imprudence.

The irony of it! That Dick, the most cautious of people, should die from his own lack of caution! He would have had time to think of all this, too, as the water slowly came up until he was out of his depth, until he had been forced to start swimming haphazardly, until he had drowned. Or perhaps, mercifully, he had been caught in a patch of quicksand or soft sticky mud and the end had come sooner.

I shuddered again. It was a brutal death for anyone. For Dick it seemed particularly unfair.

As we filed from the room, I took another look at the people who had been there.

The coroner had gone out by his own private door.

Of the rest, the policeman, the doctor, and a girl reporter from the local paper were all old hands at this game. Four of us were fish out of water: I was, and the two men who had found Dick's body, and a man from the firm for which he worked. The coincidence of the latter's name had only come upon me slowly: it was Waters. His firm was Burbidge's, the civil engineering and building contractors. I knew that Dick was working on a big contract for them, forming new sea walls and reservoirs. Waters was Dick's boss. He had not been called upon to contribute anything significant to the proceedings. He had explained that Dick worked for Burbidge's, but at the same time he had made it clear that outside his work he knew little or nothing about Dick. It is not a paternalistic firm, Burbidge's.

We dispersed outside, and I was left feeling flat. Somehow I had expected more to emerge from the inquest. But why? What else was there to emerge? Dick was dead. I had already arranged for the cremation to take place two days later. There was nothing else to it. I had booked into a hotel in King's Lynn, and now had two days in which to clear up Dick's belongings and dispose of the caravan in which he had lived.

His belongings would probably fit into the boot of my car: he travelled light. I would not have been surprised if half an hour, two or three old cardboard cases from the local grocer, and access to a dustbin would have been sufficient to deal with them. About the caravan I was less certain. Dick had not owned it, of that I was sure, but who the owner was I did not know.

It did not take me long to reach it. Once I was clear of the traffic of King's Lynn I set off on the Hunstanton road towards Sherningham, heading north and running parallel to the eastern side of The Wash. I passed the signs indicating Sandringham, a short distance off to the right and, with its royal grandeur and respectability, about as big a contrast as you could find to the dreary out-of-season caravan park, just behind the sea defences, where I ended up.

5

The keeper of the park was not difficult to find. She emerged from a tiny bungalow which looked only slightly less flimsy than the caravans which surrounded her, for all its concrete foundations and its absence of wheels.

"Number 135," she echoed at me. "Follow the concrete road round there, beyond that clump of trees. Take the next turn left, and it's on your left." I had been given the key, labelled with its number, by the police.

"Can you tell me," I asked, "who the caravan belongs to?"

"I'd 'ave thought whoever lives there could tell you that easier than what I can," she grumbled. "You can't expect me to remember the names of everyone what owns a van here, can you, when I don't see some of 'em from one year's end to another."

"I'm sorry," I explained, for I had not stopped to think how many caravans there were, nor what an impersonal business it must be, dealing with all the owners and the people to whom their caravans were let for a week or two at a time throughout the year. "I'm sorry," I repeated. "I should have explained: it's my brother who was living there, Dick Smith, but he was drowned two days ago so I've come to clear up his things. That's why I want to find out who owns the caravan - at present I don't even know who he rents it from."

"Drowned," she repeated. "That's number 133. The police 'ave already been. You've got the wrong number. Here - let me have a look." She took the key which she had now noticed in my hands. "Yes," she said, "that's a three, not a five, though the same person owns 'em both. I ought to know, 'cos I wrote it. It's the spare key the police took off of me when they was here."

"Well, who owns them?"

Muttering beneath her breath she hobbled back inside her bungalow and presently emerged with a scrap of paper on which the owner's name and address were written: D. Bassett, 13 Montrose Crescent, Peterborough. "'ere you are," she said, "But you can settle with me, if you want. I look after it."

I made no comment, but I thanked her and set off.

I found the caravan without difficulty, though the old woman's description was a bit grandiose. The concrete road was no more than a rubble track, and the clump of trees turned out to be two stunted birches. But the caravan pitches were marked clearly enough: each had a white stake driven into the ground, with the number painted near its top. The caravan on pitch number 133 was pale blue below and white above, and so were a good many others dotted about the place, including its neighbour on pitch 135.

As I parked the car and climbed out I sniffed, Dick's pitch was not a good one: it stank. Opposite was the source of the stench, a rectangular grey block with a flat roof and the words "MEN" over a door at one end and "WOMEN" at the other. Facing me though, I was glad to see a row of dustbins. I could put up with the smell - I would not be there long enough for it to worry me - and the nearness of the bins would be handy.

Two steps with a handrail led up to the caravan door. They were constructed like a miniature version of the steps which are wheeled up to aeroplanes for the passengers except that these had no wheels; instead they were supported on bricks, and as I rose from the first to the second step one corner slipped from its brick and the contraption lurched forward and downwards.

I cursed, not under my breath.

My head caught the side of the caravan, and the end of the handrail scored the paintwork just where blue and white joined.

I stepped down, re-constructed the flimsy edifice, and tried again, this time successfully.

A cupboard faced me as I opened the door. It was in a partition which separated the kitchen area on my right from the larger living room on my left. After a brief glance round I started in the kitchen, moving round methodically, opening the cupboard doors as I went and examining the lockers under the seats in the living room.

As I expected it was all as neat as could be - just like Dick!

In the kitchen were crockery and saucepans under the sink, some food in a wall cupboard, most of it in tins and packages. In the living room Dick's clothes were neatly put away in the fitted wardrobe, suit at one end of the rail and thick warm working clothes at the other. A pair of wellingtons stood on the floor below them and, on the shelf above the rail, shirts, sweaters, and underclothes. Moving round the room, there was a long shelf which ran from one side of the van to the other above the big window at the end. It was loaded with odds and ends and books. Several of the books were technical ones connected with Dick's work as a surveyor, a few were paperback who-dun-its, and two were new, their dust jackets almost unmarked, one about seabirds, the other about fishing. Laid on one of the seats, which faced each other across the width of the caravan, were a wireless set and some fishing tackle. Finally, as I completed my round of the living room, I came to the bed which Dick had been using, a double bed hinged at its bottom so that by day it could be swung up into its recess in the partition between living room and kitchen, and by night it could be lowered to sleep in. Between the two rooms was a larger cupboard. I supposed it had been designed for an Elsan, but it was not used for that purpose. It was a miniature junk room, and in it I found Dick's suitcase.

By now the dank coldness of the van and the emptiness of the deserted caravan park were seeping into me. It was a raw grey day. There had been a frost in the night, but its whiteness had worn off except in the deeper shadows. I considered lighting the gas fire, but I was afraid I might brush against it with my clothes as I moved round packing up, so I lit the oven of the cooker to take the chill away. Then I set to work putting Dick's stuff in the suitcase and the boxes I had brought. The quicker I did it the better, and when I had finished, I would take a walk over beyond the toilet block to the earthworks which defended the caravans from the sea.

It was soon done. Before long I had all Dick's clothes in his suitcase, the food in one cardboard box, the books and other bits and pieces in another, and his bedding in a third. The china and saucepans I guessed must go with the caravan, so I left them where they were.

I found two other things as I packed up: the other key to the caravan, identical in shape and label to the spare which the police had handed me, and a pair of binoculars, their strap slung round the hook of a coat hanger with Dick's working clothes and hidden in the folds of a heavy jacket. The key lay on the floor beneath the head of the bed, set back just inside the recess into which the bed fitted when it was swung up out of use.

With the bed in that position, it was quite invisible, and it was almost invisible when it was lowered to sleep on, but halfway between the two it was easy enough to see. As I picked it up and slipped it into my pocket, I wondered idly how it could have got there. It could not have fallen directly when the bed was at rest in either of its normal positions, and it seemed absurd to suppose that when Dick lifted the bed he had simultaneously leant forward awkwardly to drop the key there. No, it must have been dropped when the bed was upright and then been knocked back under the plywood which faced the room, into the recess and out of sight. It seemed an uncharacteristically careless thing for Dick to have done.

I decided to leave the stuff in the caravan for the time being. Then I removed my shoes and replaced them with Dick's Wellingtons, slung his binoculars round my neck, and set off round the toilet block towards the sea. On the way I passed my car and wondered whether I ought to lock it, but depression and inertia prevailed: there was no one about; there was nothing special about the car, a grey Cortina with a black roof; and there was nothing in it worth stealing; I had the keys in my pocket and I would not be long, so why bother?

9

Beyond the first rampart against the sea was another. The wind bit into me as I crested the first rampart: it bit deeper as I reached the second.

And there, spread out in front of me, was the scene of Dick's death.

It was low tide, and acres of flat mud stretched away, starting at the foot of the brief shingle beach. The mud was not quite uniform. In some places it was a little darker, in others lighter. Where the sun caught it in one direction it glistened at me, and a little to the left of this shining area was a much darker patch, perhaps covered by seaweed. And beyond it all, merging into the mud so that I could not see the point where one stopped and the other started, was the greyness of the sea.

I swung the binoculars round, drew them from their case, and put them to my eyes.

Now I could see the line where the mud stopped, and the water started.

I could see oystercatchers picking their way beside the water. Here and there a buoy lay in the mud, tilted at an angle and waiting for the next tide to set it to rights again. Over to the right was a slight depression in the mud with a trickle of water which marked the channel of a small stream, and in it were two boats, one grey and one white.

Raising the binoculars again, I looked over the water and beyond. There was nothing. The sky merged into the water, and it was only when I twisted to the left that I saw anything else: one or two tall chimneys and silos, dimly visible in the haze, and the jib of a giant crane.

Pushing the binoculars back into their case I walked forward down the shingle. The first patch of mud I tried was soft and I sank in over my ankles, so I retreated and tried another. This time it was firmer, and I started walking. After a time, I noticed evidence of the lugworms: little worm casts, thrown up at random. A little later, I found more evidence: footsteps and some spadefuls of mud beside a hole where someone had been digging.

The sea was still so far away that I abandoned my original intention of walking to its edge. I turned round and examined the even, deserted coast which I had left and then I started back, the chill and the loneliness and the gathering gloom clutching at me.

I found myself hurrying, anxious to get away from such a desolate spot before the murky twilight gave way to darkness.

As I passed my car, I opened the boot and arranged its contents to make room for Dick's belongings; then I went in to pick up his suitcase, the first thing, so that it would lie under the boxes which would follow.

I was preoccupied as I turned into the living room, though afterwards I persuaded myself that I had noticed a shuffling noise. In any case there would be no doubt of the next things I noticed: the strength of the arms which threw me to the floor as if I were a child, and a hand which held a pad to my face, and the featureless masked head of the man to whom the arms and hand belonged.

But that was all I noticed.

Chapter 2

Coming to was, as I said earlier, unpleasant.

My head was throbbing rhythmically, and beyond the rhythm was an all-embracing ache.

My mouth was dry and there was a nasty taste in it. My thoughts seemed to be a long way away, and it took a good deal of concentration to catch them and to start putting them in some sort of order.

He, whoever he was, had not left me where I had fallen. He had picked me up and laid me on one of the seats, and as the seat doubled as a bed it was soft and comfortable. He had even been considerate enough to leave the electric light on. I was on my back, so I turned my head gingerly to face the middle of the caravan.

It had not changed; Dick's things were still stacked on the other seat; but the new position of my head seemed to increase the throbbing, so I turned it back, gazed once again at the ceiling, and then closed my eyes in the hope that it would shut out the ceiling and the throbbing at the same time. It did not. The ceiling was gone, but the throbbing had the field to itself.

I do not know how long I lay there, struggling to gain control of my head and its contents. I did not succeed, but finally I was driven to move because I realised I was cold, so cold that the agony of my falling temperature exceeded the pain of the hammering in my head. Indeed the condition of my head seemed to improve at about the same speed as my temperature approached zero.

I rolled over, set my feet on the floor, rose, and then dropped back again. At the third attempt I made it. The upright position was a marginal improvement and my head became clearer.

I made my way into the kitchen.

The box of Dick's food, which I had had ready to take out to the car, was still undisturbed on the kitchen table. But my goodness it was cold! Just as cold as the other room.

Slowly my memories and my powers of reasoning trickled back. I remembered lighting the gas oven, and I wondered why it was so cold. The kitchen should have been warmer even if it was not up to the seventy degrees to which I had become accustomed in my last lodgings, the ones which had finally driven me to mortgage myself to a new house. The oven door was shut: I had left it open. The gas was off: I had left it on.

Instinct took over, and something approaching panic. I must re-light it. I must re-light it before I did or thought any more.

I opened the oven door.

Matches?

I was sure I had put them back where I had found them, on top of the narrow pelmet over the window in the end of the caravan. But they were not there. I looked from one end of the pelmet to the other, and I groped with my hand from one end to the other. No matches. No matches on the other pelmet either, the one above the window over the sink.

Suddenly my whole being was bound up in that box of matches. It no longer mattered, for the moment at least, who had knocked me out with the chloroform, it no longer mattered why he had done it, and for the time being Dick's death receded into the past, an unimportant and remote event in history. These things could be studied later. Just now all that mattered was one small box of matches.

Round the cupboards I went again, under the sink, sifting through the china and pots and pans. I looked in the grill, on the tabletops, in the wall cupboard. No matches.

The cardboard carton came next. I pulled things out and dropped them on the table next to it, reversing what I had done so carefully only a short time before.

And then the air, pent up in my lungs hissed out with relief. I found them wedged between a can of luncheon meat and the side of the box.

How stupid! I must have thrown them in without thinking after I had lit the oven, even though I remembered deciding there were too few to be worth taking with me.

This time I lit not only the oven, but also the rings and the gas fire in the living room. Then I lay down again, shut my eyes, and waited. Further thought was postponed until I had thawed.

But further thought ignored its postponement.

Who had been waiting for me? And why?

I was a complete stranger to the district. I knew nobody. I had no friends or acquaintances, still less enemies, in this God-forsaken part of the country. Nor, to my knowledge, had I any enemies anywhere else, not of the kind who would hide behind a wall and then creep up and put me out with a pad of chloroform. And why chloroform? Wouldn't it have been easier just to have hit me on the back of the head? Almost any weapon would have served for that - no need for any preparations, just seize the first brick which came to hand. But chloroform? People don't walk round with it in their pockets in case it should come in useful. Whoever did it had made preparations.

It did not make sense.

I tried another approach.

Either he had intended to get me, for a reason which I still could not begin to guess, or he had meant to get someone else. If so, who? Dick - he was the only possible person. He was the only person who used the caravan - probably the only one who had used it since the end of the previous summer season, months ago. But surely if someone knew Dick and his movements well enough to waylay him in his own caravan he must also have known that Dick was dead?

So it looked as if I must be the target after all. But, again, why? I was getting nowhere.

After an interminable length of time, I began to feel warmer and the throbbing was dying away. My thoughts continued to go round on the same track, muddled and inconclusive and, by now, automatic. I abandoned my unsolved problem for the present, opened the door, and made my way uncertainly as far as the road, noticing with relief that my car was still in its place and that someone had been considerate enough to close the boot. I returned to the caravan and sat down again to think.

I ought to go to the police, I told myself. After all, that is what they are for. But at the same time I knew I would have to be pretty desperate before doing that.

What else could I do?

I went through it all once more, working out that whoever it was could not have wanted to get Dick, and as I was the only other candidate he must have been after me. The reason was something which I myself did not know, not yet, so how could I find out?

Putting it this way made it simpler it must be something to do with Dick, so I must start with his things. It would give me something positive to do even if I found nothing.

I opened the suitcase first and searched every pocket of every garment he possessed. My reward was a five-pound note.

Next came the bedding. There was nothing in it.

Finally I came to the box of books and papers and other bits and pieces.

I took each book out, flipped through its pages to see if they held any loose papers, and laid it in a pile with the other things I had already searched. Dick's notebooks I put aside. They would take some time to go through, and it seemed more sensible first to look through the odd scraps of paper and letters.

But there was nothing significant among them; a bank statement showed he had a healthy balance in his account, as I would have expected with a cautious person like Dick, single, earning a good salary; a shopping list, including matches, showed a sensible order of priorities; and that was about all.

I started on the notebooks. There were two of them, of which one was full of technical stuff, a kind of memorandum about articles and papers which Dick had found interesting, with notes about what they contained in some cases. The other was a diary. It was the first thing to come out of the box, as it had been lying on top, and the last which I started. There was not a great deal in it, as it was still early in the year, so I began at the end and worked back. It was a business, not a diarist's, diary, but surprisingly full.

I examined every entry twice, once at its face value and once, as it were, crooked. It was slow, tedious, work and I was thankful that it was still only February and I did not have to go through a full diary from December backward. My efforts to read crookedly, to find sinister implications in innocent notes, were as unsuccessful as my efforts to find anything of interest by taking the entries at their face value.

I was about to give up when I came to the pages of addresses and telephone numbers at the front of the diary.

And there I found it: the last entry was my own name and telephone number, accurately, and my own address - a complete fabrication. 1, Panel Row, West End, Hants.

I shivered involuntarily. Dick was a sensible, uncomplicated, straightforward man. He was reticent to a fault, but I knew him well enough to recognise that there was nothing deep or sinister about his reticence, that it was born of shyness and a lack of assertiveness, not deviousness or obtuseness, as some people had been known to assume when they met him.

So what in heaven's name had he been up to? He had let himself be drowned in the most careless of ways, completely out of character with his usual caution. He had been associating with someone who had knocked me out for no apparent reason with a chloroform pad. And the most recent of a good many addresses in his diary was my own, which he knew by heart anyway, with a bogus address which I could only assume must be some kind of clue for me to follow up. Dick might have enjoyed melodrama and Sherlock Holmes as a spectator, but for him to join in the action was the last thing I would have expected.

1, Panel Row, West End, Hants.

I stared at it stupidly. Memories of schoolboy stories with clues in code came to me. I seemed to remember one in which every fifth letter meant something. But if I took the fifth letter, or even every third or second, the message could not be very long, and Dick had a lot of explaining to do. Every fifth letter produced E-W-N-T, ever, third A-L-W-S-N-A-S, and every second P-N-L-O-W-S-E-D-A-T. I needed another key to break down the fresh codes.

1, Panel Row, West End, Hants.

There was, I knew, a West End in Hampshire, somewhere near Southampton. So perhaps Hants was only added to make the address look realistic.

West End? West end of what? Practically everything had a west end or side, so by the law of averages half the things in the world must have a west end. Not very helpful.

Panel Row? Row of panels?

What, I wondered, had a row of panels in it and a west end? In particular what, associated with Dick, possessed these two features?

I looked round at his belongings, the boxes of books and clothes and food.

They all had west ends, and the individual items in them would have west ends, too, though not now the same ones as before I had moved them. About the only thing I had left in the same place was the caravan itself.

And that had panels! They were all round me. The interior walls were made of panels.

I recalled the map of The Wash to my mind, enlarged it, set the caravan on it, and superimposed the points of the compass.

The West was the living room end. The big window was across it with the shelf of books and odds and ends over it, and there were panels above and below the window, held in place by beading secured with Phillips screws. With a Phillips screwdriver it would be easy enough to take the panels off and replace them without damaging the van, but I had no Phillips screwdriver.

I looked at my watch. Shops would be shut by now. Most garages would be shut, too. Pubs would be open, but in my experience they do not sell screwdrivers.

I could go back to King's Lynn, asking everyone I came across if they had a screwdriver they would lend me. Anyway I could think of nothing better.

And there was something else I had begun to recognise with a sinking feeling. When I had arrived at the caravan park my objective was to pack up Dick's things, dispose of the van, and leave the desolate place and its stinking toilet block again just as quickly as I could. Now, though, things were different. I liked the place no more than before: it was just as desolate, just as smelly, and much much more sinister. But events had moved on since then... and Dick had left me a message. I could not turn my back on it, however much I was now scared by the whole business. With a feeling that fate was taking a hand I acknowledged that my bed for the night was in the caravan.

I looked round the van before I left it, wondering if I had overlooked anything which I should take with me. I slipped Dick's diary into my pocket, drew the curtains, left the lights on, locked the door, and drove slowly away. Was it a mistake to leave the light on? Would it attract or repel boarders? I just hoped that the masked man had finished with me now. He had, after all, had a chance to do anything he wished with me and the van, and it was not exactly as if he had let his opportunity go by default.

As I drove, I was so immersed in my thoughts that I almost ran into the old Morris Minor which was standing at the edge

18

of the road, even though its lights, muddy and dim, were on. As I drew out and round it I saw a figure standing in front of it. Instinctively I pulled into the kerb and stopped. It was a deserted stretch of road, beyond the caravan belt and not yet in the village of Sherningham.

In my mirror I could see the figure apparently bending towards something on the road, silhouetted against the side lights of the car. I got out and approached warily. I was a changed man already from the one I had been that morning, no longer open and trusting. As I came near the figure stood up. It was a girl, and she looked first at me, and then down again. A large hare, its hindquarters limp and its front legs damaged, twitched desperately in its efforts to escape. As I came up its eyes focused on me, full of fear, before it redoubled its dying efforts to get away.

The girl had unrolled a bundle of tools on the road. She was holding the biggest of them, a wrench, and what was more she was holding it strongly, as if she meant to use it. Without a word I removed it from her hand, planted myself between her and the hare, took careful aim and, thank heaven, caught the hare squarely on the back of the head. It stopped struggling and lay still.

I lifted the animal's body and laid it beside the road.

I put the wrench back with the other tools, rolled them up in a bundle and, at last, looked at her, standing at the door of her car, as I handed it to her.

"Thanks," she breathed, and I knew she meant it.

She was short, with a wide forehead which caught the red light from my car. She had a small narrow mouth.

"It's horrid, isn't it?" I answered, "and the bigger the animal the worse it is."

"Yes," she answered simply. She was obviously still watching in her mind's eye as the animal lay twitching on the ground, but she pulled herself together. "I'm so grateful," she went on,

19

"I suppose I might have done it myself, but not like you, not cleanly and quickly like that." I was not so sure. She had been holding the wrench as if she knew how to use it, and she did not seem the panicky kind. But she was still talking "Thank you," she said again, "it doesn't seem enough, just to say that...." her voice trailed away.

"Of course it's enough," I replied, and then I hesitated before I went on "but if you wouldn't mind there's something you could do which would be a great help to me. You have a Phillips screwdriver in your tool kit. I need one, and I'd like to borrow it. May I, please?"

"Yes, of course. In fact, why don't you keep it? I never use it. Three cars went by without even stopping, you know."

I removed the screwdriver and rolled the bundle up again for her. I refused to let her give it to me. I made a note of her name and address and I promised I would let her have it in the next day or two. Sally Anderson, 5 New Road, Sherningham. She lived in the village towards which we were both heading only a mile or so on.

The people in the hotel in King's Lynn in which I had booked a room were not pleased to see me go. They would not fill the bed again at that hour of the evening. On the other hand they had other empty rooms, as I pointed out to the hotel receptionist when she turned indignant, so I had lost them no business.

By now I was beginning to know the main road and its family of names which ended in 'ham': Sandringham, Dersingham, Snettisham, and Heacham. It did not take me long to get back to my caravan - Dick's caravan. No, mine now.

Learning from Sally Anderson I armed myself with a spanner. Then I locked the car and approached the van. The door opened outwards and I withdrew to the bottom of the steps before I pulled it, standing warily with my spanner at the ready as it swung open. But there was nobody there, nobody hiding round the corner either in the kitchen or the living room.

I locked myself in. Then I inspected the van. No change. I turned my attention to the panels.

Before touching them or the screws I examined them carefully, and what I found did not give me much cause for optimism. I could not be sure, but those screws did not look to me as if they had been touched since the caravan was put together. True, if Dick had decided to hide something behind them, he would have done his best to avoid leaving any traces to show that they had been disturbed. But there is a difference between leaving the screws unburred and the ply panels undamaged, and putting back dirt and grime into the cracks and into the star shaped slots in the screw heads.

I set to work on the panels below the window.

There were two of them, one on each side, each of them half covered by the seat on its side of the van and by the locker below it. Some of the screws were inside the lockers, awkward to get at.

I had the panel on the right off first. I took the screws out and the beading off, and then I prized away the panel not, I feared, as neatly as Dick had done it.

If he had done it.

He had not. There was nothing to see except the ribs of the caravan and the inside face of its outer skin.

Without re-assembling it I started on the other side. Nothing there, either.

The panel above the window was more difficult because the shelf had been fixed against it. I had to loosen the shelf, leaving it hanging from a strut in the ceiling, before I could get at the panel. But finally I had it off, too.

Nothing there, once again - but by then I was not surprised: the battle to remove it had already convinced me that Dick would not have used it as a hiding place.

It was while I was replacing the panel over the window that there came a knock at the door.

It made me jump, I had heard no footsteps. Then it made me prickle all over, and the butterflies started in the pit of my stomach. I had not known them like that for years, not since that time the police got hold of me.

Who on earth would be knocking at the door at this time of night, and at this time of the year? I had seen nobody about - apart from the man in the mask and the warden of the caravan park.

I armed myself with my spanner again, sliding it into my trouser pocket where it was easily accessible. I unlocked the door, stood back from it as far as I could, and pushed it away from me.

The person outside knew about caravan doors, too. He knew it opened outwards, and he had stood back for it.

"'Ullo Mate. Got any matches? I'm down to my last."

The light from the van shone out on his pale, square-jawed, thin-lipped face, topped with short fair hair which receded from the forehead. It was an alert but expressionless face, and it reminded me of a Scandinavian I had once met, a Finn.

"Yes," I had bought some more at the hotel in King's Lynn.

I went into the kitchen, found the half empty box, and turned to take it to him.

He moved fast and silently, that man.

By the time I had turned round he was in the caravan, standing just inside the door, and I had heard nothing.

"Thanks, mate," he said as I handed them to him, and before I could take another look at him he was out of the caravan and on his way.

I stopped to see where he went. It was to the next van, number 135, the twin of my own. I had seen no signs of life there earlier in the day.

Chapter 3

It did not take long to refix the panels, although by the time I had finished it was obvious they had been tampered with. But then I am not much good with my hands, and Dick used to be; he could have done the job so that no one would have noticed they had been touched, at least on a casual inspection.

I had intended to open a couple of tins and make myself a meal in the caravan, but by now I had had enough of it. The sheer dreariness and depression and dankness of it had got into me, and when that was coupled with the worry and fear of a person or persons unknown who lurked round corners and put chloroform pads over my face for no known reason, I wanted to run away, screaming. I had noticed a fish and chip shop in Sherningham as well as a few pubs. Between them I must be able to find something to eat.

I left the light on again in the caravan. Even if it kept no one away it would make the place a bit less depressing to return to. Just before I locked up I looked round and noticed the screwdriver. I might as well return it now as later so I picked it up and took it with me.

Lights had been turned on in a few more caravans as I drove away - not many, but the place was not quite as deserted as I had thought. Perhaps it was not so odd, after all, that the one next to mine, which I had presumed was empty for the winter, had its lights on and shadows of movement against the curtains.

New Road, Sherningham, was easy to find; the first person I asked when I reached the centre of the village directed me without hesitation.

The road must have been built about seventy years ago and it was lined with solid, roomy, red-brick, houses. Number 5 was semi-detached, and walking through the front gate towards the door I had an impression of respectable comfort and stability. The garden, as much of it as I could see in the light of the street lamp opposite, was cared for and the edges of the grass trimmed. Its centre-piece was a clump of pampas grass which rose from a perfectly circular bed, and at each boundary were full-grown ornamental trees and shrubs. Sally's Morris Minor was parked in a kind of lay-by beside the timber garage, whose doors stood open revealing an empty space inside.

Sally herself opened the door. She did not recognise me at first, which was hardly surprising as we had only met in the semi-darkness of our car sidelights, but when she realised who I was she tried to compensate by insisting that I should come into the hall even though by then I had explained what I had come for and there was no need. However I had no objections; it looked an inviting house and it could only soothe the raw edges of my nerves after the caravan park.

Besides, I was not against having a better look at the girl herself.

She was younger than I had thought, early twenties probably, perhaps even late teens. While she stood at the newly-painted front door, the porch light shone down on her at an angle which did not catch her face fully but showed up the colours of her pale fawn pullover and red skirt, and the light in the hall silhouetted a neat, slim figure. Beyond her I could glimpse marks of comfortable affluence: polished mahogany furniture, a silver salver, and black and white prints in old gilt frames on the papered walls.

It was a pretty picture, I thought. An attractive girl, a substantial cared-for house, no doubt a solid, respectable, prosperous family, well-known and established in the neighbourhood. Everything I had never had!

But when she turned the picture crumbled. It came as a shock when I saw her walking away from me with the exaggerated movements of hip and leg forced on her by a club foot. The trappings of respectability and comfort were all about her - for the rest of her family they must have been the real thing - but for

24

this girl they were flawed. "Disadvantaged" was the word, and it covered a multitude of sins. I should know.

"Are you staying near here?" she asked. "I don't think I've seen you before, have I?"

"Just for a couple of nights. I'm in one of those caravans near the beach. I came to the village to see if I could find something to eat."

"It can't be much fun in this weather." Then she brightened. She looked quite different when she smiled, she did it with her wide blue eyes rather than her mouth, which was too thin and nervous to do the job well. "I was just going to make myself some cocoa. What about scrambled eggs? Will they do? Come on." She did not wait for an answer. She led the way across the hall to the kitchen, past a door which stood open to reveal bookcases and a teak desk untidily piled with papers and books, past a white-painted shelf on which stood two framed photographs of girls of identical ages with a strong family resemblance, one of them clearly Sally, taken when she must have been about thirteen.

"You're not on holiday, not at this time of year, are you? Nor just for two days?" she asked as she started to take out eggs, saucepan, and milk from the neat rows of kitchen units. "What are you doing? Here on business?" Her questions could have sounded inquisitive, but they did not. They were put too artlessly to give offence.

"No," I answered slowly. "No. I've come because my brother's just died. He was working up here and living in the caravan. You may have heard about it. He was drowned a few days ago ... went out looking for lugworms and was caught by the tide..."

Sally stopped in the middle of what she was doing. White of egg dripped to the marbled work top.

"Oh," she exclaimed, and then: "yes, I did hear about it. It must be awful for you."

I stood there dumbly. I am no good at receiving sympathy. I am not used to it.

25

But she was a nice girl, Sally, sensitive as well as sympathetic. She realised I did not know what to say. The egg continued on its way and she turned from me to busy herself at the electric cooker. After a pause she went on, without turning back to me:

"He'd been here for a few months, hadn't he?" She was speaking softly, almost as if she were talking to herself. "I read about it in the paper, and people round here have talked about it, too, but no one I've come across seems to have met him."

"I'm not surprised. Dick kept himself to himself."

"What was he doing round here?"

"He had a job with Burbidge's. He was a surveyor."

"Working on those reservoirs they're building in the sea?" She glanced at me momentarily. "It's a big thing, that, isn't it?"

She was right. Dick had explained something of it to me. Three immense reservoirs were being constructed across the southern end of The Wash: they were building embankments against the sea round the edges, and then dredging out the middle. Once they were full of fresh water there would be enough to supply people for miles round, and to pipe it to other parts of the country in a drought.

"I gather it is, but I don't know a great deal about it. How do you come to have heard of it?"

"Everyone in the neighbourhood has, that is everyone who takes the least interest in what goes on round him. The conservationists are all worried about what will happen. They say you can't tamper with nature to that extent without side effects. Where will the tides go? And what about the fish and the birds which live on the marshes there at present? And what will happen to the silt? Dad never stopped talking about it when it all started, and he was forever going to meetings. But it all made no difference. They went ahead just the same."

"Why should he worry? What's his job?"

26

"Oh, he teaches. History's his subject and he loves it!" Suddenly she was speaking with an added warmth in her voice, she was fond of her father, there was no doubt about that. "That's why he's out this evening. He's giving a talk to the History Society in Norwich: 'King John - good or bad?' That's the title of his talk. I'd have gone with him if I could have done, and that's where the rest of the family are. But he's doing it again in Lynn tomorrow and I'll be able to go then."

"King John? - bad, surely? I don't know much history, but I can remember that, at least."

"But that's where you're wrong - at least nowhere near as bad as everyone thinks, that's what Dad says."

"But why couldn't you go, too?"

"Oh, I do this visiting. Once a week I go and see Mrs Thornton. She'd miss me if I didn't go, and she can't get out at all now, so she'd never forgive me," She sighed, and I wondered why: because she had not been able to go with the rest of her family? Sympathy with Mrs Thornton? Or perhaps it was the association of ideas, perhaps Mrs Thornton's infirmity, whatever that may be, had reminded her of her own infirmity. As if she knew what I was thinking she went on: "She's not all that old, either, but she's quite crippled with her arthritis. It makes me realise how lucky I am. My foot doesn't stop me getting round, not like her...."

"But it must be pretty grim, all the same, watching other people doing the things you can't do?"

"It's a nuisance sometimes, but you get used to it. We all get used to what we can't do, don't we? After all, I don't suppose you worry much if you can't run a mile in four minutes, or if you can't play the piano. It's a matter of degree." She spoke lightly, as if these were every-day truths, as if anyway it made no difference.

She had finished her cooking and she set a large plate of scrambled egg in front of me, first moving to one side the screwdriver which I had brought back to her.

"What did you need that for?" she asked, changing the subject. "Surely the caravan hasn't fallen to pieces since you moved into it, has it?"

"It's a complicated story." I stopped, wondering where to begin, whether to begin at all. But she had sat down at the table with me now, sipping her cocoa, her wide blue eyes on me, listening. After all, she had answered all my questions, she was giving me food, it was she who had lent me a screwdriver when I wanted one, and she was a nice girl. Why shouldn't I tell her? To hell with my ingrained habit of reticence!

Her eyes widened when I told her of how the man with the stocking over his head had waited for me and had got me with his pad of chloroform.

"You poor boy!" she exclaimed. "How terrible? You must go to the police. Why don't you ring them up from here? They'd be round in no time to look into something like that."

"No," I answered quickly. "No!"

Fool that I was! Why had I told her all about it? I had known it was a mistake, and I just could not explain why I would not call in the police.

"But you must! This man ought to be caught and punished. He might do the same to someone else; he's not safe to have around."

She was right, of course, but how could I explain? How could I tell her the police would never believe me? - that I had a police record myself? Of course, I knew I had no regrets about what I had done, but it was not something I wanted to explain to her, still less to the local police.

"No," I answered again. "No ...they'd never believe me...."

"Of course they would. Why ever not?"

"Well... what evidence is there? The effect of the chloroform has worn off now, and I have no bumps and bruises."

And then, in a flash, it came to me: that was why the man had used chloroform - to avoid any traces of violence on me.

28

That was why he must have aired the caravan, too, why when I had walked round afterwards I could detect no traces of it.

"But even so, why shouldn't they believe you? There's no reason why you should make up a story like that, is there?"

"But there's no motive for it, either," I went on. "No one knows me round here. Nothing was stolen, nothing was even disturbed. So far as I could tell everything was just as I had left it." Except for the matches, I thought. It was funny about them. I had persuaded myself at the time that I must have thrown them into the box, but I knew I had not. Why had they been moved? The man in the mask had not needed to use them, in fact the opposite was the case, it was he who had turned out the gas, not lit it. "No," I went on. "They just wouldn't believe me."

Sally was still looking at me. She did not agree. Obviously nothing I said would persuade her, so I must get her off the subject.

I did, with the first thing which came into my mind. I went on with my story and explained why I had needed a screwdriver. I told her about the diary entry and about taking the panels off, and I succeeded in one thing: she stopped talking about the police. She might have gone back to them, but before she could do so there were sounds from outside as the rest of the family returned.

When she heard the car she stood up and cleared away the dirty things. I watched this shapely girl as she stomped in her awkward, graceless, way round the kitchen. I watched her as she opened the door into the hall and greeted her family.

She did it warmly, and they greeted her just as warmly, and then she introduced me to them.

"I don't even know your name?" she exclaimed.

"George," I answered.

"This is George," she said to the rest of them, gathered together, rather squashed, in the hall. "He rescued me this

29

evening. I ran over a hare and half killed it, and he came to the rescue of the lady in distress: he put it out of its agony for me."

They seemed to be all round me as we went through into the lounge, a bubbling, lively, family. Sally's sister Margery I recognised easily from the photograph, attractive, too, but with a hard edge not present in Sally. Mr Anderson was slightly built but tall, with sandy hair which receded and was starting to turn grey. His blue watery eyes were fixed on me, and I was sure that anything I said would be analysed with cool academic logic, any loose or inaccurate statements would be challenged as a matter of course.

Her mother was different, but no less polished and part of the family; she was a handsome woman, not so talkative as the others, but self-possessed and thoughtful, offering me coffee while the others were chattering round us, too full of what was inside them to keep it there. She fitted perfectly into her house, I thought, middle class, solid, respectable, and the lounge (or drawing room, as I started calling it to myself, too, as soon as I heard them do so) was especially her room: inlaid antique furniture, pastel portraits of her children, ivory ornaments and cut flowers in a vase, immaculate loose-covers, and the whole thing with a feeling of being both tidy and used, as if this was the room in which, for all its perfection, she really lived and was at home. What a contrast, I thought, to the study I had glanced into from the hall, with its modern furniture, its book-cases, and its academic untidiness. That must be Mr Anderson's room, definitely not his wife's. But the drawing room? - they both fitted in it, Mr Anderson as I could see him fitting into his study, but perhaps, there, with his hair a little ruffled and carpet slippers to his feet: I could picture him as two different men, the enquiring academic of the study, the polished host of the drawing room.

While Sally's mother was talking to me I could hear Sally in the background asking her father about the lecture, about how it had gone and about how the audience had reacted. It had been a success, apparently. Was everything this family did a success, I wondered? And for all the efforts of Sally's mother I felt less and less part of it. Sally was all right, she was human; she had a club foot; she knew what it was like to be different. But the rest? I shied away.

They were just what I had imagined when I first saw the house with Sally standing at its front door, assured, clever, polished, and with no chinks in their armour.

They were too much for me.

I turned to Sally's mother and said, more abruptly than I realised "I must go. Thank you, but I won't stay for coffee."
And suddenly they were all silent and giving me their attention, even though I had not spoken loudly, even though they all appeared to have been talking at the tops of their voices.

"But must you?" they said. 'We've only just come in; we've only just met you."

I could not stand it. They seemed to gather round and converge. But for me there were just two of them now: Sally, and the rest. Sally, who I began to know, and the rest who were not my scene at all. A pity, but it could not be helped. I ought to be used to it by now. It was life - my life, at least.

***

By the time I returned to the caravan park most of the lights, even those which had been lit when I had left, were out. That went for the light in the neighbouring caravan, too. I approached my van carefully again, holding my spanner and standing back as I opened the door, but once again my precautions were unnecessary, and after I had locked myself in and examined the inside of the caravan I could find no sign that anyone else had been there while I was out.

I made myself some coffee. It was disgusting powdered coffee, powdered milk, and stale water which tasted of the plastic which

31

had contained it. But I was not going outside again to fetch fresh water, not for anyone, not in the dark and at that hour. Anyway, for all its nastiness, I was more at home with it than I would have been drinking much better coffee with Sally's family.

It seemed a long time since I had been able to sit back in peace and think, and I had plenty to think about.

I had a day and two nights before Dick's funeral, a day and two nights to try to get to the bottom of this business, if I was ever to do so. I made up my mind that until the funeral, like it or not, I owed it to Dick to do all I could.

After the funeral - and only if I had done all I could in the meantime perhaps I could leave it if I had had no success.
But if I shirked the job during the next day and two nights ... then perhaps I would find I could not give it up after all. It was all quite senseless, this reasoning, if you could call it reasoning, but I was certain of it, just as certain as if I had been given my orders.

So how should I go about it?

It was late; I was tired; and I could think of only three things which I must do. I must go to Dick's office to see if he had any personal things there which I must remove. I must get in touch with D Bassett of Montrose Crescent, Peterborough, to pay off the caravan. And I must get some sleep. Sleep came first. Without that I could do nothing else.

Chapter 4

Waking in the morning was an odd sensation. Drowsiness gave way to panic when I realised I was not in my own bed, secure in my new semi. Panic gradually subsided as I recognised where I was, and panic gave way to anxiety, and fear, as I remembered the events of the day before and my resolutions for that day. In the evening it had seemed easy enough to decide I must get to the bottom of Dick's affairs and find out why I had been attacked, but that was yesterday, when I had known that a night's sleep lay between me and the implementation of my resolution.

I climbed unsteadily out of bed into the icy air inside the caravan. I lit the fire, the oven, both rings, and the grill, and then I jumped, shivering, back into bed. Dick's bedclothes were certainly efficient.

When the temperature had risen from near arctic to sub-tropical I got out. I dressed, turned the fire down and the cooker burners off, swung the bed up into its alcove, and thought about breakfast - and coffee.

I could not put up with the same disgusting brew again, and as it was now day I was prepared to brave the outside world and any attackers who might be lurking in wait for me. If they attacked me at that hour they would do it sooner or later anyway, so they might as well get on with it.

It did not take long to refill the water container, and there were no signs of life to be seen. I hardly let the van out of my sight while I fetched the water and I knew no one had approached it, so I had no need for my precautions with the spanner. As I mounted the steps, though, this time with an almost care-free heart, I had forgotten the other trap: the front corner of the steps again slipped off its brick, banging my head and the corner of the handrail against the side of the caravan.

Again I cursed.

It was only when I had set the water down for a moment and was putting the steps back where they came from that I gradually became aware that something was different.

The handrail had scarred the outside of the caravan almost as before, but not quite. Last time it had scraped and dented it where the blue paint met the white. This time it was below, it was all in the lower half of the van, the blue half. But it was not the new scratch which made me stop and wonder, it was the old one.

It was not there.

It was not a sudden discovery, it was a gradual realisation, which came to me, I suppose, at about the same speed as my slow-moving early-morning mind turned over. And with it came something else which seeped in at about the same speed: an instinct that somebody was watching. Twenty-four hours earlier such an idea would have been preposterous. Now it seemed not just possible but probable, even natural.

And to show that my body as well as my mind had accustomed themselves to this new world of shocks, suspicion, and fear, I found that just as instinctively I did not stand back, scratch my head, measure the new mark with my finger and point to the place where the first one should have been. Instead I found I was replacing the steps on their bricks just as if I had noticed nothing. No outward tremor or movement of my body indicated that anything was amiss, not until I was once more in the safety of my van, with the door locked. Then I sank limp and trembling on to one of the seats.

My slow-moving early-morning mind was now racing, but it went through its paces logically and step by step. If the scratch was not there now one of three things must follow: either I was mistaken in believing there had ever been a scratch, but I was not yet so far gone as to accept that - it had happened the day before, in daylight and I put my hand to my head to feel the two tender spots where it had hit the side of the van; or someone

34

had repaired and repainted it - but that was ridiculous, and there would be a patch in the paint to show for it; or it was a different van. It did not take genius to decide that the third was the likeliest option, unlikely though it seemed, but to decide why would have needed genius, and genius is a quality with which I am aware I am not endowed.

Anyway it provided an answer to two questions which had been lurking at the back of my mind and, I realised with a start, there was a way of proving it, too. The mystery of the matches was solved: my assailant had tossed them from the pelmet where I had put them into the cardboard box with the food, and had then forgotten to replace them on the pelmet of the new van after he had transferred its contents including me from one to the other. And the gas oven; he had forgotten to re-light that, too.

The proof was the keys. I had two of them now, the one the police had given me and which the caravan park keeper had told me was the spare and the other which I had found under Dick's bed. The spare had been on the table when I was attacked, easy for my assailant to change, but the other had been in my pocket.

I laid them side by side on the seat next to me. Their labels were identical, and the keys should have been identical, but they were not. The spare the police had given me fitted the door of the van I was in, I knew, because that was the one I had been using. It was possible, I supposed, that the lock was such a cheap and shoddy affair that both keys would fit it, so I tried the key I had found under the bed. It would hardly go into the lock, still less turn.

If the van had been changed there must still be some traces of the move outside on the ground. They would surely confirm my suspicions, although I already regarded it as a certainty. I set out for the toilet, locking the van door as I went, sauntering slowly across, eyes to the ground as if I were still no more than half awake.

The ground between the van and the road was covered with shingle; it would be; a vehicle would leave no track on that. But between the shingle and the so-called concrete road I found a slight depression, hard underneath and with a thin film of sediment on its surface. I recognised the footprint of a wellington in one place as I walked over, probably made by me, but none of the tyre marks I was looking for.

Inside the toilet block I peered for a moment through the window towards the van, and the van next to it, number 135.

On my way back I took a different route, passing about halfway between my van and 135. Again I sauntered sleepily, eyes to the ground. The sediment in the depression was different. It had been scraped over recently so that a casual observer would have seen nothing, but it had not been done carefully enough for me: the print left by the edge of a tyre was clear in one place, and the tyre pointed towards my van.

Sleepily I climbed into the van again. Wide awake, I peered between the curtains, still drawn, towards the caravan beside me, number 135.

They were twins, so far as I could tell with my unpractised un-caravanning eye. Its curtains were drawn, as mine were, and as most of the curtains in the park were. Its curtains were the same pattern as mine. And, I remembered, the park keeper had remarked that the owner of both caravans was the same person, D Bassett, 13 Montrose Crescent, Peterborough.

How could I tell if there was anybody in that van?

No car was parked beside it. I had noticed that on my visit to the toilet. But then, I had noticed that no car had been parked beside it on the previous evening, when its lights had been up and its occupant had come to me for matches.

If he could come to me for matches, why should I not go to him? After all, they were my matches. I saw no reason why I should not ask him for what was left of my own box.

I did not bother to lock up this time, but I hid the box of matches I had bought at the hotel in King's Lynn, and I turned off the fire. Just in case he should follow me back I did not want it to be too obvious that my need for matches was a fabrication. I could always say that the ones I had were damp. I was amazed at my own deviousness.

I dropped the key I had found under Dick's bed into my pocket.

The door to number 135 was on the far side. I had already noticed that someone could easily enter or leave it without my being able to see him.

I knocked, two firm knocks, and then I stood back, waiting and watching the curtains in the windows. No sound. No movement.

I knocked again, three harder knocks. No reaction.

I put my hand in my pocket and grasped the key. Then I dropped it, I would give one final knock before I tried it.

This time I battered at the door. I hit it at least a dozen times, each one harder than the last. And my hand was actually on its way to the door, key towards the keyhole, when a voice came:

"What the hell!" it shouted angrily. "Can't you leave a man to sleep?"

"Matches," I yelled back. "Have you got my matches?"

A muttering and growling followed and then, slightly louder, "Yes. I'll bring 'em round in a minute. When I'm up."

He came, and this time I was ready for him. I stood in the door of my van to take them and to stop him having another look inside, to stop him feeling the warmth and realizing that I had had the gas on already. He was fully dressed, and when he had handed them over - without a word to me - I watched him walking away, up the concrete road, towards the entrance to the camp.

Where had he gone? What for? For how long? And would I have time to try my key in his van before he returned? There was only one way to find out.

As soon as he was out of sight I was round at the door of his van again, and this time I did not knock. The key went into the lock, and it turned, and there, next to the door, was a scratch in the paintwork just where the blue joined the white. I must have been too preoccupied to notice it when I was knocking and waiting for an answer - I had been watching the windows, searching for a face peering out.

I opened the door and looked each side of the partition first to make sure that no one else was there, lying in wait for me as before.

As I did it I saw the change: the place had been ransacked.

I closed the door, locking myself in. If the man returned I would hear him as he put his key in the lock. I did not know what I would do, but whatever it might be I had given myself a little more time to do it.

The living room end was in the greatest mess. The cushions and mattresses had all been cut open and their stuffing covered everything. The man must have had an uncomfortable night, sleeping, like me, on the double bed, but in his case on a broken mattress in a sea of kapok. It was odd though: there were no blankets or sheets or sleeping bag.

Having slit the mattresses open he had started on the van. He had not been so thorough about that though. Like me, he had removed some of the panels lining the walls, the ones at the Western end, below the window. He had not done it as neatly as I had, for he had broken the woodwork of the seats on each side of the van instead of taking out the screws and sliding the plywood panels out. Having removed those panels though, he had stopped, so he must have found what he was looking for, whatever that was.

And, I realised sickeningly, it was I who had led him to the panels! Dick had told me where to look in a way which no one else could have understood, not unless they knew something about me and where I lived, but like a fool I had led this man straight to the hiding place by letting him see where I was looking when he came round for the matches.

If only ...

It was probably too late, but the least I could do was search to see if I could find whatever it was he had found. It would have been easier it I had known what it was, as he must have done. All I knew was that it must fit into a space about two feet wide by three feet high by an inch and a half deep.

I started in the living room. I looked in a fitted cupboard beside the wardrobe, in the wardrobe itself, and in what was left of the lockers under the seats. The wardrobe had a thick coat in it and a black stocking mask pierced with eyeholes; apart from that there was nothing. The kitchen had even less: crockery and cutlery, matching the equipment of the other van, and nothing else, not even any food, and that explained where the man had gone, either to fetch food for his breakfast, or to eat it elsewhere. If he was fetching it he might be back soon, if he was eating out I was all right.

He was fetching it. I saw him through a chink in the curtains walking back along the concrete road, swinging a plastic bag which he had not held as he set off, and whistling carelessly. The door to the van was already in full view of him as he approached.

I was not used to this kind of life. I had never hit anyone in anger, still less had to fight for it or get a knock-out blow in first. My pulse soared again and I could feel the adrenalin at every corner of my body. It was a sensation which I disliked more each time I experienced it.

A frying pan was the best weapon I had found in my search. It was too light, but I decided that the china tea pot, which was heavier, was too clumsy, a bad choice. I had no confidence that l would have time for more than one blow. The man looked stronger than me; indeed I was now convinced that I knew from experience that he was stronger.

He would go into the kitchen first, so I must hide in the living room, which was awkward because he had left the double bed down and I would have to stand on its yielding mattress. The chances of my moving silently up on him in the kitchen, I thought, were nil. I would do better to flatten myself against the partition, standing on the bed in the living room, and then hit him from above as he went through into the living room. The only other thing I might do was hide in the big cupboard in the partition, the junk room in which I had found Dick's suitcase, but I had doubts about that. If he found me there he would have me at his mercy, however much I caught him by surprise. I would have no room to swing a cat, let alone a frying pan, or a tea pot. Besides, if my heart beats continued at the same pitch they would give me away soon enough: to me their noise was deafening.

I watched until the last minute as he approached. He was still whistling cheerfully, swinging his bag, apparently without a care in the world. He turned half left off the concrete path, cutting the corner of the neighbouring pitch, and heading straight for the door. It was time for me to take up my hiding place on the bed in the living room.

But then he changed course. Suddenly and without warning, he swung to the right towards the toilet block.

I hardly remember unlocking the door, re-locking it, tearing round the far end of his van and back to my own, and stopping only when I was safely in it, watching through the window as he emerged from the toilet block and made for his van.

It was only then that I noticed that I was holding the frying pan still. Too bad if he had planned a fried breakfast.

***

I wanted to know more about the man whom I had already christened the Finn to myself for lack of a better alternative, and I wondered if my time would be well spent if I waited in my caravan and then followed him when he left. But I was not practiced as a sleuth, trained to follow somebody through a deserted out-of-season caravan park without being noticed. Besides, by now I was beginning to feel that it would not work for another reason: if he was there to watch me he would never leave; and if he were only to leave in order to follow me there was not much hope of my being able to follow him!

There were two things which I had to do; I must go round to Burbidge's to clear up any personal things which Dick may have left behind there, and I must locate D Bassett in order to pay off the van. The warden of the caravan park told me I could pay her, it was true, but instinctively I did not quite trust her, perhaps because she must have had contact with my enemy, the Finn, when he hired the neighbouring caravan from her. I preferred to deal with D Bassett direct.

I had already locked the van and was about to get into my car when I had second thoughts. I climbed into the car just the same, as if I had never had any other intention, but I did not drive away immediately as I had intended.

I backed up towards the van until I was as close as I could go. Then I opened the boot and loaded all of Dick's stuff into it, before I locked up again and drove slowly along the track towards the entrance to the park.

It was not kind-heartedness which made me want to give my assailant a day off from watching the van by showing, as clearly as I knew how, that I was going for good. I still had every intention of returning for the night. But I reckoned he might be less guarded if he thought I was gone, that if I could not find out what he was up to in any other way the best thing might be to encourage him to give himself away. With me apparently off the premises he might be less careful.

41

When I reached the caretaker's bungalow I drew up and knocked. Even if I did not leave the key with her I must look as if I had done so for the benefit of the Finn if he was still watching. She appeared to be just as grumpy at being disturbed as she had been the day before.

"I've cleared up my brother's things," I told her. "I'll get in touch with the owner, Mr Bassett, today."

"You'd better leave me the key then."

"I'd rather get in touch with Mr Bassett first," I answered. It was a feeble reason for keeping it, but I could think of no other. "I see the van next door is occupied, number 135?"

"No. Someone's had the key to look at it for a friend, that's all."

"Has he decided to have it?"

"Dunno yet, he hasn't been back." She was grumbling again; she enjoyed it and it made her talk. "I'll 'ave ter go and get it off of 'im this evening, I suppose. Anyway it shouldn't be difficult as 'e lives in another van. I expect 'e's only waiting for me to go an' fetch it, lazy bastard."

"Oh," I said, doing my best to sound as if it was of no interest to me, as if I was just going on talking because I enjoyed a chat. "That would explain it: it struck me as funny that the lights were only on for a short time early in the evening, as if he'd either gone to bed very early or just been visiting. Where does he live, the fellow who's been looking at it? Where is his van?"

"Just round the corner, number 47. The worst pitch here, I reckon. It's cold and it's windy and it's out of the way. But there's some as likes that sort of thing, I suppose."

"Yes, no accounting for taste, is there?" I had got more out of her than I had expected: it seemed too easy. "Anyway, it's a nice place you've got here, isn't it?"

"It is that. You should see it in the summer, it's a bit livelier then, I can tell you. There's some as 'ave been coming here for years, and not just for the 'olidays, but every weekend, regular

42

as clockwork, right through from Easter till the winter. You can understand it too, when you know the places they come from. Nothing like a breath of fresh sea air if you live in the middle of a town, is there?"

While talking I had had an eye on the track out of the park, but I could see no signs of my watcher, nor could I see any signs of him as I left the caretaker and drove slowly away. Perhaps I was only of interest to him while I was in the caravan park - but if so, why? Or could it be that now he had found whatever it was that Dick had left for me he no longer had any need to bother himself with me?

Once in the village I stopped at a telephone kiosk. I dialled 192 for enquiries, and while I waited for a reply I watched the traffic thundering through. Eventually my call was answered and I asked for the number of D Bassett, 13 Montrose Crescent, Peterborough.

She could find no number.

Perhaps I had the initials wrong: the old woman at the caravan park was quite capable of making a mistake. The girl at Directory Enquiries was helpful, as helpful as I could have wished, but after she had told me she had looked through the rest of the Bassetts and had noticed none who lived at 13 Montrose Crescent I had to conclude that D Bassett was not on the telephone. I was not altogether surprised, nor altogether disappointed. I had time to go to Peterborough and back during the day; I was not averse to meeting D Bassett, and there was another call in that direction which I thought I might make if I had time.

I did not go straight to Burbidge's. I stopped in King's Lynn on the way, just to make sure that the arrangements for the cremation were all correct. I ordered an extra bunch of flowers for Dick. I suddenly had visions of finding that the wreath I had already ordered would be the only one, for though I knew Dick well enough I did not know a great deal about him: he was too reticent for that. When I came to think about it I was not aware

43

whether there would be a dozen other bunches of flowers or one, a dozen other mourners or none. He had friends, I knew, but I did not know how close they were, nor - because Dick himself was so reticent - whether they would be equally reticent and just not come to the funeral.

It was a slow business. By the time I had succeeded in parking and found my way round King's Lynn the best part of two hours had passed.

I had been told that Burbidge's depot was off the Sutton Bridge Road, not far short of Sutton Bridge itself. I had no difficulty in finding the turning off the A17 as an enormous sign indicated "Burbidge's - Construction Traffic" and the side road had the hallmark of all such roads: a coat of dirt and grit which had fallen from lorries as they turned into it.

The road had been widened; there must be, or have been, a lot of traffic to justify that.

I had only just started down it when a rhythmic bumping, gentle to begin with but rapidly increasing until I was in no doubt what was causing it, told me I had a puncture. I slowed and then stopped.

The near-side rear tyre was flat.

I took out the jack and spanner, felt for the hole under the car into which the jack fitted, and started to unscrew the nuts. But they had been tightened with a power-driven spanner and two of them would not move. Try as I would, all I managed to do was bend the spanner: the nuts were stuck fast.

I straightened and looked round.

On the opposite side of the road, about fifty yards back, was a group of farm buildings opening out of a small courtyard with one of its sides to the road. Parked in the courtyard was a blue car, so with luck there would be someone around, even though I could see no farmhouse.

44

I walked back up the road, carrying one of the nuts which I had succeeded in dislodging so that I could try it for size if I was lucky enough to find a source of spanners.

The buildings on two sides of the yard were obviously used for storage only. The third had double doors at its front, and between them a glimmer of electric light. I banged, and waited, and then pulled one of them. It swung open.

A man was approaching the door in response to my knocking. He was only two or three yards away from me, a farm hand, dressed for the winter weather on an open, windswept, fenland farm.

I explained why I had come, and he took the nut from my hand, went to a bench at one side, and started trying it in a series of big, workman-like, spanners hanging on a wall behind it. While he was busy I looked round.

I could not have found a better place to come. The shed was a workshop. A space inside the door, big enough for a piece of farm machinery, was surrounded by the paraphernalia of the trade: benches, power tools, a welding machine and, overhead, a gantry for lifting engines and other heavy parts in and out of machines. In a corner at one side of the doors I noticed, as I started to leave with the spanner which the man had picked out for me, a jumble of equipment which I did not immediately identify. As I walked back towards the car carrying the spanner I had been lent, I realised what it was: mine-detectors, of the kind you buy in the shops to find metal objects under the ground.

I glanced at them again when I went back to return the spanner. There seemed to be a lot of them, many in pieces. I pointed as I went out and said conversationally:

"Do you use them? And do you ever find anything?"

"Not me," he answered. "Them's Mr Holden's toys; he plays with them." He gave me a gap-toothed grin, and I thanked him and returned to the car.

Burbidge's depot consisted of a large enclosure containing huts, vehicles, plant and equipment. It was surrounded by a high chain-link fence topped with a still higher angled piece of fence threaded with barbed wire. At intervals round the perimeter were floodlights fitted to tall posts.

I drove through the gates and parked.

The huts were at the same time both shabby and smart. Their structure was shabby, their plywood sides patched and the ridges undulated from end to end. But they had been painted recently, so that the general effect was of glossy new orange paint.

I made for a door labelled 'Enquiries.' I asked for Mr Waters and was told that Eric was in the far hut on the opposite side of the compound. The girl spat out the last letter of his name in a way I had never met until I came to King's Lynn, a sharp click from the back of the mouth, coming just when she appeared to have finished saying the name.

I asked for Mr Waters again when I reached the hut, picking my way between puddles spotted by drizzle, and this time I was told that Eric, with the same delayed action click, was in 'there'. I went through the door indicated by the jerk of the head, and found him.

"What can I do for you?" he asked when I had reminded him who I was. "I've been clearing up Dick's belongings and I came round in case he had left any of his private things here."

"We'd better have a look."

Mr Waters seemed impassive and impersonal, but he also seemed to be a man of action. He had attended the inquest, and now he lost no time in leading me across to the table in another hut which Dick had used as his desk. As I had expected we found nothing apart from a few drawing instruments and a photo of Dick at work evidently taken by the local press at some stage. Waters insisted on giving them all to me.

"A bad business," he commented when we had finished.

46

"I shall miss him. In fact I wouldn't be here now if he was still alive."

"You don't work here normally then?"

"No, I'm based at our Head Office, that's in Malden, though I've been up here for a few weeks now. What about you? You don't live round here, do you?"

"No, but I come from Surrey, too, near Guildford."

"And you'll be going back there as soon as the funeral's over?"

"I suppose so."

"You'd better," he rejoined. "There's nothing to do up here at this time of year. I expect you'll have a job to get back to as well? Are you in the same line of business as Dick was?"

"No, I'm a draughtsman, an electrical one." I saw no reason to add that I might have been in the same line of business if I had been any good at passing exams. But I had not the persistence, the clear-headedness of Dick. He had gone through all the technical exams without any hitches: it never occurred to him or to me that he might fail them. He worked steadily and methodically, he remembered what he had learned, he could churn it back to them on paper in the examination room, and he was a qualified surveyor.

But I had ploughed the first paper I had tried, and then I had been offered a job, so I had taken it. It suited me well enough though. I was competent at it now and, at last, I knew it. So, fortunately, did enough people who came to me with work to be done. Being freelance and self-employed now I could keep myself to myself, which suited me, and I could work hard when the work came in, and I need not pretend to work hard when it did not. I used to worry when it did not come, but now I found I had to work hard most of the time. However I enjoyed it, and since I had got myself a telephone extension to a local electrical contractor, who took messages for me when I was out in return for which I buckled down to his work when he wanted it in a hurry, I had found my life was much better managed. I could get away from it when I wanted, and I had only to tell the office that I was 'out' and I could settle down to an urgent piece of work undisturbed if I needed to do so.

When we came out of Dick's hut I looked out of the gates, northwards, towards the sea. An arable field, tinged green with winter corn, separated us from the inevitable earth embankment. There was nothing else to be seen, except sky, grey, lots of it.

"Where are those reservoirs you're making?" I asked. "Over there?" I nodded towards the embankment.

"Yes."

"How do you get there?"

"We have a jetty for small boats near the mouth of the river. It's quite convenient, just up the road." He looked at his watch. "I must get on," he said. "I have to see to a few things out there, and if I don't start soon the tide will be against me. It takes much longer then." He held out a hand towards me, but I did not take it.

"That's all right," I answered. "I'll come too. You don't mind a passenger, do you? I'd like to see what Dick was up to." I was suddenly curious to see these reservoirs which Dick had been working on, and I should still have time to get to Peterborough and back before dark.

Waters looked as if he was going to refuse to take me and just because I thought he was going to do so I started to prepare my counter-arguments to persuade him, beginning with his duty towards Dick. But either I was wrong or he changed his mind.

"Come on, then," he said, but he did not say it with a good grace.

We drove to the jetty, all of a hundred yards. It was a narrow pontoon, rising and falling with the tide and kept in position by stakes driven into the riverbed. The boat to which he led me was open, no more than a dinghy, but it had a motor, and as we emerged from the river mouth I was able to appreciate the thickness of the vivid orange coat which Waters insisted I should wear. It matched the colour of the huts and had Burbidge's name printed in large letters across its back.

"You'll freeze without it," he told me, and he was right: even with it I was not far from freezing.

As soon as we emerged from the river mouth I could see the reservoirs, one on each side of us with the river channel dead straight between them. The one on the right had the appearance of being more nearly finished. Its side seemed to have a regular, straight, top to it, while the one opposite was irregular and it looked rough and muddy.

Waters turned right, away from the river, passing close to the south side of one of the reservoirs and leaving on our right a low-lying marsh cut by random muddy channels running through the sea-covered vegetation.

Before long we stopped at another pontoon, fixed to the south side of the reservoir, and we climbed concrete steps to its top. It was immense. At its far side was an ant-like figure beside some machinery, and further away was a break in the reservoir wall, looking as if the sea had already started to demolish Burbidge's work before they had finished it. But as we came nearer the whole thing looked much more as I would have expected: cranes, drag-lines, huts, and silos, together with a coaster which was moored and delivering materials.

"I expected to see dredgers at work," I said to Waters.

"We don't use the kind of dredger you're thinking of," he answered. "There's one of ours," he pointed to it, "it's really a big turbine: it has a hose which stretches to the place where we are working, and then another which goes out to sea. It pumps sand and water and small rubbish to wherever we want to put the stuff. That's why we haven't finished the side of the reservoir over there." He pointed to the gap which I had already noticed. "You have to allow the water to come in again so that there's enough inside to be pumped out with the mud and sand through the dredger."

We stood in silence as Waters looked round. "I'd like to go as far as the dredger," he said, "It's a bit windy out there. I'll pick you up on my way back. OK?"

"No, I'll come with you," I answered. If I was going to get cold anyway I might as well have a change of scenery. Waters was annoyed, and for a moment it looked as if he would tell me to stay, but he evidently thought better of it, so we set off.

"Will you be reclaiming those marshes?" I asked, nodding towards the muddy expanse beside us.

"Not us," he answered "at least, it's not part of our present contract."

We started again, back the way we had come, but turning right when we met the main channel from Wisbech instead of left. We chugged northwards for some time between the two reservoirs until finally reaching the sea, bounded by dim shapes on each side, Lincolnshire to the left, Norfolk to the right. Waters turned right, hugging the seaward side of the reservoir, stopping where there was an iron ladder and bars for mooring. He tipped out fenders, tied up, and climbed the ladder with me after him, and then introduced me to Barry, the man who had seemed so ant-like from a distance but was enormous close-to.

"How's it going?" Waters asked him as he turned to me to explain: "We've been having trouble with the dredger recently. There's a mesh cage over the inlet to catch anything which might jam the pipe, and lately it seems to have been more sensitive.

"It's better," answered the big man, "We've hardly lost any time today," but at that moment the tone of the engine changed: it was struggling and overloaded, and Barry stopped to close the throttle.

From where we stood the dredger's pipe dived off the wall, held on the surface by floats, and at its end, about a hundred yards away, was a contraption which looked like a cross between a raft and a boat. Sitting in the middle was a figure, clad in the inevitable bright orange coat. As we watched he rose from his seat and took a few steps away from us. Presently he stood again, waving some small branches from a tree towards us. These he dropped into the boat beside him, together with another object we could not identify from where we sat.

Meanwhile Waters had opened a box he was carrying. From it he took a new guard for the end of the dredger's hosepipe, tied a cord to it, and threw it to the man in the boat, who had been concentrating so hard on his work that he had not looked at us.

When he looked up he was as surprised to see me as I was to see him.

It was my neighbour from the caravan park, the Finn.

Chapter 5

It took an hour to reach Peterborough, and it was not a pleasant hour. It was not quite raining, but it was a damp, soft, day. The windscreen washer had to work hard, and before I was halfway, I was peering through a patch of glass edged with thick mud. Everything was grey: sky, fields, road; even the air was heavy with greyness.

Montrose Crescent was on a municipal housing estate, not one of the modern ones pushed up in a hurry by the Development Corporation, but a row of uniform dirty stucco houses. They were set well apart and must have been more spacious than some of the houses I passed on my way, but they were marked by the same monotony. However it was relieved, as far as number 13 was concerned, by the neighbour's front garden, laid out exclusively with exquisitely tended roses: bushes, trees, climbers, ramblers, each with a neat circle of farmyard manure at its base.

Rather to my surprise D. Bassett was in. Also to my surprise D. Bassett was female.

She had heard about Dick. She had noticed his name in the local paper. Such a nice boy, she told me, and who'd have believed it? But there now, these days you just couldn't tell what was going to happen, could you? She didn't know what the world was coming to. She knew what it was like for me though. She had had death in the family, only last year, when her husband had died. A good man, he had been; he'd looked after her proper for 38 years almost to the day, and even now he was still looking after her; those two caravans down at Sherningham Beach, they were a real comfort, they were. They weren't no trouble, for old Mrs Ackroyd who looked after the caravan park fixed her up with people who took them all through the summer. She didn't have to worry about them at all, for Mrs Ackroyd was that good; and it was just as well, wasn't it, seeing as how she'd had to give up the car since her husband had died? Not that she could drive even if she had been able to keep it on - and to get to the caravans by bus was pretty near impossible; they only ran every two hours as far as Lynn, and then you had to take the Hunstanton bus as far as Sherningham, and even when you reached Sherningham there was still a two mile walk down to the Beach, and at her age she couldn't be expected to do that every day, could she?

Still, I put in, wishing to make my own contribution to what had become a monologue, it must be nice for her to be able to go there for a week or two in the summer?

Not a bit of it, she wouldn't go there no more, not now her husband was gone. It was he as had liked the place. Of course she'd gone along with him, seeing as he'd been so fond of it, but no, she wasn't going there no more. She was born and bred in Peterborough, she was, and she'd rather stay there. But because of the caravans she had enough money and to spare, and when she wanted to go down to Swanage to stay with her grown-up daughter, the one what had married the boy in the army, she could do it without wondering where the pennies was coming from.

"Funny," she said at last. "You're not a bit like your brother. He was big, wasn't he and dark? Fact is, I'd never 'ave known you was from the same family. Still, there's one thing you've done the same: you've both come to see me, and there's not many as takes the trouble to do that, I can tell you."

"Dick was always thoughtful, and he kept the caravan beautifully," I answered, and then I went on: "what happens about repairs when they become necessary - and replacing broken crockery, and that kind of thing?" I pictured slashed cushions and ripped panels, as I spoke, and a sea of kapok covering everything.

"Mrs Ackroyd looks after all that," she answered. "She's that good, she is, I don't 'ave ter worry about nothing."

I wondered if she would be left without worries this time. They were not ordinary run-of-the-mill repairs which Mrs

Ackroyd was going to have to deal with. But I saw no point in telling her. After all, the van which had been broken up was not on my pitch, it was on number 135, next door, and even if I told her, what could she do? She'd be worried to death, and if I said nothing Mrs Ackroyd would have the damage attended to and then let Mrs Bassett know afterwards, when it would no longer be such a worry.

"And the van next door, is that let at present?" I asked. "Or has it been let in the last few months, since Dick was there?"

"No. I've been lucky to have one of 'em bringing in the money in the winter, let alone the two. Funny, though," she added, "your brother asked that, too."

So, if Dick had come all the way to Peterborough to ask about the van next door it looked as if he might have been watched from it too, and as if he also had come to regard Mrs Ackroyd as a source of information not altogether to be relied on. It was a funny thing about her: I could not put my finger on it, but instinctively I felt a need to verify what she told me. Dick had felt the same.

I left Mrs Bassett eventually, still standing in the same place outside her front door. She had never asked me in, and if I had not left then she would have stood there just as happily for the next hour in the same way, as likely as not repeating the same things.

***

I did not drive straight back to King's Lynn. I followed the signs for the A1, and once I had reached it I turned southwards. At St Neot's I turned off again and made for the Council Offices.

"Le Poidevin?" Yes, there were two council properties occupied by people of that name. An uncommon one, wasn't it, at least round here? But with so many people from London you got all sorts nowadays. I did not trouble to say that it was a common enough name in the Channel lslands.

"I know them both," I said, "parents and son. They moved up here from London a year or two back. It's the parents I want. Can you give me their address?"

St Neot's was another London overspill town, and I knew that the two households had moved up together.

"Can't tell, I'm afraid. But they're in the same road so they can't be far apart."

I was given the addresses, and set out, once again driving through rows of houses designed by GLC architects.

I chose the right house first time.

Nance opened the door, and when she had got over her surprise she was all over me.

"Well I never! Years without a sight of either of you, and now you both turn up on my doorstep within three weeks of each other!"

"Dick's been, too, has he?"

"How long ago would that be, now? Three weeks did I say? - more like two."

"Have you heard about him, since then?"

"Heard? Heard what?" The bounce was suddenly out of her. She could see in in my face that there was something behind my question. I told her.

"Dick!" she exclaimed. "It's not possible."

And suddenly, then and there, she burst into a fit of uncontrolled tears. Gathering her apron about her eyes she made her way back into the house, tottering through the door into the immaculate sitting room, slumping into a chair, to sit there, sobbing. I sat too, in the chair opposite her, waiting.

She was just the same, I reflected, but older. Her emotions were still just as near the surface. She was still just as concerned about Dick as she had been on the day he had been delivered to her by the social worker, a scruffy, silent, bullied twelve year old. He had stayed with the le Poidevins for four years, and she had been the nearest thing he had ever had to a mother, kind and caring, spoiling and stupid. But she was concerned; she was concerned about everything to do with Dick, just as she had been concerned about everything to do with all her foster children, about everyone she had ever come across. If it had been I who had drowned I did not doubt that the flood of tears and the fit of sobbing would have been just the same, and no less genuine for that, even though she had never fostered me.

Eventually the sobs which jerked the big comfortable body gradually became fewer, and then they stopped altogether. After that I had to tell her all about it, not once but twice, and then once again.

By the time I left she had written down the date and time and place of the funeral. Percy would take her to it, she told me, and I did not doubt it. Her son would take a day off work when he was told to by his mother and the three of them would be there, Nance, her husband Fred, and Perce. Perce's wife would have been there too, except that she had to stay behind to nurse the latest arrival, their fifth child, born only two weeks earlier.

"I'll tell Dick's father, too," she said as I was leaving.

"Dick's father?" She must have made a mistake. Dick's father had ceased to exist as far as I was concerned, as far as Dick was concerned, so long ago that I had put him completely out of my mind.

"Yes," she answered, "Dick's father. He suddenly turned up. Didn't you know? Didn't Dick tell you?"

Dick's father! It could not be true. He had no business to turn up like that, in fact it was positively sinister, that he should have disappeared from Dick's life when he came into the world only to reappear when he left it again.

"He came round only a couple of days ago," Nance went on. "He told me who he was and he asked ever so many questions about Dick: where he was, whether he was married, and about his friends, and so on. He said he'd go straight on to Dick, seeing he wasn't so far away. I suppose he must have done, but I never saw Dick again, so I don't know. Then he gave me his address - he said it would be just as well in case I ever needed to get in touch with him."

"Strange. Why should he want to do that if he was on his way to see Dick?"

She was rummaging in a pile of papers she had taken from a cupboard against the far wall of the living room. "Here it is," she exclaimed, "here's his address," and she handed me a piece of paper.

"Laurence Smith," it said, "c/o Midland Bank Ltd., High Street, Islington."

I handed it back. I was still stunned by what she had told me; that Dick's father had turned up after all these years. It did not seem possible. What was more, it did not seem right. It was just like everything I had imagined about him too; a faceless man, with a name so common that no one would notice it, leaving nothing more traceable than a forwarding address. It was in character with someone who could not be bothered with his own son and found it more convenient to abandon him for other people to bring up. But why should he turn up now? It was uncanny that he should do so just as Dick had died.

"I'll write and tell him," she said. It suited me. I don't think I could have brought myself to write to him, even though I knew I ought to do so if I had his address. Nance had taken the task out of my hands though, and I need have no doubt that she would carry it out; you only had to meet her once to realise she was the kind of woman you could rely on.

As I approached Sherningham again it was dark as well as wet, but at least the drab greyness of the weather was hidden by the night.

I decided to eat in the caravan. If I could not stand my own company for the evening I would go into King's Lynn to the cinema, or bury myself in one of Dick's who-dunnits ... or even reconnoitre. I might take a look at the isolated caravan in which my watcher lived.

I stopped in the middle of the village to buy some food.

The shop was stacked high. It was divided in two by a set of shelves which rose as far as the ceiling and I had to pick my way round the inadequate gangway left between shelves and walls, careful not to knock over piles of merchandise for which no space had been found on the shelves. Outside the shop door, as I set off with my purchases, I nearly bumped into Sally. She was followed by her mother.

Her eye fell on the frozen cottage pie I held, and on the tin of peaches. "You're not going off to eat those, all on your own, in that miserable caravan?" she exclaimed. "Come and have a meal with us."

"Yes, you must," her mother chorused as she came up beside Sally.

"Well..." I said, it was tempting. I had forgotten all about Sally during the day. But here she was, small, lively, greeting me with those big, expressive, blue eyes of hers. The contrast between her warm bright home and the dank unheated caravan towards which I was going, would have been enough to make anyone hesitate. Just looking at her made me forget my preoccupations. It was a luxury just to do that, and here they were inviting me - urging me - to take a longer look.

"Well," I started ... habits die hard, and caution was a habit with me almost as much as with Dick. "Well, I've just bought my supper. And I've things I must do." Things? What things?

"Come on," she persisted. "They can wait. It must be awful, that caravan, at this time of year. Come on."

"But I've got to go down there, just to sort things out." I remembered that I had removed everything that morning and I would have to put them back, at least the ones I would need for the night. "I must, really."

58

"And when you've done that you must come straight back to us. Promise?" She would not be put off. "Come on: promise?" "Well...."

"Good," she broke in promptly. "That's settled, then. And just to make sure you can't have second thoughts, I'll take charge of those, shall I?" And quickly and firmly she leant forward and took the things I had just bought from my hands.

"All right," I felt relieved, light headed. "You win." I touched her hand as she reached for my tin of peaches. "I'll come - if I can. I'll be right back." And I was not dreaming: there really was a look of anxiety in her eyes when I said "if I can".

The caravan park seemed just as deserted as ever, with only a dim light in Mrs Ackroyd's window and two of the caravans. My neighbour's van, number 135, was plunged in darkness.

I parked quickly, drawing up with the boot of the car not far from the van.

The parking lights shone dimly on the door, enough to guide my hand with the key as I pushed it into the lock.

It would not go.

I pulled it out and tried again, pushing harder this time. It did not fit.

Definitely, it did not fit.

I descended from the steps and examined the key to make sure I was using the right one. I was. It was the key which my attacker had thoughtfully left for me in the place of the one which the police had provided me with.

I looked up at the door, and then I ascended the steps once more and examined the side of the van. The scratch made by the steps when they slipped was there - but it was on the join between the white and the blue paint.

The vans had been changed again! And with this discovery came all the anxiety, and the empty feeling in the pit of my stomach, with which I now associated the caravan and the park.

I had not even taken my old precaution with the spanner, but now I did so.

I returned to the car and dropped it into my pocket, handy, just at my finger-tips. Then I returned to the door with the other key.

It fitted.

What if somebody was waiting for me again? In the dark, and standing above me, he would have me at his mercy. I had no torch, nor even matches. But of course: the matches must be in the boot of the car, along with the food and other things I had taken from the kitchen.

It did not take long to find them.

I unlocked the door, pulled it open, and stood back, my fingers on the spanner. There was nothing to see, except for the black void of the doorway.

My hands shook so much, with fear as well as cold, that it took me some time to strike a match.

Shielding its glare from my eyes I held it in front of me, slowly approaching the door of the van. By the time it burnt out I had held it inside the doorway, and I had been able to see that there was nobody in view from there.

Two matches later I had looked as far as the kitchen, and turned on the electric light. Nobody was there, nor in the living room. But the van was just as much of a wreck as it had been last time I had seen its slit cushions, broken panels, capok everywhere.

At least my pulse rate was going down again.

Two things struck me. One was that a night in that caravan would be impossible.

The second was that this broken van was mine again now, the one I must return to Mrs Bassett, or Mrs Ackroyd.

First things first: if I was not to sleep in my van it would have to be in number 135. I had its key, too, and it did not take me long to establish that, apart from its position, it was unchanged from the morning. It would be bad luck if my attacker decided he must renew his watch by joining me in his (my?) caravan. I did not like that idea at all, and I blessed Sally for insisting that I should at least come up and have a meal with her. After that perhaps I would find a hotel, but first, even with my nerves once again on edge, I was determined to do one other thing before I left the park.

I locked both vans. I drove slowly towards the entrance, then veered left and turned round to face the way out of the park. I stopped beside the track, switched out the lights and locked up. Then I set off, keeping away from the track, and moving as silently as I knew how towards the spot which Mrs Ackroyd had indicated as the regular pitch of my watcher.

It was not far, and its lights were on. Keeping my distance I went round it, looking to see if there were any gaps between the curtains through which I might look. I found a small chink in the middle of the big window which every caravan had at one end.

Cautiously I approached, careful not to scrape my feet on the ground or kick any loose stones.

It was a small crack, but big enough to see through. And the thing which greeted me was the sight of the man whose face I knew all too well by now, the face which I had last seen looking up at Waters from the raft in the reservoir. He was coming in from the kitchen at the far end of the van, carrying two cups.

Instinctively I ducked.

He could not have seen me, hidden by the dark, but the impulse to hide by shrinking below the level of the window was overwhelming. Then slowly I straightened again.

He was out of sight. All I could see was a pair of hands at each side of the table, men's hands, each cradling a cup which held some steaming liquid and which disappeared from my view intermittently as each was borne upwards to its owner's lips.

I must have been only three feet from them. I stood, and looked, and waited, and listened.

For some time there was silence. Then a voice came. It was slightly muffled, but I could distinguish every word clearly; caravans are not built for soundproofing.

"He's gone, then? You're sure of it?"

"That's what I said."

I recognised one of the voices, the one which spoke second. I had heard it before, asking for matches, returning matches, shouting from a raft ...

"How do you know he's not back? Or that he's not coming back?"

"He wasn't there half an hour ago. And if he came straight from the reservoir he'd have been back hours ago. Eric must have set him on dry land all of four hours ago, I'd say." Eric, I repeated the name to myself in the way I had just heard it, this man, whoever he was, was no local; he did not spit out the hard c in the way the King's Lynn people did, in the way the people in Burbidge's offices had done. The voice went on "Besides, he took his stuff with him this morning. I told you that. I reckon we must have frightened him off. He must be staying in a pub for the night."

"He won't be far away at all events. He won't leave before the funeral, but after that we'll be free of him."

"All the same, Eric shouldn't have taken him out to the dredger today, that wasn't clever."

"Eric said he couldn't help it, not without having a row. He said the man insisted, practically forced himself on to the boat."

"Mm ... He shouldn't have allowed it."

"Anyway," the voice I knew said, "if the man does come back he won't have much of a night of it, not with the van in the state I left it. You should have seen it. Practically pulled it to pieces, I did."

"That wasn't too clever, either. You should have left it till tomorrow, when we know he'll have gone. Still, with any luck it won't do any harm, it's the kind of thing any vandals might do, and it'll probably be some time before old ma Ackroyd finds it - lazy old bitch."

A silence followed which was broken this time not by the voices I had been listening to, but by the arrival of a car. I had heard it approaching, but I had paid little attention standing, as I was, in a side alley of the caravan park.

When it came round the corner of the track though, its headlights were turned full up and pierced the air like a pair of searchlights, catching the moisture in it and flickering across an arc as it rounded the bend in the track, creating deep shadows here and dazzling patches of brightness there.

Again I ducked instinctively, and as I did so I heard the caravan's occupants struggling along the bench seats to stand up clear of the table between them.

I thanked my stars that the big window was at the far end, facing towards the sea and away from the track, so that I was not caught by the headlamps, helpless as an aeroplane in the beams of a searchlight.

The dark shadow cast by the van moved sideways as the car approached and drew up on the far side.

As soon as it was stationary, I moved. I dashed away, keeping in the long shaft of shadow, trusting the dying noise of the car's engine to drown any sounds I made, away and up the bank of the sea defences. At the top I threw myself to the ground, flattening myself against its surface and slithering down the other side. Then I lay still.

I heard the car door slam. I heard footsteps approach the caravan, and at the same time I heard the caravan door open and I heard muffled voices, the words no longer distinguishable. But though the words were not distinct I could catch their general tone: no excitement showed through it, and I breathed more easily as I made sure I had not been noticed.

Now that I was out of sight of the artificial lights, I was conscious of the damp greyness of the air about me, laden with moisture near the ground but clear enough above for me to distinguish a hazy cluster of stars immediately overhead.

I was between the two banks built to keep the high tides out. Beyond one was the caravan I had just left, beyond the other the sea; either it was so calm that it made no noise, or the tide was out and the nearest water a mile away, beyond the mud. Underfoot the ground was covered by short grass, broken by patches of shingle and bigger tufts of vegetation.

Cautiously I started walking. I walked southwards, parallel with the embankments, towards the main body of the caravan park.

When I judged I had gone thirty yards or so I crawled up the landward embankment and peeped cautiously over it.

To my left were the car and the caravan which I had just left in such a hurry. The track towards them, along which the car had arrived, must veer away from me, obliquely, until it was hidden by some rough ground. Further to my right was the black mass of the toilet block.

The driver had left his sidelights on, and I watched the caravan windows darken and the car lights flicker as black shadows passed to and fro. Then I heard the engine start and I watched the car turn, backing in front of the caravan, before the headlights came up once more and it started on its way along the track.

But it did not go on.

First it slowed, then it stopped, then it backed again. It halted at a slight angle to the track.

Through the tops of some birches, I could see why, the headlights of the car shone straight at another car parked beside the track, a grey Cortina with a black roof: mine.

There were noises of doors opening and slamming and a figure, two figures, appeared in the beams of the headlamps, examining my car and peering through the windows. Then they retired from the brightness, and I could hear the low sound of voices.

They did not continue for long. Presently I heard more opening and shutting of doors, the engine started again, and this time it did not stop until it had faded into the distance.

But what I did not know was how many were in the car now. It had started with three in it, of that I was sure, for I had seen them leaving the caravan before turning its light out, but for all I could tell it might have continued with two, or even one, my old friend having been left behind to continue the task which he had apparently been set and which they had thought, until they saw my car, he had finished. I cursed the fact that I had not left it in a more inconspicuous place; even if I had left it on my own caravan pitch it would not have been noticed.

Anyway, of one thing I could be sure. My eyes were by now accustomed to the dark; the eyes of anyone left behind by the car would still be conditioned by the blinding artificial light of its headlamps. If my watcher had stayed, now was the moment when I ought to move, when I had the advantage over him. If I did that the watcher could be watched, but if I delayed I might be too late.

I hugged the ground as I slithered over the top of the embankment, exposing myself for as short a time as possible on the skyline. In any case, I thought it unlikely I would be seen there, the ground mist would help to obscure me, and the chances of the watcher happening to look that way, and of his eyes yet being good enough to see me, were remote. Once over, I made my way forward as quickly and as silently as possible.

I had already seen the branches of trees, silhouetted against the car headlights when it had stopped to examine my car, and I was dimly aware of a small patch of broken ground in which they grew. It was in a corner near the toilet block, too small and awkward in shape to accommodate a caravan. It was just what I wanted - if it did not trip me up.

I came to its edge, a jumble of black shadows hardly relieved by any bright patches. So I skirted its edge, keeping to a track along the side of the toilet block. Then, when I was nearly at the front of the toilets, I slowed, sank to the ground, and edged to my left, crawling, creeping, and finally lying against the trunk of one of the small trees. I felt breathless but triumphant. If there was anybody in front of me, waiting and watching, I would be astonished if he had seen me or heard me. Not bad for someone who had never been a boy scout, who had never practiced stealth in his life before!

Waiting was a cold business. The chill and the damp seeped in, and after a time I started to wonder if my teeth could be heard chattering. I wore an anorak, but I was not dressed for a motionless night out in February. I comforted myself that it must be just as bad for the other man, perhaps even worse, for he did not know I was there and for all he knew he might be condemned to a whole night out, fruitlessly spent watching an empty car.

Or was I the one who was doing that? Maybe they had all gone on. Maybe I was the one who was fruitlessly watching an empty car - and foolishly, too: watching my own empty car, too frightened to get into it.

And what if the watcher was there? Why should he want to stop me? Surely all he would want was to be sure that I had gone. Would he not be only too thankful to see me gone? Then he would be able to go too. Then he would be able to get out of the freezing cold night, back into the warmth of his own caravan.

But even as I told myself this, I knew that things had changed.

After the initial attack all he could have been watching me for was to see that I had gone and that in the meantime I had discovered nothing; found nothing behind the panels, nothing of what they were up to, nothing of who they were.

But now the game had changed. They had seen my car, parked no longer in an innocent position, and they must be wondering why. It was no good repeating to myself how foolish I had been to leave it there, surreptitiously, instead of openly and where I had every reason to leave it; how, if I had done the obvious and sensible thing, I would have no reason to be afraid. I had done it. And my watcher knew it. And I was afraid.

Moreover if he was waiting out there in the darkness for me he must know as well as I did that the game had changed. It did not take much intelligence to guess that I must be around, that if I was around I had probably seen him, that I may have overheard things and seen what company he kept.

He was probably armed once more with his chloroform pad, or with a brick, or with something worse. And perhaps it was not just 'he'. Perhaps two of them had stayed behind to make certain of me.

I do not know how long I waited. It seemed ages, but it was probably no more than half an hour.

Then he gave himself away.

I heard him first.

I heard the chink of gravel as he moved. He was somewhere over on the far side of the track, I thought, and he must have moved just to get himself in a more comfortable position.

I nearly jumped out of my skin when I suddenly found he was only six feet from me.

He was padding with soft feet along the strip of clear ground at the edge of the track, between the stones of its broken concrete surface and the gravel of the caravan pitches where they bordered it. He was crossing in front of me, from left to right, leaving my car, half left and on the far side of the track, and making his way slowly and silently away from it between the track and the toilet block.

67

Once again I felt the adrenalin flowing to every corner of my body, that painful sensation which I still disliked as much as ever, and which I had been halfway towards for the last hour.

I crept forward until I was three feet from the edge of the track. I looked up to my right, peering into the murky gloom, trying to pick out any clue, any shadow, which might show that he had stopped and was waiting for me. Nothing. All I could hear was the occasional drip as moisture fell from the twigs where it had settled and condensed from the air.

Infinitely slowly and silently I rose, turned left, and imitated his movements in the opposite direction to the one he had taken.

I prayed that he would be on his way to my caravan to see if I had returned there. That, surely, would be the natural thing for him to do if he had waited and watched for half an hour and heard nothing to indicate that I was still near the car.

But what if there were two of them? The second would be lying in wait for me at the car. He would have the benefit of surprise. If he attacked me I would not stand a chance.

Perhaps I ought to abandon the car and walk back to the village and civilisation. I could be sure of creeping away without being seen, whereas I could not be sure at all of regaining the car. Indeed, if there were two of them, I could be sure that that was just what I would not do; I could be sure of a brick on the head or a pad in the face, and of all that would follow it, whatever that might be.

I suppose one's judgement must be conditioned by one's physical condition more than one can appreciate.

At that moment I became a betting man, though I had never laid a bet in my life before. I laid odds of ten to one against their having left two watchers behind, and I laid odds of ten to one that the single watcher had gone off to inspect my caravan rather than that he had moved just to lure me into moving too.

Did that make the odds 100 to 1? Or 20 to 1?

I did not know, and I did not care, and I did not stay longer to think about it.

Purposefully but still as silently as I could I took five more paces beside the road, and four paces across it. By the time I reached the door of the car I had the key in my hand. Feeling for the keyhole silently with my left hand I guided the key home between finger and thumb, turned it, and in an instant I had opened the door, jumped in, slammed it behind me, and locked it. The stab of light which came on when I opened the door was blinding even though I knew from experience how dim it was. Blinding and revealing: anyone within a hundred yards must have seen and heard me.

I fumbled with the ignition key and the engine started first time. I switched the headlights on as I began to move. They were startlingly bright, but much more so for the other man, hurtling towards me down the middle of the track. His arm shot up to shield his eyes from the glare and he veered to one side, so I saw him only for a moment. Then I had swung to the left and was making for the entrance to the caravan park and for the road to the village. If he followed he would have a two mile run, for I had noticed no second car parked near his caravan. My only surprise was that it was Barry, not Jason; maybe they took it in turns.

Chapter 6

"That took you long enough," Sally started as she opened the door, pretty as a picture and silhouetted once more against the lights in the hall. Then she gasped. "Phew!" she exclaimed, "what on earth have you been up to this time?"

I glanced down the front of my clothes to see what she was staring at. When I saw the dirt clinging to the front of my anorak and trousers I grinned carelessly. I felt relaxed, artificially relaxed, after the strain of the last hour.

"Just crawling around," I grinned at her. "I've been playing cowboys and Indians down at the beach. Quite exciting. I'm not sure who won - not yet."

Her look of concern faded a little when she heard me joking like that. But not altogether.

"You'd better come in," she said, and at the same time she turned and the charming picture changed into the crippled, hobbling, girl.

I followed.

Voices came from one of the rooms.

I'm afraid we've started," she explained. "Dad's got to get off, and the rest of the family too. I'm afraid we couldn't wait any longer." Then she changed tack. "Come on into the kitchen," she ordered me. "We'll clean you up and get you your food."

Cleaning up consisted of my removing the anorak while she brushed my trousers with her hand to remove the loose dirt. I liked the attention. Then I washed my hands and face at the sink while she hung up the anorak and took a plate from the oven.

"Ready?" she asked, inspecting me.

"Lead on," I answered.

It is strange how a little excitement can buoy you up so far, but no further. Up to that moment I was feeling so full of myself, so exhilarated after the strain, that I would have said and done things which I would not have dreamed of in normal circumstances. If the opportunity had presented itself I am sure I would have gone on my knee and proposed to Sally - and so powerful was my feeling that everything was going my way that I was convinced at that moment she would have caught my mood and accepted me.

But the moment passed as soon as we crossed the threshold into the dining room.

They were all there, gathered round the table, with Sally's father at its head and her mother at its foot, all so prosperous, so assured, so secure.

And in a trice my euphoria was gone.

Sally's father rose from his chair, the polished host welcoming his guest.

The rest turned and looked at me, and their conversation died.

"Come on in," said her father. "Come on in and sit down." He indicated a chair for me between Sally's mother and the place where Sally had obviously been sitting before she had got up to open the front door to me. Then he sat down too, and picked up the spoon and fork with which he had been eating. They had reached their second course, while I was about to start my first.

"I'm so sorry we couldn't wait for you," Sally's mother went on as her husband started eating again. "You see, Don's giving a talk this evening, it's in King's Lynn and it starts at 7.30, so we just had to start. I'm sure you understand, though, don't you?"

"I'm so sorry," I answered. "I had no idea I'd be so long. If I had known I would never have said I would come." I sat down "You're all going, I suppose? I really am very sorry..."

I was interrupted by Margery. She looked alert and eager, and a smile hovered about her mouth. "What happened?" she asked, "Were you beaten up again?"

"Margery!" This was her father. Last time I had seen them none of them had used her full Christian name. He spoke so suddenly that we all looked towards him. "I'm sorry," he went on, realising the effect of his words, "but you know we were to keep it to ourselves. If ... if George says he doesn't want it to go any further it is up to us to keep his confidence." He turned to me. "That's right, isn't it?"

"Well," I answered, a little hesitantly. I had told Sally about it, but I had not actually asked her to keep it to herself; I had not stopped to think about that. On the other hand I realised, now that I really was thinking about it, that she had been quite right if that was what she had told them. The last thing I wanted was for it to reach the ears of the police. To have the police sniffing round me ... again ... no! Once was enough. "Yes," I said, "I really would rather it went no further if you don't mind." I glanced to my side, towards Sally. She looked relieved, I thought, to have her words - her guess about my own thoughts - confirmed in this way.

"Sorry." It was Marge speaking again. She still had that smile on her lips as she stretched across the table for the sugar. "No harm meant."

This time the smile was directed at me, and it was a clever one. She had all Sally's attractions, and no club foot, and she knew it. I said nothing in reply; I felt it would be disloyal to Sally to do so, and I felt Marge was dangerous: too slick, too gifted, too attractive. Definitely dangerous.

"We ought to leave in five minutes, I think." Sally's mother was a tactful woman, and practical. "If you all go on I'll stay while George finishes his supper." She turned to me. "Why don't you come, too? We could follow after the others in Sally's car. We would still be in time, and the others could keep seats for us."

"Nonsense," her husband retorted at once. "George doesn't want to come."

He had looked at me as he spoke, but now he said to his wife. "Winifred, I've told you before: you really must not suppose that because we are interested in the subject other people will be as well. If you can come on later, come by yourself; George might like to spend the evening here." He turned to me again.

"It would be more comfortable than that caravan of yours. What about it?" He was pressing and persuasive. I almost said yes, but Sally spoke first.

"No, I think you'd enjoy it, George. And as you're living in the district now, even if it's only for a day or two, you ought to take an interest in local things." She spoke in a more calm and matter of fact way than her parents. Then she said to her mother: "You know you can't manage that car of mine, Mum. I'll stay with George. It won't take him long to finish and we'll be with you quite quickly."

"I'd like to come," I said. "Thanks for suggesting it." I was about to add that I would take Sally in my car, rather than the other way round, when it occurred to me that if I did that I might be landed with her mother instead. That would never do.

And so it was settled. Marge said invitingly, "See you later," as she tripped from the room. Mrs Anderson had made a half-hearted attempt to persuade her to remain and come on with Sally and me, but she was not having it. And Mr Anderson had one more try at stopping me altogether - over-doing it, I thought. "Don't you bother to come," he said as he reappeared, clad in his coat and ready to go. "Don't you bother: I expect you'll only be bored. Why don't you just stay here and make yourself comfortable? There's some beer in the sideboard." He turned to Sally. "Come on, Sally. You come with us."

Mr Anderson's efforts to discourage me from coming really did seem to go beyond the normal solicitation of a host for his guest, and in order to do it he had come near to giving his wife a dressing down in front of a stranger, a stranger young enough to be their son. It seemed odd at the time, and inexplicable, though later when I recalled the incident I was able to make it more understandable.

Sally looked at me doubtfully for a moment after her father had spoken, but when I said firmly once again that I would come the contest was over. Quickly the rest were gone and just the two of us remained. I sat back and relaxed.

"That was kind of you, Sally. Thank you." I said to her.

"Not a bit. I really do think you'll enjoy it. Dad's a good speaker, and it's an interesting subject, you know. But he's diffident about it, too, and he can't believe sometimes that other people can be as interested as he is."

"No, I didn't mean that. I was thanking you for asking them to keep it to themselves, this business of my being knocked out. I might have said it myself, but I didn't. You must be a thought reader."

"Not me: it's Dad you must thank for that, too. It was he who insisted that if you didn't want to go to the police we should all keep quiet about it, even though I think you're wrong."

"Well, it was good of him, and I'm grateful. But you are a thought-reader, you know. I really do want to come, though it's nice of your father to suggest I should have the run of your house for the evening, especially as he doesn't know me from Adam. By the time you all came back I might have been gone, complete with the family silver." And, I added less flippantly to myself, if he only knew my record that was exactly what he should have expected.

But Sally was not listening.

"Now," she said in her calm way, turning her clear blue eyes on me. "Now you can tell me what happened? Why the mud on your clothes?"

I told her, more or less. I told her about the caravan, about how it had been changed for the one next door, broken up, and then returned to me. And I had to tell her something about my snooping round in the dark and the cold and the damp. But I did not quite tell her everything. I made light of the man who had been left to watch my car, of how frightened I had been, and of

74

how I was convinced that if I had been caught worse would have befallen me than last time. I did not tell her I had seen my watcher during the day at the reservoir. And I did not tell her about my trip to Peterborough and St Neot's, and about the reappearance of Dick's father. I had forgotten that last point for the time being, but it came back to me again: there was something wrong about it, something which did not ring true.

"Phew!" she said when I had finished. "You seem to attract it, don't you?

"You should be more careful, George. And one thing's settled, too: you can't go back to the Beach for the night, not with the choice either of a broken caravan, or of one which someone else might walk into at any moment. No: you're staying here tonight." When I started to protest she repeated it. "No, you might as well accept it - there's nothing else you can do. And what's more, we'll get your things into the spare room now, so that you can't argue afterwards. Come on."

There was no stopping her, and anyway I did not try very hard. I went through the motions, but I was half-hearted about it. And she knew it! I could see it in the sparkle of her eyes, and in the briskness with which she got up from the table and started me on my way to fetch my bags from the car while she went swiftly but awkwardly upstairs to make the bed.

But there was one fight which I did win. She capitulated quickly enough when I told her she was coming with me in my car. And when I made a point of leaning across, close to her, to fasten her seat belt she made no effort to stop me.

***

On the way to King's Lynn she started asking me about myself. Where did I live? Family? Job? It was not the conversation I would have chosen but she made it easy: she did not persist and probe when she came up against my reticence, she just worked round in another direction.

75

"But do you mean to say that you've never had a home, not until the last year or so?"

"Oh yes, I had one - until I was four. That was when my mother died."

"Since then though? You say you've been in foster homes? What have they been like? Surely they've been homes for you? That's the whole point of them, isn't it?"

"Sure, that's the point," I agreed with her, "but it doesn't always work out like that, you know. The worst one I was taken to ... I can still remember it vividly. Mrs Parker was the name of the woman, and she was all over the social worker who left me there. Too good to be true, she was, and I think the social worker suspected it, as well - but I daresay it's not always easy for them to find foster homes, nor to see through the ones they do find. Someone's always got to be the guinea pig, hasn't he? Anyway, as soon as Mrs Parker was left alone she locked me up, just like that: she said she had to go out for an hour or two. That was quite early in the morning. They came home in the evening, she and her husband. By then I'd cried my eyes out and I'd lost my appetite, even though I could have eaten a horse earlier in the day. But they made me eat: the husband stood over me until I did. They weren't stupid, those two. They knew they had to keep me reasonably well, or else I'd have been taken away from them, but they made it quite clear that all they were interested in was the money they got for me. When they were at home I had to keep out of their way, but I had to stay in the house - no running away, they said - and when it suited them they went out and locked me up. It was their good luck and my bad luck that the social worker never called when they'd left me behind - but then, I don't know if it would have made any difference if she had. By then I was cowed; I was so frightened that I doubt if I'd have raised my voice even if I'd known she was at the door. Anyway I couldn't have seen her from my room, and for all I knew it might have been a neighbour, or it might have been Mr or Mrs Parker come back just to make sure I really did keep quiet when anyone knocked. They'd told me they'd do that, and that they'd skin me alive if I made a sound. No, they had me where they wanted me."

"So what happened?"

"In the end I did run away. I hadn't intended to, but one day when Mrs Parker was at home I found I was outside when she wasn't looking, so I just went. I didn't think of the consequences. If I had I wouldn't have gone. And once I was out of her way I went for miles before I dared to speak to anyone: I was scared to death of being taken back if I hadn't gone far enough."

"And they didn't just send you straight back?"

"No. I think the social worker had her doubts. And anyway I must have been pretty convincing; I was that terrified."

"So then what?"

"A council home, and then another foster home."

"Better?"

"Much better, only I didn't realise it. I'd been so scared I didn't trust anyone. They tried hard enough, and looking back on it I don't think they were to blame.

"But after that I kept to myself. I did what I was told, and I kept out of the way. I still do that - at least I keep out of the way, even if I don't have to do what I'm told any longer. Not usually, anyway."

"And Dick? What happened to him?"

"He was luckier than I was, I think. At least he ended up with some nice people, but he was a bit like me: he kept himself to himself, too."

"Did you see much of each other?"

"It varied. When we were teenagers we did, and after that we were always good friends."

"But you weren't close?"

"Mm ... no, I suppose not, though I don't know of anyone who was closer, not unless Dick had friends I didn't know about, which would have been quite possible because we didn't see that much of each other."

Sally was sympathetic. "It doesn't sound much of a way to start life to me," she commented. "But you seem to have survived it all right?" She turned to me enquiringly, urging me to go on talking.

"Survived, yes," I answered. Then we drove in silence.

Chapter 7

The lecture was in a school. Sally knew her way, and she directed me to park in front of the building in a position reserved, according to a large notice, for staff only. It was dark and damp and chilly.

Inside she guided me along bare and echoing passages, limping beside me, until we came to the lecture room.

The door was in the side of the room. As we entered someone on a low platform at the end on our right rose to introduce the speaker, and the voices which we had heard as we approached died down. Hastily we found seats for ourselves. We were too late to join Sally's family at the front, so we sat at the side, near the door through which we had entered. Sally's mother had seen us come in and waved. Sally waved back.

I was glad we were not with them. I never go to the front, myself, and besides, I was not sorry to be away from Sally's family. They were the kind who would ask questions at the end and I would have felt like a fish out of water beside them.

The man on the platform had a soft voice, so soft that it was like a continuation of the murmurings of the audience before it died down.

The talk, he told us, was to the members of the King's Lynn and District History Society. He welcomed Mr Anderson, who was obviously well known to them, and he told us that the subject was 'King John: good or bad?'

Sally had told me that her father spoke well. Judged by the way he held attention for some time, even though I knew nothing of his subject and had no interest in it, she must have been right.

"King John was not a good man, he had his little ways..." he started. Then he went on to explain how that impression had grown up mainly through the accounts of two historians of the time, one called Roger of Wendover and the other Matthew Paris. But it seemed the first of them had not started writing until ten years after King John had died, a full twenty-five years after the beginning of his reign and thirty or forty after his earlier life. And Matthew Paris had not even been alive when John came to the throne and he had merely re-written, more dramatically, what Roger of Wendover had set down.

And that was not the end of it, either. It appeared that this Roger of Wendover was a baron's man, prejudiced against John, and that he happily mixed up fact and fiction, so that in one breath he was telling a fable - how a small black sucking pig had sucked an old washer-woman dry because she had done something wrong - and in the next he was giving 'facts' about King John which had then been passed down and believed by later historians.

It made me wonder what the historians had been up to.

But then Mr Anderson went on to say that recently people had been reading the contemporary records much more, and although they contradicted a good deal of what the two historians had written and made it clear that King John was not as bad as he was made out to be, he was no saint either. This digging into the old records produced a good deal of factual information, some of which Sally's father referred to later.

Before that though, my attention had wandered.

Sitting where we were, rather less than halfway down the room and at its side, we were looking straight at the audience rather than the speaker, and it was to them that my attention had gone.

First I counted them: thirty-five including Sally and me, but not counting the man who had introduced her father.

Then I looked at those of them whom I could see, making guesses as to what they were like and what their occupations were.

Some were obviously school children, perhaps the ones taught by Sally's father, or maybe they had history exams coming up. There was one group like that straight opposite us, and another further back. Both fidgeted.

Dotted about were a number of elderly people, men and women, respectable looking and very attentive. Middle class, retired, I thought, most of them probably colonels or the widows of colonels.

Another group was not quite so easy to pick out, but I was sure they were school teachers. I could not make out what it was about them which convinced me, but I was in no doubt about it.

That was about all the neat classifying I could do; but it left some untidy edges, the kind of thing I dislike. The untidiest edge was at the back: two men in thick duffle coats. I could hardly see them because they were in a dark corner and half hidden by other people.

A little further forward was a man sitting by himself. I could not place him. He too looked as if he spent a lot of time out of doors, but he was too well dressed to be a working man. Anyway he could concentrate. He looked as if he was not missing a word of the lecture.

Forward of him again, but at the opposite end of the row, was another who did not fit into my groups: slight, glossy black hair, neat suit, watch chain. He could have been a city gent, only King's Lynn is a bit too far from the City.

Occasionally I heard a word or two of the lecture, but I did not follow it. Too much of it pre-supposed some knowledge of which, of course, I had none: names of barons and bishops, references to other kings. I did not even know which countries some of them were kings of, let alone what they had to do with King John. Finally the lecture ended - and that was when it became interesting again. One of the retired colonels started it.

"King John's treasure," he asked, "where is it?" He must have been a colonel; no one else would have spoken in that way; it was more like a command than a question.

"Treasure?"

"Yes, the treasure he lost in The Wash."

"If I could tell you, it would no longer be in The Wash." Mr Anderson got a laugh for that, and Sally turned to me and whispered: "there's bound to be someone who asks about it."

"Of course The Wash was very different then," Sally's father went on. "It was bigger because a lot of land has been reclaimed since then, and the rivers which go into it were not the same as they are now." He looked at his watch and when he continued he spoke faster.

"At the end of his life John had a civil war on his hands. The French had landed in the South of England and the Scots had come down from the North as far as Cambridge. But then some of his rebel barons started drifting back to him, and that seems to have spurred him into marching to and fro across the middle of England, showing the flag so as to divide his enemies and encourage more rebels to come back to him, and plundering the estates of those who did not come.

"He spent a night in Lynn - this was in October - and from there he set out for Swineshead Abbey, going through Wisbech on his way and leaving his baggage train to follow. John travelled on firm ground to Wisbech, keeping well to the South of The Wash and perhaps crossing the Ouse at Wigginhall St Mary, but his baggage train cut the corner. It travelled from East to West just South of The Wash as we know it today, and that meant crossing the river which flowed North through Wisbech and on into The Wash.

"Today that river is called the Nene, and it's a neat, navigable, straightened river. In those days though, it was called the Wellstream, and it was not the same river at all. It was much bigger because it drained a good deal of the water which is now drained by the Ouse through King's Lynn - the course of these rivers has changed a lot since then - and it was anything but neat. Its estuary must have been four and a half miles wide where they would have tried to cross it between Cross Keys and

Long Sutton, and at high tide it would have been more like an extension of the sea than a riverbed. At low tide it would have been an expanse of mud flats, rather like the edges of The Wash at low tide today, with the river flowing North across it, probably in one or more shallow channels which it had scooped out for itself through the mud.

"It was on October 12th that the baggage train set off from Lynn. Low tide that day was at about midday, high tide at 6 pm., about 45 minutes after sunset."

Sally nudged me.

"He's off!" she whispered. "He loves this."

"Right at the start of their journey," her father went on, "they would have had to ford the Ouse at Lynn, and although the Ouse was a much smaller river in those days, I doubt if they could have done it at anything approaching high tide, particularly as spring tide was only two days later, on 14th. So what time did they leave?   Nobody knows, but it's unlikely that it could have been any earlier than half tide, at about 9 o'clock in the morning. It could have been later.

"Then we come to another factor: the size of the baggage train. Again, no one really knows, seven hundred and fifty years later, how big it was, but a few intelligent guesses have been made. Of course the king's treasures only formed a small part of it; most of the carts and wagons and pack horses would have been carrying more mundane things: probably a certain amount of food and wine and household goods, certainly the royal wardrobe and chapel, and some of the royal records, spare weapons and equipment, and so on. It has been estimated that this procession might have been two miles long once it was on the road, and that the fastest it could have travelled was about two and a half miles an hour.

"Now it's seven and a half miles between Lynn and the point where the estuary of the Wellstream started, at Cross Keys. At 2½ miles an hour it would have taken 3 hours for them to reach

Cross Keys, and a fourth hour before the last of them got there. So if they left Lynn at 9 a.m. and all went well the vanguard would have arrived at Cross Keys at midday, exactly low water. They would have been able to cross the estuary while the tide was well out, the mud at its driest and firmest, and the Wellstream at its lowest for fording. By the following half tide at 3 p.m. the last of the baggage train would be reaching firm ground on the Lincolnshire side of the estuary at Long Sutton.

"But it didn't. Something went wrong, badly wrong. What?

"To start at the beginning again, they may have been slow getting away. It would not have been the first or the last time that a journey has started late because people are not ready. And besides, my estimate that they could have forded the Ouse at Lynn at half tide may be wrong: perhaps the river was still too high then, and they had to wait a little longer. Remember: spring tides were only two days ahead.

"Next, there is the road between Lynn and Cross Keys. If the baggage train could make two and a half miles an hour in fair conditions, how fast would it travel in poor conditions? You all know how bad a farm track round here can become in the autumn after a period of heavy rain, and the main roads in those days were probably no better than farm tracks today; indeed, some of the land on the way, at Terrington St Clement for instance, is very heavy, terrible stuff to walk across when it is wet. A few boggy patches of road, maybe a small bridge put out of action by heavy rain and lack of maintenance (no County Surveyor's Department in those days to send a lorry for immediate repairs!); perhaps a break-down, if one or two of the wagons lost a wheel on a narrow part of the road there would be delay while they were being repaired or dragged into a passing place so that the others could go on. All sorts of things might have happened to slow them down and, as the journey was exceptional, we can judge that some sorts of things did happen.

"So ... instead of arriving at Cross Keys at midday at low tide perhaps they were late and the leader had a hard decision to make. Should he play safe and stop, and wait for low tide on the following day? Should they endure the delay and discomfort of remaining at Cross Keys? Or should they push on?

"Maybe other factors entered into it. The King was not one to suffer fools gladly, and perhaps he had given orders as to which day they should cross, and which day they should reach their destination. Perhaps the leader of the vanguard was the very man who, by his slothfulness or inefficiency, had delayed the start of the journey - if they got across straight away all would be well, and the king might never hear of his misdoings, but if they stopped, prudent though it would be to do so, the king could not fail to hear.

"Whatever the reason, we can assume that they arrived later at Cross Keys than they would have wished, and that they pressed on into the estuary.

"And having once left firm land a whole new set of misfortunes could have overtaken them.

"Of one thing we can be certain though. Disaster did not overtake them immediately. If it had done so, the rear part of the baggage train would not have been lost as well, for it would still have been on firm land. The chroniclers agree that the whole of the baggage was lost, so enough time must have passed for the rear of the train to have been well clear of Cross Keys - say an hour or so - long enough for the vanguard to have reached the ford across the waters of the Wellstream itself.

"So what really did happen?"

Sally's father stopped, looked round, and chuckled. I glanced at Sally and I could see that she was smiling as well.

"He loves this!" she said to me again.

"The usual explanation is that they were caught in the mud and the quicksands, and held there until the tide overtook them. The incoming tide could have converted what had been firm enough ground into quicksands, into which the baggage could have sunk without trace even before the tide went out again.

"Undoubtedly this could have happened. If, another possibility, the fog which is by no means uncommon in these parts in the autumn had come down then the rearguard would have been unaware of the vanguard's difficulties and all would, so to speak, have piled into the same black hole."

Suddenly my mental picture of all those men and animals and their wagons groping across the endless mud, lost in the fog, changed. Now there was only one man, alone but just as lost, just as doomed: Dick. They had found Dick's body. Perhaps they had found the bodies of some of King John's men, too, but they were not important, and seven hundred and fifty years later there would be no record of it, no coroner's inquest and report. And, I reflected, it was only two or three hours since I myself had been groping in the dark in the caravan park, consumed by the dank depression of it all. I had found that bad enough, but it was a thousand times worse to picture myself transferred a mile to the west, the fog more impenetrable, the raw air colder, the mud softer, the water nearer, the tide rising ...

Sally's father was still talking.

"But," here he frowned and looked puzzled, " ... I sometimes wonder. Two miles of baggage train is an awful lot to disappear without trace. And Civil War was raging ... and the king was not without enemies. Why, I sometimes wonder, when the vanguard ran into difficulties, should the people at the settlement of Cross Keys - probably a small enough number to keep a secret, especially if it was worth their while and if the penalty for failing to keep it would have been their lives - why should those people not have seen the vanguard in difficulties and seized their opportunity to cut out the rear guard? One ruthless, dominating, man at Cross Keys would have been enough to start it, and by then the rest could have been so implicated that they felt they had no alternative but to follow his lead. Maybe some of the valuables found their way back to Cross Keys, and then to Lynn, and perhaps abroad from the port. Or maybe some remain at King's Lynn even now, hidden in a safe place in the cellar of a merchant's house such as that of Mr Stevens. His house was probably built about that time, and enemy bombing during the last war exposed cellars whose very existence was unknown. Perhaps there are others, still not found, still containing the treasure hidden there seven hundred and fifty years ago."

Mr Anderson paused and it was evident that Mr Stevens was present in the room, but I failed to pick out which he was. "The thieves would have kept the valuables, of course, but the rest, the tell-tale remains of the royal wagons and their guards, they of all people would have known where to dump them - in the quicksands."

Mr Anderson looked up and grinned at his audience. His grin seemed to reach to the very back of the room. "Of course it's only speculation," he added, "but who can tell ... ?"

Then he remembered the retired Colonel whose question had started him off. "Does that answer your question?" he asked mildly.

The colonel, I think, had by then forgotten that he had asked the question to begin with, but he was not deterred. Presence of mind is something which I suppose they cultivate in the army.

"Er ... which of these explanations do you favour?" he asked.

"Oh, there's no doubt about that," answered Mr Anderson without hesitation. "I enjoy speculating, I admit it, but it is no more than speculation. No, I think there can be no doubt that King John's baggage train is submerged somewhere on the direct route between Cross Keys and Long Sutton. The land is all soft silt down to a depth of twenty feet or more, even allowing for the shrinkage which has taken place since it was drained. It's the kind of thing which could be converted to quicksand by an incoming tide. Maybe one day when the land has sunk a little further, some lucky farmer will turn it up with his plough, just as the Mildenhall Treasure was turned up. But of course in seven hundred and fifty years, during which the rivers have altered their courses, storms and currents and tides have shifted mud and sand from one place to another and back again, and men have reclaimed acres of land and cultivated it - well, it might have been moved anywhere. But I don't think so. I don't believe it will be far off the route which they took - but that's just my opinion: yours may be better."

He stopped and looked down on his audience. Then he spoke again: "What do you think, Mr Holden?" he asked. "Do you think; you'll be the lucky man? Do you think you'll find it on Bower's Farm? Do you think that one day you'll walk into Lynn wearing the crown which the Empress of Germany, King John's grandmother, used to wear? And carrying her gold wand, and with Tristram's sword buckled to your side?"

Sally's father grinned, and there was general laughter in which a voice could be heard saying "bit small for 'im", but it was not shared by Mr Holden himself.

He was one of the people in the audience I had been unable to place, the weathered man wearing good clothes, but all at once he had been explained to me: a moment before he had been a mystery, now I knew all about him. He was a farmer, a working yeoman farmer, well-to-do and old-established, and it was at his farm that I had stopped on my way to Burbidge's place earlier in the day: Bower's farm. The only thing which did not seem to fit into his personal jigsaw puzzle was his presence at the meeting. It was understandable that he should be interested, certainly, but that he would go out of his way to attend a rather academic meeting of the Historical Society on a cold winter evening - that did not add up.

"I should hope not," Mr Holden replied after a pause. He spoke grudgingly, as if he would not have spoken at all if he had not felt himself forced to do so by the silence and by the way everyone was staring expectantly at him. "It'd only be Treasure

Trove if I did find it," he went on, while in the background a voice could be heard saying "you could melt it down!" "and I'd have every reporter and every treasure hunter in England trampling over my farm. It's hard enough to earn a living as it is, the way things are going up, without having my land beaten down by a pack of trespassers."

"Nonsense, man," the colonel was bubbling with indignation. "You ought to be proud to recover your sovereign's treasures ...Narrow self-interest ..."

"Only last week fertilisers went up ten per cent..."

The colonel looked as if he might choke at this further evidence of bigoted self-interest.

"And cattle cake looks set to follow suit."

Sally leant towards me, looking at once worried and amused. "I'm afraid Dad can't understand it," she whispered. "He can't believe anyone wouldn't be pleased to discover historical evidence. He's baited Mr Holden before, quite unintentionally, just like that. In fact I can't think why he's here this evening at all, I'd have thought he'd have heard it all before, and nobody'd call him an academic type!"

Fortunately for the colonel's health someone else was asking a question. It was one of the half dozen or so colonel's widows.

"I read an article recently in the Geographical Magazine," she said in an educated voice, almost refined but not quite. "It was all about sea levels, and how the tide is much higher now at the mouth of the Thames than it used to be. I wonder, would the level of the sea in The Wash be different now to its level in King John's time? And if so how much more mud would be exposed at low tide in those days?"

Her last few words were partially drowned in a scraping of chairs and fidgeting in the back row. Some of the school children turned round to stare.

One of the men in duffle coats was responsible, but I could not see what was going on. Besides, I was interested in the question. If sea level was lower in those days the expanse of mud and sand must have been immense. I wondered if half The Wash might be exposed at a low spring tide. But Mr Anderson was a historian, not a geographer.

"I can't answer that," he replied. "Like you, I've heard that sea level has risen in the last two or three hundred years - or the land has sunk - but what happened before then I simply do not know; it's an interesting point, though, an interesting point. I must make enquiries."

There was a noise of some kind from the colonel's wife, presumably to thank Mr Anderson for failing to answer her question, and I wondered how long Sally's father could keep up his "very interesting..." and "yes ... yes's". But he was saved by the soft-voiced president of the Society who now appeared on the platform with the speaker. He did not seem to stand up and mount the platform: he just appeared, materialising softly like his voice.

"I ...now call upon Mr Stevens ... vote of thanks..." and just as inconspicuously he melted away again.

Mr Stevens rose briskly, moved just as briskly to the side of the hall where Sally and I were sitting, and having positioned himself so that he could see everybody except for the two of us and so that they could see him, he began.

I was delighted. I had by now given up hope of placing the smart city gent, yet here he was, standing within arm's length and, I hoped, about to explain himself or be explained.

I was not disappointed.

"Mr President, ladies and gentlemen," he began; his delivery was brisk like him, clipped, proper. "I am honoured to have been invited to propose this vote of thanks honoured in anticipation, yet more honoured after listening to the superb lecture with which we have been favoured by Mr Anderson, for I make no exaggeration when I say that his lecture has been quite brilliant, a magnificent combination of learned erudition and accomplished delivery."

I sat back on my chair and looked at Sally. It seemed to me that we might be in for another talk, just as long as Mr Anderson's and with a fraction of its interest. Sally winked at me, sharing my misgivings.

"I am, as you all know," the city gent went on, "myself the President of a Society, in my case the King's Lynn and District Conservation Society, and of course I and my Society have links of common interest and purpose with the History Society. While the History Society is concerned with matters which, shall we say, are mainly of academic interest, I think I can claim without risk of contradiction that my own Society, the Conservation Society, is in some respects wider in its appeal, more immediate in its objectives. While the History Society is as it were the back-room research department, the Conservation Society is the striking force: a multi-disciplinary, socially committed, activist body of men and women, dedicated to the protection of all that is worth preserving of this great heritage - which is ours...." There was more of it, much more, tenuously related to Mr Anderson's lecture, the general gist of which was that we should all join the Conservation Society, put on our armour of self-righteousness, and have a go at whatever we found in our way. He was grateful to the History Society, when he remembered that it was at its meeting that he was talking, because it helped to point the way to things which should be preserved, though what there was still to preserve about King John which had not already been preserved I could not understand. Not much more was likely to appear after seven hundred and fifty years, surely?

Eventually he finished and the clapping took its place, for Sally's father, not for the city gent.

"Who on earth is he?" I asked Sally as the clapping went on, "And what does he do with himself when he's not giving speeches like that?"

"Local councillor," she whispered back, "belongs to every committee that's going."

"And when he's not being a councillor?"

"Antique dealer in King's Lynn. He has one of those lovely old houses in King's Street, not far from the Custom House. He's sandwiched between offices and things like that, but they say he has a good business. At least the stuff in his window looks expensive."

Soon after that the meeting started to break up. As Sally and I were in chairs by the door we remained where we were, waiting for her family to reach us rather than fighting our way against the current to meet them. For that reason we had a good view of the people as they went out, a view in retrospect more significant than I found it at the time, and even at the time I found it interesting enough.

Mr Stevens, the city gent turned antique dealer and general committee-man, was nearest to us, but he did not leave immediately. Nor did he go towards the front of the room to talk to the platform party, as might have been expected of a local dignitary who had just proposed a vote of thanks. Instead he made a beeline for the farmer, Holden.

It was obvious they knew each other. There was no preliminary handshake of the kind I would have expected from someone as self-important as Stevens appeared to be. Far from it: he put his arm across the back of Holden in a gesture of commiseration and comfort for someone who had just undergone a nasty experience. But their conversation was too far away and conducted in voices which were too low for me to be able to catch any of it.

In any case, by then I had noticed someone else, one of the duffle-coated men who had been hidden from me at the back of the room. I did not see him until he was about three paces from me. Then I looked in his direction and we recognised each other simultaneously. We were both surprised. It was Waters, Burbidge's man. Behind him was the Finn.

As soon as he had got over his surprise he greeted me. He did it well, as if he was pleased to see me, but I was sure I had not been deceived: in that split second between his recognising me and his putting on his expression of greeting there had been another expression: dismay? surprise? I was not sure - I would have appreciated a re-run so that I could assess it again, but the slow witted are not given re-runs. I would have to make do with what I had, and that was a warning signal.

Waters took my hand.

"Nice to see you again," he said, "an enjoyable evening. No practical interest, though, eh?" He still held my hand as he spoke. When he let go, at the end of his last words, I shook it involuntarily and looked down. It was white from the pressure of his grip.

"See you tomorrow," he went on. "After that you'll be getting back home, eh?" He stared into my eyes. If my hand had still been in his it would have been reduced to pulp.

"Yes," I answered. I get your message: I'm to go home. But why? That would not be a tactful question, would it?

I had forgotten Sally for the moment. As Waters turned back towards the centre of the room she said to me:

"A friend of yours?" She was looking up enquiringly.

"Certainly not." I shook my hand again to get the circulation going.

"But you have ... interests in common?" She was determined to pursue it. "No more than he has with other people," I answered. "Look."

She followed the direction of my eyes. Waters was greeting someone else: Sally's father. It might have been a repetition of his greeting of me: a handshake and a few words, but Mr Anderson was not wringing his hand; their encounter seemed to be a friendly, not a threatening, affair.

"Looks like your Dad has interests in common with him, too, doesn't it?" It was my turn to look at Sally enquiringly. But she took no notice. "Who is he?" she asked.

"Name of Waters. He's with Burbidge's, making those reservoirs. He was Dick's boss. Heard of him?"

She had, but she did not say so straight away.

"So that's him, is it," she muttered to herself, and then, to me, she went on: "I've heard Dad mention him," she explained. "I think he has something to do with the Conservation Society - Dad belongs to that too - but I've not met him myself."

"Do you want to, now?" I asked her, "now you've seen the Conservation Society connection getting the same treatment as Dick's brother?"

Suddenly she relaxed and grinned up at me. "Not much," she said.

For an instant a thoughtful frown returned to that wide forehead, but it had no time to stay there.

"Well, Sally, this is a pleasure."

It was Stevens who interrupted our conversation, sailing into it with his hand outstretched to Sally, brisk, proper. "And what an occasion! Your father is remarkable, quite remarkable, Sally. No one else could make the subject so interesting, could he? And it's not just what is written in a few history books, is it? He's really gone into it - really knows his subject." He released Sally's hand and turned to me. "And your friend here ... I don't think I have had the honour..."

Hastily Sally introduced us.

"So it was your brother who was drowned? A bad business, that, a bad business. Most distressing, most. And the funeral is tomorrow, is it? And after that no doubt you'll be on your way home. A pity you are not staying longer in the district: we badly need people who are interested in their environment. If

94

you had longer here you could come and see my own premises, they are in the old historic part of Lynn. In fact," he went on, and for the first time I had the feeling that he was actually choosing his words instead of merely turning up an appropriate bit of his internal tape-recorder, "in fact I have in my shop at this very moment some articles which are very apposite to this evening's lecture: silver pennies, minted in the time of King John, just the kind of thing which his negligent servants probably lost for him in The Wash. A pity," he repeated "if only you had a little more time up here you could call and see them."

"And buy them," added Sally unkindly when he was out of earshot, while I reflected that at least Stevens was preferable to Waters in one way: Stevens had urged me to stay in the area, whatever his motives; Waters just did not want me around at any price.

By the time Stevens had done with us Sally's family were approaching. But there was one more diversion before they reached us. Her father suddenly moved off to one side and I was surprised, after Sally's words, to see him go up to Holden of Bower's farm and speak to him. Less surprising, again after Sally's words, was the way in which Holden himself did not appear to relish the encounter. From where I stood, out of earshot, l had no difficulty in realising that Holden was giving monosyllabic replies to anything and everything which was said to him. The last thing he wanted was a conversation with Mr Anderson.

Chapter 8

On the way back to Sherningham Mrs Anderson again suggested that Margery should come with Sally and me, but either through uncharacteristic tact or inclination she refused. As I again stretched across to fasten Sally's safety belt I nearly took my chance and kissed her. The opportunity was there; and if Sally had wished to avoid it she could have fastened the belt for herself. But I hadn't the nerve. I was so angry with myself that we drove in silence while I tried to work myself up to make up for lost time when we reached Sherningham.

Sally interrupted my thoughts. "What's your job?"

"I'm a draughtsman."

She thought for a minute. "There are all sorts of draughtsmen. What sort are you?"

"Electrical."

"So ... what happens? You work for G.E.C. or some firm like that, drawing pictures of gigantic turbines? Or you work for your local neighbourhood electrical firm?"

"Neither - or both!" There was no doubt about it, there was definitely something about the way Sally asked her questions which put me at my ease. I had found it before, and I was finding it again now. Here was this chit of a girl, sitting in my own car beside me, grilling me with questions in a way which, if it had been anyone else, would have driven me straight into my shell. And yet, here was I ... answering them. And enjoying it!

"You're becoming addicted to mysteries, aren't you? How come?"

"I'm self-employed, so I do both - turbines and small works."

"Ah, that explains it! But you haven't always been self-employed? How long? How did you manage to get going on your own?"

"I worked for a small firm first, then for a nationalised industry, then another private company - until it went bankrupt."

I stopped to censor the next thing I might have told her, not a difficult decision: this was no moment to explain my contacts with the police. I was half inclined to tell her all the same, for I had a feeling that if I did it in the right way and at the right moment she would understand. Not here, though, and not just now. I went on: "The firm I'd last worked for was in the middle of a job for a customer who I'd got to know, and they asked me to finish it off for them so I did - but on a self-employed basis."

"So you work from home, do you? Or have you a big office with glamorous secretaries?"

I laughed and glanced at her, but she was looking straight ahead, expressionless.

"Jealous?" I asked.

"Of course." She flashed a smile at me.

"Then stop worrying! I don't have a secretary to myself. I don't even share one. All I have is the left-overs, what remains of two girls when other people have finished with them." I stopped to give her time to think about that.

"Go on."

"One's a peroxide blonde."

"And the other?"

"She's a brunette." I hesitated while I struggled to think of one of Sue's features which would characterise her for Sally. Whatever I said Sue would not be flattered. "She goes in for nail varnish, a different colour for each day of the week." Not quite true, although she did wear red varnish sometimes.

"So what do Peroxide and Painted Nails do for you?"

"They take messages and make appointments and generally run me."

"And what happens to them the rest of the time? What do they do then?"

"They work for the estimators of the firm which employs them, the one I was telling you about, which came up with some jobs when I needed them. It's a good arrangement actually: it

97

suits both sides. They get first call on me when they have urgent work, but they don't have to employ me full-time and they don't have to provide an office for me. I get a telephone answering service during working hours; I get a buffer, if I like, between myself and people who think they want to get hold of me more urgently than they do; and I get bread-and-butter work from them while I can look elsewhere for the jam. And incidentally if I'm tactful I can get my typing done by Painted Nails after hours."

"Very nice. So they're keeping people at bay for you while you're up here?"

"That's right," I wondered if Sally could use a typewriter. If she could she would make a very competent secretary; better than Peroxide. Probably better than Sue, too, and she was not half bad.

"And where do you do all this?"

"Somewhere in Surrey," I answered mysteriously as we drew up outside her house.

I was too slow. Before I could lay my hand on the catch of her safety belt she had undone it herself, slipped from the car, and was halfway to the house. It was small consolation that she put her hand into mine as we approached it.

"Thanks for the lift," she said, pausing and looking up at me as I held her hand before we went in, but time stopped and paralysed me, and then she was through the door and I was following - cursing myself again.

***

I had a full time-table the next day. Dick's funeral was at 12.30, and there were at least two calls which I wanted to make first.

I came downstairs early. I had had a good night's sleep, the product of tiredness, a comfortable bed, and security. The drab coldness of the caravan and its plumbing arrangements seemed a bad memory, even though it was only twenty-four hours old.

Sally and her parents were already at breakfast when I appeared. Sally helped me to porridge and tea, they all said good morning, and then they went on with what they had been discussing.

It was Mr Anderson who continued the conversation, which clearly he had never stopped thinking about when he broke off to wish me a good morning.

"But he's the president," he said, "I can't go behind his back."

"He wouldn't hesitate to go behind yours, dear, would he, if it suited his purpose?" rejoined Mrs Anderson calmly, rather as if she were talking to a small child.

"I dare say, I dare say," Mr Anderson was looking troubled. But you know, two wrongs don't make a right, and one should do these things in the proper way. If one doesn't it only rebounds sooner or later. And it's all arranged now: I don't believe it's possible to change it at this stage."

"Well, don't say I haven't warned you, dear," Mrs Anderson shrugged her shoulders. "It's happened before, and I dare say it will happen again, and you'll still be surprised, won't you?" and she smiled affectionately at her husband while he continued to look down at his food, worried and pensive.

I did not discover what it was about at the time, though later I guessed, because after that she turned to me to ask how I had slept, and to suggest I should stay there another night if I wished. However I assured her that the funeral was early enough for me to get home that day, even though I remembered that I still had to pay off the caravan. "If I may," I added, "I'll leave my things here and pick them up in the afternoon: I'll have to come back to Sheringham to deal with Dick's caravan, but it won't take me long."

I got away as soon as I could.

In King's Lynn I first found a long-stay car park. Then I made for a telephone kiosk. Sue - Painted Nails to Sally - answered. Everything was under control: no crises; one appointment had come in which was fairly urgent, a site meeting to sort out a disputed account, but she had persuaded the other people involved to leave it until the following morning. "I tried to put it off until the next day, just in case you had to stop up there a little longer," she told me, "but they were very pressing so I gave in. O.K.?"

"O.K." I answered.

Next I returned to the car and took out Dick's fishing rod and tackle.

I felt foolish, walking about with it as if I knew what it was and how to use it. But no one stared at me, so either I did not look as foolish as I felt, or a lot of people in King's Lynn were fishermen and one more person with a fishing rod was neither here nor there.

I had noticed the shop which sold fishing tackle when I first came to King's Lynn. It was not in the modern pedestrianised malls, but down a nearby side street which had escaped the fate of whatever building had stood on either side of the malls before the new shops were built.

The shopkeeper was middle-aged, with grey thinning hair, rimless glasses, and an efficient no-nonsense look about him. His shop was not confined to fishing but most of the space on my side of the counter seemed to be devoted to fishing equipment of various sorts. I was particularly interested in a container in which a quantity of earth seemed to be mixed with a heaving mass of long, whitish things: lugworms.

"Can I help you?" he asked.

I pulled myself away from the lugworms.

"This fishing rod," I said slowly, raising Dick's rod and placing it on the glass topped counter.

"Yes?"

"Can you tell me, was it bought here?"

He looked down at it. "It might have been. That make of rod, and the tackle, I sell it all here." He pointed to a rod which was displayed on the wall at one side of the shop. The only way in which it differed from Dick's was that it was assembled, ready for use. I was surprised to see how short it was.

"That's the same kind," he said.

"Where would you use it?" I asked, thinking of the long, whippy, rods I had watched fishermen using, casting for mackerel from the shingle beaches of Dorset.

"Anywhere off the coast round here," he answered.

"Off the coast?"

"Any boat will do - so long as you're careful not to go out too far in bad weather, particularly if it's a small one."

So Dick must have arranged the use of a boat, perhaps the grey or white one I had seen in the mud off Sherningham Beach. That explained the question which had lurked at the back of my mind, un-answered because it had never been properly asked. The impossibility of fishing from the gently shelving beach at Sherningham had been subconsciously evident to me, but simply because it was subconscious my mind had never taken the next step of asking where Dick had planned to fish if it could not be done from the beach, as in Dorset, the only other place where I had watched sea-fishermen in action.

"It's new, isn't it?" the shopkeeper said. "I doubt if it's ever been used."

"Yes. Do you sell many of them?"

"A fair number. What can I do for you?"

The stage of small-talk was over, and I must get to the point. But I was still undecided as to how far I should go with the next stage.

"Would you remember people who've bought rods from you recently? Would you recognise them again if you saw them?"

101

"Probably. I've a good memory for faces, and it's a personal business, this. What are you getting at?" There was a hint of impatience in his voice.

I put my hand inside my jacket, into the breast pocket. Out of it I drew the photograph of Dick which I had been given, along with the drawing instruments, at Burbidge's depot.

"Could it have been him?"

The shopkeeper looked hard and long at it.

"No," he answered. "I don't think so. He doesn't look familiar." Then he looked up at me, and asked the question I had been expecting, and hoping would not come before I had got the answer to the one I had asked. I had prepared my story but it was rather a thin one.

"What is all this? What are you after? You sound like the police, the way you've been going on - but I don't think you are."

"No," I answered, "I'm not. The rod and tackle belonged to my brother, but he died not long ago and I thought that if I could find whoever sold it to him he might take it back. You see, I've no use for it - I don't fish, and I don't know anyone who does." The shopkeeper looked satisfied with my explanation, which in a sense was not far from the truth. "Anyway," I went on, "I'm sorry to have troubled you, but perhaps you can tell me if there's anyone else in King's Lynn he might have bought it from."

There was, and he gave me directions for finding it. "And there are shops in Hunstanton and Wisbech," he added for good measure, telling me where they were.

His directions were good, and I found the second shop in King's Lynn without difficulty. Neither the shopkeeper nor his wife had any recollection of having seen Dick. Besides, there was one item in the tackle which they did not normally stock, so it was unlikely that Dick had bought the stuff there. A novice like him would not have gone from shop to shop to locate the exact sort of cast which he required.

When I emerged I looked at my watch. If I went to Hunstanton I would be back soon enough for the funeral, but it might leave me without enough time to make the other call I wanted to make. On the other hand if I made the other call I would be cutting it too fine to go to Hunstanton and back with any certainty of returning soon enough. Hunstanton had to come first.

It was a fruitless trip, except in a negative sense. But with each try the negative became more positive. It was a pity I had no second photograph to take with me, or rather a handful of second photographs to use like an identification parade.

When I returned to King's Lynn I parked on the quay. I walked past the Custom's House and on down King Street.

There was only one antique shop in the street, on the side nearer to the river. Sally was quite right: the antiques which I could see from the road all looked good ones. And although there was plenty to see in the window the general impression it gave was of a slightly cluttered, civilised living room rather than a shop window.

I entered.

No one appeared to be in the shop, or in the little room which looked like an office beyond, so I walked slowly round. I stopped in front of a glass topped display case.

"I think that's what you're looking for, sir."

The voice in my ear made me jump, but there was no mistaking it. Mr Stevens, antique dealer, councillor, committee member, and prominent citizen was at my elbow still looking exactly like a city gent, still talking in his clipped, positive, authoritative, voice.

"Two King John pennies," he said, opening the case and removing them so that I could look more closely.

He did not pick the coins up: he took out the plush tray on which they were resting. "Not bad condition," he went on, "not bad at all."

"Are there many of them about?" I asked.

"Not many, but they're not too uncommon either. Coins in better condition than these have been found."

"And where did you find these?" I asked.

He did not answer. Instead he winked. It was an exaggerated, wink and its meaning was perfectly clear: he was not telling; but its conspiratorial exaggeration conveyed a revolting kind of slyness. Or was it just my own prejudice?

"They get picked up from time to time," he said, "not often, but just occasionally..."

"But if so shouldn't they be handed in? Aren't they Treasure Trove or something of the sort?"

"Not really. 'De minimis non curat lex', eh?"

He looked up and sideways at me to see if I had understood. I had not, which pleased him.

"The law does not bother with trifles," he translated. "So if you find the odd coin or two it doesn't matter, not unless they're something special. If you dig up the Mildenhall Treasure, though, you ought to hand it in. That is, if you're honest, but I'm afraid that doesn't apply to everyone, eh?"

I wondered how far it applied to him.

"Interested?" he asked ambiguously, looking down at the coins.

"Interested - yes," I answered. "But not, I'm afraid, in the market to buy." I laughed uneasily as he put them back in the case. "I wish I could afford it, but in any case I'm not a collector."

He shut the door of the case and locked it.

"This is a handsome old house," I said. "I suppose it was built for a wealthy merchant originally, along with the others in the street?"

"Yes, it was a prosperous town then. That's why we have so much that's worth preserving. In fact the town's usually been prosperous, right from the beginning. You heard what Mr Anderson was saying about it in King John's time, didn't you? It was an important place then too."

"Is anything left of it from those days?"

"A little. There were houses along here then. This one was built on the foundations of a much older building."

"Are there any traces of that?"

"In the cellar, yes." He looked at his watch. "Just enough time," he said. "It's people like you who ought to be encouraged to become active. You should join your local Conservation Society, make it bigger and more important, affiliate to the National Association of Conservation Societies. It's national importance we need as well as local activity." He broke off suddenly from his well-worn speech. "Come with me," he commanded.

He led the way briskly towards the back of the shop. We passed through his little office, out of it again through a door at its side, into a small lobby with doors leading from it on two sides. One of them gave on to a side alley which I had noticed before entering the shop; I could see daylight under it; so ill-fitting was it that the streak of light smothered the dim bare bulb hanging from the ceiling.

Facing it, and through another door, some stairs led downwards.

Switching on a light he led the way. At the bottom we were in a handsome brick-vaulted room. At least, what could be seen of it was handsome and brick-vaulted but it was so cluttered down each side with old chairs, tables, packing cases, and bric-a-brac that much of the walls and roof was hidden.

"This is the same age as the house," he explained. "Through there it's older, much older."

As I stood looking at the black, low, arched, opening which he had indicated there came the jangle of the shop doorbell. Clear but faint, the sound appeared to penetrate by the route we had used, through the small office and the lobby, and down the rickety stairs.

"Damn," he said vehemently and positively, like everything else he said.

"That's that, I shan't have time to come down again." He squeezed past me and started up again. "You must come another day."

He was halfway up the stairs when my sleeve caught the corner of a tray perched on top of a small packing case which was, itself, placed somewhat precariously on top of a table. The tray was laden with small cardboard boxes which tumbled against me before falling to the floor. By their weight I knew they were empty.

Stevens paused long enough to see what I had done.

"That doesn't matter," he said. "No harm done. Leave them: I'll clear them up when I come down again."

"But I upset them, so I ought to pick them up. It won't take a moment."

Stevens hesitated. It was more than he could bear not to attend to his customer promptly. On the other hand he did not want to leave me there. It all happened in a trice, however, and it was only afterwards that I realised the way he must have been torn between his two choices.

The customer won and Stevens left me picking up boxes. It took only a few moments and then I started to follow in his footsteps up the stairs.

I switched off the light at the top, and I switched off the light in the small lobby as I passed through the door and into his office.

The corner into which the door gave was half hidden from the main body of the shop, so I could hear Stevens' voice but I could not see him. He was still busy with his customer, so I would do better not to hurry; I might interrupt him just as he was clinching a deal. I stood and waited therefore, one hand still on the handle of the door from the lobby, ready to shut it and continue into the shop as soon as I heard Stevens' customer leave.

The office was packed untidily with the smaller bric-a-brac of the trade, rather as the cellar had been. A cardboard box labelled 'English Apples' stood on a shelf near me. The flaps were down over its top, and as I waited I casually lifted one of them and peered inside.

King John pennies! Not just one or two, but half a box full - hundreds!

On top of the pile three had been cleaned and the silver shone up at me. The rest were dark and dirty, crusted with mud and grit.

Not my business!

Hastily I let the flap fall again. Then I slammed the door from the lobby into the office whose handle I still grasped in my other hand and walked on into the shop. Mr Stevens was facing me, returning from the front door through which his customer had just left. I had been just in time.

"I've picked up the boxes," I told him, "and turned the lights out."

"Good," he answered. "Thank you. You must come again ... join the Conservation Society. Big plans afoot, you know, for widening its scope ... more members, more influence; then we'll really be listened to." By this time he had ushered me to the door. As I passed through it he said once more: "Come again," and I saw him locking it behind me as soon as I was through.

Outside, I turned to the right, retracing my footsteps to the car. I passed the end of the alley which ran down beside the building. If that side door were broken down the contents of the shop, cellar, and office would be easily accessible. I wondered whether Stevens, or anyone else, lived on the premises. The door was well sheltered: unless someone passing the end of the alley actually turned to look down it nobody would notice a break in, and there would not be much activity in King's Lynn at night. And the cellar ... I suddenly remembered Mr Anderson's comment at his lecture: Stevens' cellar, he had said, was just the kind in which King John's treasure might have been hidden if any of it had found its way back to King's Lynn. His treasure had included silver pennies. Could that possibly be where Stevens found his pennies, in his own cellar, brought there, as Mr Anderson had suggested in his lecture, by someone from Cross Keys who had plundered the baggage train? It seemed unlikely, but where else could Stevens have laid his hands on so many pennies - pennies still encrusted with dirt as if they had only just been found?

Chapter 9

I made sure I was in good time for the funeral.

Dick's coffin was still in the hearse outside the doors at the end of the mortuary chapel when I arrived, and mourners were leaving the chapel by another door from the previous funeral. There were about twenty, and I watched them filing out and gathering round a group of flowers and wreaths while I parked.

As I approached the chapel the undertaker came towards me, efficient, deferential, black-coated. He led me into the chapel, seated me in the front pew, and then returned to his team of bearers.

For a minute or two I was the only occupant of the chapel. Then Dick joined me, placed by the undertaker's men on a platform at the front. When they withdrew, Dick and I were alone together, the first time for ages.

I talked to him, noiselessly.

I'll find out, I told him. I've not done it in the time I originally set myself but I have a few leads to follow up now. I'll do what I can. That note you left for me in your diary will not be wasted. Don't worry. Don't you worry.

Other mourners came in. Seated at the front I had to turn round to see them.

Burbidge's were well represented. There must have been half a dozen of them, led by Waters. They included one other familiar face: my sparring partner who looked after the business end of the dredging machine, watching me in his spare time in the caravan site, and attacking me when I was not looking. But the big burly man who had operated the dredging machine itself was not there.

Good, sympathetic, mourners, I thought, killing two birds with one stone: watching me and representing the firm. Or were the birds they were killing Dick and me? My stomach heaved.

Not long after they arrived another, noisier, party came in and I turned round again. It was Nance and her family. She was followed by her husband, Fred, diminutive as he tucked himself down inside his overcoat, and by Perce and two of his girls. I was surprised. The children looked too young to be dragged off to a funeral, but then Nance was always one for an occasion.

The service did not last long. The parson did his best, I suppose, to make it sound different from the last one, but to him it must have been just the same: after all, he had never seen the only real difference, now encased in a wooden box.

Dick descended noiselessly into his platform. That moment was the one which seemed final and I was surprised how moved I was, for I thought I had already accustomed myself to his death. I found myself renewing my vows to clear up the mystery surrounding it.

Then we filed out, just like the previous funeral, and stood round a smaller group of wreaths and flowers. I noticed the next hearse outside the front door of the chapel, complete with its coffin and an undertaker going to meet someone who had just parked his car. The vows I had made to Dick inside the mortuary chapel already seemed more distant and unreal, less binding.

Then, suddenly, our funeral became different from its predecessor and its successor.

Nance started it. As the group broke up there she was, between us and the parked cars, holding one of those instant cameras to her eye. I did not actually hear her say 'smile please', or 'watch the birdie', but everything else about her indicated the words, and soon after she was pressing a newly developed photograph into my hand. "It's nice to have something to remind you, dear, isn't it?" she said.

And then I noticed another difference.

Sally was standing, self-effacing, at the back of the group. She smiled wanly at me when she saw that I had noticed her, but before I could go over to speak to her Nance was upon me, powerful, overwhelming.

"There's one person missing today," she said to me. I looked back at her blankly.

"Dick's father," she explained, "I sent a wire to him through the address he left. I thought that if he'd taken the trouble to leave that address I ought to let him know, but I wasted my time, didn't I?"

Once more I had completely forgotten the existence of the man, no more than he deserved after the way he had deserted Dick, but Nance did not leave me time to reflect on it; she was already on to the next thing.

"Come along," she commanded. "What we want is a little bit of something to pick us up. I noticed a pub on the way. It's just what the doctor ordered."

Burbidge's party would not come with us, something for which I was thankful.

I shook them all by the hand as they left. Water's grip was twice as powerful as any of the others, and I did my best to return it with interest.

"So long," he said to me. "Safe journey. You'll be off home straight away, I suppose?"

"Yes," I answered, and then as an afterthought I added: "unless I stay around for a day or two; I might do that." I said it casually, throwing out the idea light-heartedly, secure by now in the certainty that I would be safely back at work the next morning at the meeting Sue had arranged for me, and forgetting completely my recent vows to Dick. I was, I suppose, trying it on instinctively, but my instincts were sharper than I had bargained for.

"I shouldn't do that if I were you." Waters spoke slowly so that what he said could sink right in. Up to the hilt. "You've no cause to stay longer, have you? You'd better be off home, mate."

111

His words alone were harmless enough, a bit of friendly advice for the bereaved brother of a former employee, still suffering from the shock of sudden death in the family. But his tone of voice did not go with friendly advice. Nor did it go with a good night's sleep, nor with an easy life free from butterflies in the stomach.

I was glad I was going.

The pub was a dreary one, but it was enlivened by Nance, and Sally.

When we reached it, I looked at the photograph Nance had pressed into my hand. I was disappointed: plenty of Burbidge's men, not a trace of Sally. She was hidden behind the others.

But she was with us, life-size, at the pub.

"Are you really going back today?" she asked. "Has Painted Nails got her talons into you so hard you have to go?" She grinned. "There's the Conservation Society meeting tomorrow. Why don't you come along to that? After Dad's lecture you know more about it than most of the locals."

"Sorry," I answered. "Painted Nails not only has her talons into me, she's fixed a date for me tomorrow morning and she won't let go until she's dropped me right in the middle of a cosy group of hard-headed contractors who are each going to blame me for what they've done wrong." But I had reckoned without Nance.

"Go on!" she broke in. "You can't refuse an invitation like that, George. Never heard such nonsense! If they're that hard-headed a day or two here or there won't make no difference to them. Go on! Go and ring up and put 'em off straight away. There's a phone just outside; I saw it as we came in."

Sally and I both grinned. I did not take much persuading and by the time I had got through to Sue nothing would have put me off.

Nance practically knocked me over when she dug me in the ribs with her elbow after Sally had left. "You keep on to her," she ordered me. "I know something good when I see it, and no mistake."

I recalled what Waters had said while I was driving out of the pub's car park. I savoured its full flavour now that I had it to myself. Delicious! I felt like turning right instead of left and driving straight back home.

If my decision to stay had not been made in public I would have turned right too. But it had been. Nance, Sally, Sue they all knew what I had said; and by now Sue would have altered my appointments again, and it would not be long before Sally had told her family.

I had no choice, I had to stay. I was driven to it not by any bravery in ignoring Waters' threat, far from it, but by weakness in not wishing to be seen to change my mind for no reason.

I was too distraught to follow Sally back to Sherningham, and anyway I had told her I would not be coming straight away. They would not want me around for the rest of the day, and although I was all for Sally's company the confident vitality of the rest of her family was more than I could stand for any length of time just at that moment - or at any other moment, for that matter.

Then I remembered the fishing shop at Wisbech; I had not been to it yet. Wisbech was ten or fifteen miles away and it would settle my nerves to drive there even if nothing came of it.

It took me some time to find the shop. The place was full of closed roads and diverted traffic, and by the time I had asked half a dozen people the way and driven round the town three times, my nerves were feeling a good deal less frayed.

The shopkeeper stocked the same kind of fishing rod and tackle as the ones I showed him, but when I produced the photo of Dick he looked blank. It meant nothing to him.

I replaced the photo in my pocket. It would not go so I had to remove the rest of the things to make way for it, and I found the photograph of the funeral which Nance had given me had

113

jammed across the pocket. Without thinking I put it down in front of the shopkeeper.

"What about them?" I asked, pointing at Burbidge's contingent. Could it be one of them?"

"No, I can't remember seeing any of them."

It was no more than I expected, so I picked up the photographs and left.

I set off again, back towards King's Lynn.

That fishing rod: it must have been bought locally. There was no reason why it should have come from anywhere else, and it was so new it was hardly likely to have been sold through an advertisement in the local paper or a card in a newsagent's window. The obvious place for Dick to have found it was in King's Lynn, mid-way between where he worked and where he slept. I had already ruled out one of the shops in Lynn because it did not sell both rod and tackle like Dick's. That left only the first shop I had tried.

I had forgotten about Waters and the butterflies he induced in the pit of my stomach. The puzzle of where the rod and tackle were bought had driven them out of my mind and smothered my qualms about returning.

The shopkeeper recognised me.

"Back again!" he greeted me, not very welcomingly, I thought. "More questions?"

"Only one," I answered as I laid the new photo in front of him, "Was it one of them who bought the rod? They're friends of my brother's."

He did not hesitate. "That's him." He pointed to the second of Burbidge's men who had been approaching the camera as Nance took her photo. It was the Finn, my watcher from the caravan site, "He bought something else, too," he added pensively. "Now what the Dickens was it?" He paused, thinking hard, and then he suddenly brightened and looked at me again. "I know. It was a couple of books..."

"One about how to fish the other about birds," I prompted.

"That's it; you knew all along. Anyway, why don't you ask him?" and he jerked his head down towards the photograph of the Finn which still lay on the counter between us.

"I hadn't thought of it until now," I explained quickly and I hoped plausibly, "but I'll talk to him. Thanks." I replaced the photographs in my pocket and started for the door.

"Haven't you forgotten something?" The shopkeeper stopped me in my tracks.

I turned, puzzled and enquiring.

He did not help. He stood there waiting for me to speak.

"Forgotten what?"

"Forgotten what you first came in for." Still I could not understand.

"You wanted to ask if I'd take the rod back - remember?"

"I think I'd better have a word with the friend first. Maybe he'd like it back himself." I was not convincing and I did not convince him. I was altogether too slow in the uptake. It could not be helped though. I had found out what I wanted. "If he doesn't want it I'll be back." I escaped before he had time to say any more: he was sharper than I liked.

Everything pointed in the same direction, all the clues which I had assured Dick I would follow up.

I was still puzzling over it as I retraced my tracks towards Sherningham, which was just as well because puzzling kept the butterflies at bay.

I did not stop at the Anderson's house. I drove straight past and on, towards the Beach. I knocked at the door of the old woman who looked after the caravan park.

"I've come to settle up for my brother's caravan," I explained to her, holding out the key which the police had given me and which she had already seen in my hand before.

"That's all right. He paid in advance. I expect you're due some of the deposit, unless he broke a lot. We'd better 'ave a look,

115

I suppose." She did not relish the prospect of turning out of her warm bungalow.

"I'm afraid a lot of things are broken," I answered. "Though it wasn't my brother who broke them. Some vandals have been at the place. You didn't know?"

She looked startled. "It 'appens sometimes, but not at this time of year, not generally."

I drove her round.

She was upset. "Cor!" she exclaimed. "Would you believe it! You'd 'ave thought they'd 'ave better ways to spend their time than go round doin' that kind of thing. Cor!"

"Is it insured?" I asked.

"Not when it's empty, it's not."

"But it wasn't empty," I answered. "I spent the night there. Does that make any difference?'"

"I 'ope so. I'd better get on to them an' find out. Cor, what a mess! And all this lot'll 'ave ter be put right 'afore Easter, too. The lettings start then. Cor!"

I remembered Mrs Bassett. She would not have budgeted for a loss like that if she was not covered by insurance.

"I'll leave you my address," I said to the woman. "You'd better let me know what happens and whether you need my evidence that the van was occupied."

We locked up and I took her back to her bungalow. "Have you any idea who might have done it?" I asked.

"Not the least."

"So this kind of thing hasn't happened before?"

"Not like that, no."

"There are not many people here at the moment, are there? Could any of the ones living here be responsible, do you think?"

"Not as I know of."

I hesitated. I did not want my questions to sound as if they were prepared.

116

"What about the man who borrowed the key to look in the caravan next door? Could he have done a thing like that?"

"Dunno. Can't think why anyone would 'ave done a thing like that."

She had a point there! It was not for lack of trying that I, too, had failed to come up with an answer to that one.

"He lives in the caravan round the corner, doesn't he?" I went on. "The one which is set apart from the others. Why does he live here? Is he working locally like my brother? Do you think he'd be at home at the moment?"

"No, 'e wouldn't be at 'ome now. 'e works on them reservoirs they're making in the sea. I reckon 'e'd be over there at the moment, doin' 'is job."

"And he's alone? He doesn't share with anyone else?"

"Not as I know of."

I had discovered what I wanted, or rather all she knew of what I wanted.

I gave her my address, handed over the key, and left. I retained the spare key for the time being. It might come in useful for all I knew, and I could always send it on to her later. I was becoming crafty.

I drove out of the caravan park and past a shop which was closed at that time of year, but instead of turning right towards Sheringham at a T turning just beyond I turned left and back towards the sea. Soon after I swung off the road into a big public car park. In the summer it would have been filled to overflowing Now it was empty.

I turned the car before parking it, and then I left it in a corner as close to the sea embankments as possible.

I locked up, carefully, armed myself with a torch and a spanner, and set off up the embankment separating me from the sea. The other embankment was on the inland side of the car park, so I had already crossed it on my way in.

The tide was out again leaving a vast expanse of grey flatness, and a silence which seemed unnatural on a beach, broken only by the occasional calls of gulls. The waders must be far away at the edge of the water, where I had seen them before through Dick's binoculars.

I turned left and started walking.

The light was already going, but I could see enough to avoid clumps of weeds. I kept to the top of the beach and the bottom of the embankment where the walking was easiest, made difficult neither by the loose pebbles of the beach nor by the vegetation and slope of the embankment. From time to time I climbed up it to see how far I had gone.

Before long the second embankment swung in towards the first, so I crossed the near one and walked between the two. The going was still easy, although there was a certain amount of rubbish to avoid as well as more natural obstructions. I started mounting the inner embankment instead of the outer one in order to check my progress.

It was not long before the corner of my caravan park came in sight, the corner occupied by the isolated caravan. It was growing darker now. Lights would have shown if anybody had been at home, but the van was in darkness.

I crossed the embankment and approached. I saw no reason to be surreptitious.

I walked up to the door and knocked. I was so certain nobody was inside that I had not even troubled to prepare a story to explain my presence in case it should be needed.

There was no need.

I tried the door but it would not move; it had a lever lock like a car door, with the keyhole in the handle. I pushed the windows, but they were all fastened. I fingered my spanner, but then remembered some of the rubbish I had passed between the embankments on my way.

I returned and picked up a piece of galvanised pipe, one inch in diameter and about four feet long. With four feet of leverage it was not difficult to force the lock but I was puzzled that the occupier should have entrusted the contents to something so feeble. Perhaps, though, the contents were of no interest, and this was a wild goose chase? Time would show, at least I hoped it would.

I shut the door behind me and unfastened the flimsy catches at either side of a window opposite. I would have preferred it to have been the big end window, since that was the one which was hidden from anybody approaching along the road, but it was fixed. If a car came I would have to bide my time until it was drawing up beside the van, and while the driver was getting out I would have to escape through the window which, by then, would be hidden from him by the van. I would have to rely on his slowness in leaving his car and in reacting to the broken lock and unfastened window to give me time to get clear.

I dared not turn on the lights. I drew the curtains and used my torch, shading it with my hand as best I could, and at the same time keeping my ears alert for sounds from outside.

I might be interrupted, so I started in the most likely places. First the cupboard.

I threw everything from it to the floor. They had had no qualms about wrecking my caravan so why should I bother to keep theirs tidy? I had not enough time to cover my tracks. At intervals I stopped to listen for sounds, and to peer through a corner of the window facing the approach road, but there was no movement, not a whisper.

Clothes and shoes were in the cupboard, nothing else. It would have been easier if I had known what I was looking for.

Next came the shelf over the big window at the end. All these caravans must be designed in much the same way - at least that went for the ones I had come across so far. I found a few

119

books, and some papers which I stuffed into my pockets. I could examine them later in peace.

When I again stopped to look and listen I could see the glow of a car's lights round the corner outside the caretaker's bungalow. I had not heard it approach.

If it belonged to the owner of the van I was searching it would not take him long to reach me.

I left the van by the door.

I withdrew towards the nearby embankment and waited. If the car came on I could slip over the top of the embankment, concealed by the shadow of the van from the approaching headlights - I already had experience of that move.

It was night by now, damp and dark and so still that I could hear the low murmur of voices as a man left the caretaker's bungalow, walked along the path to his car, and opened and slammed the door as he entered it.

The car started forward into the camp.

But then it stopped, reversed, and drove slowly away again.

I returned to work.

The lockers beneath the three seats came next.

I threw the cushions from one to another and picked up the hatch which covered the access hole in the top. Inside, the space was crammed with old clothes, dirty and smelly. I pulled them out one by one, shook them, and threw them in a heap on the floor. To begin with I went through their pockets but I found nothing so I soon stopped doing that and relied upon shaking and handling to reveal thing which might be there.

When I reached the bottom I replaced the hatch and cushions and repeated the process with the second locker. It was not so full and its contents were at least clean, spare curtains and bedclothes. Again I shook them out and threw them aside. The pile on the floor grew inconveniently large, so when I reached the bottom of the locker I filled it again, stuffing filthy clothes and clean linen into it together. It gave me a simple kind of satisfaction to contaminate the clean things with the dirty, though it was poor revenge for the mess they had made of my of my own van - revenge probably taken on the wrong person, the owner rather than the occupier.

I replaced the hatch, put back the cushions, and repeated the process with the third and last locker.

Spare cushions and pillows: it did not take me long to pull them out and throw them on the floor, but I found nothing of interest.

I refilled the locker, lowered the bed from its recess in the partition wall and examined the bedclothes. The idea of making an apple pie bed crossed my mind, but that would have been too gentle; a man trap would have been more appropriate.

In the big cupboard between the two rooms I found a tool box, one of the kind which open out to reveal echelons of steel trays. It was well stocked, but with nothing more exciting than tools.

I had heard and seen no more since the car which parked near the caretaker had driven away. I began to hurry I could not have much more time, now that it was dark and normal working hours were over.

It did not take me long to search the kitchen. Again I removed the contents of all the cupboards, throwing most of them on to a table in one corner. I found nothing.

As I left the kitchen I flashed the beam of my torch round for the last time.

Something glinted from the pile of utensils on the table, probably the stainless-steel cutlery. I had searched everything now, so the pressure to hurry was easing and I returned to the table and rummaged through the pile, pulling out the shining piece of metal. It was not cutlery: it was in the middle of a pile of small plates, an odd one, slightly larger and more dished than the others, and the glint came from the edge of the rim. I turned it over, but by torchlight it was not easy to see it. It had

121

been badly treated, it was misshapen and twisted, and the rim had been flattened at one point by a blow which had turned the metal up. It looked to me like pewter.

I dropped it back on top of the pile on the table and it clattered on the crockery, knocking some to the floor so that I kicked plates and cups aside as I crossed to peep through the corner of the window facing the road and check that the coast was still clear, not a sound, not a movement.

On the way from window to door my torch travelled over the table again.

It was odd, the plate, in two ways. It was odd that there should be this one damaged plate that did not match the clean lines and primary colours of the melamine crockery which went with the caravan, and it was odd that it should have been brought in to augment the furnishings and equipment provided. Clothes, food, personal washing things had obviously been introduced by the occupier but sheets, pillows, cushions, crockery, cutlery, saucepans - all these were of a standard pattern, all must have been provided by the owner of the van; all were undiluted by the personal belongings of the occupier, except for the pewter plate.

I picked it up and found it just fitted into one of the front pockets of my anorak. It was easy to carry, so I left it there.

It was time to go. The owner of the caravan would surely be back soon.

I left as I had come, by the door, taking my length of galvanised pipe with me. I crossed the embankment and started on my way.

I went slowly to begin with. Although there was a nip in the air it was not as cold as it had been, and my exertions in the caravan had warmed me. After a time I discarded my piece of pipe and crossed the second embankment, so that I was walking at its base with the sea to my left. The tide was coming in. I could see the reflection of a low moon in the water further out, and where before there had been silence, now I could just hear the waves muttering on the mud they were overrunning. I stopped for a moment and turned to look and listen and admire.

I stopped again as soon as I turned back; something had moved on the embankment further on.

It was too big for a bird, and anyway no birds were about at that hour. A dog perhaps? But dogs do not crawl over the tops of embankments at night on their stomachs, keeping a low profile. An enormous snake might have moved like that, but I doubted whether there were any pythons and boa constrictors about, and anyway it was excessively fat and short for a snake. I could only be a human being, but a human being on his stomach. Why?

I followed suit, sinking down on my own stomach and lying there, thinking and looking.

Whoever it was had crossed the embankment not far from the place where I would have to recross it, just about opposite my car. I wondered if I would be wise to cross it where I was, instead. If the person had come down on my side I would miss him. If he had descended on the far side ... either I would miss him, or he would be lurking in the shadow cast by the moon from my side. I regretted that I had thrown away my piece of pipe. It would have made a better weapon than the spanner.

In any case I had better get over here.

I looked back at the spot where I had seen the movement. I could not be sure where it was now. I continued, searching with my eyes backwards and forwards along the crest of the embankment, and the longer I searched the more difficult I found it to identify the same place again.

Until it moved.

That was why I could not find it, the skyline had changed shape, and whoever it was, was just lying there, waiting - for me? From the far side, where the car was parked I would have missed him, but from the position where I lay below the bank my skyline was the near side of its crest, exactly the place occupied by the bulk of his body. In keeping off the skyline from the far side he was doing for me, in my position, exactly what he was trying to avoid.

I was surprised to find how calm I was. I must have become used to this strange lifestyle which to begin with I had found so alarming. Or, more likely, when it came to action I was all right - at least when the opposition so considerately gave away its position to me. It was when I was threatened, when I was reduced to waiting in suspense while I wondered where the next blow would come from that my confidence evaporated and I just wanted to run for cover.

One thing comforted me, whoever it was could not have seen or heard me. If he had he would not have stayed where he was, silhouetted from me against the skyline. I had two advantages: firstly that I knew where he was, secondly that he was not even expecting me to come from the side where I was lying.

If I simply crawled up to the top of the embankment and over there must come a time when from my watcher's position I would myself be on the skyline. Perhaps he would not be looking at that moment. The faster I crossed, the less time he had to turn and see me. I remembered a man I had once met who professed to a habit of applying this theory to the crossing of road junctions in a car. The faster he went, he told me, the shorter the time he was exposed to oncoming vehicles at right angles to him, and therefore the less dangerous it was. He had said it with a twinkle in his eye, but he ended up in a coffin.

No; greater finesse than that was called for.

I looked round at the moon, so recently my ally, now my enemy.

Help was approaching. A small bank of cloud was drifting across the sky.

I lay and waited. As soon as the moon was dimmed by the cloud I started crawling. When I was near the top of the embankment I adopted the other man's method: very slowly I eased myself over the crest, and by the time the moon came out again I was in the shadow on the far side. I looked back and could see no sign of my watcher.

So far so good, but what next?

I would be within my rights to walk openly into the car park from the public road, enter the car, and drive off. Nobody could stop me ... well, not legally.

But I had a feeling that the fiat of the law might not be impressed very deeply upon the car park at that hour.

My watcher would be getting cold lying there motionless for hours at a time.

Serve him right! I would do better to keep moving and keep warm. I set off, on foot, discreetly and silently at first, cheerfully and nonchalantly when I was out of earshot of the car park, but ready at any moment to drop into a ditch at the side of the road if a car approached from behind.

There was no need, however, for the roads were deserted that night. Perhaps at that time of year they were deserted most of the time. If so it reinforced my lack of confidence in the maintenance of law and order in the car park.

Sally again opened the door, neat and trim, in a white blouse and a black skirt. It always seemed to be her. Coincidence? I hoped not.

I was hot and dishevelled and once more covered with mud, and she stared at me.

"Cowboys and Indians again, I suppose?"

"Yes, but no horses."

"Who's winning now?"

"Nobody. It'll go down in the history books as an indecisive engagement. The Running Battle of Sherningham Beach, perhaps. That sounds quite good, doesn't it?"

"It sounds a good deal better than you look." She sighed. "Will you never learn, George? You'd better come in and be cleaned up again."

I was about to follow her meekly, ready to receive my punishment and enjoy it, when sounds of voices came from the lounge. Immediately I had visions of the rest of her family, bright, talkative, friendly ... and questioning. My heart sank. But then it rose again.

"It's only on the surface," I told her. "If I take the outer layer off I'm clean and neat as can be. I'm dressed up, specially to take you out." Specially, yes - for Dick's funeral, actually.

"But you're expected for supper here."

"So are you - that makes two of us."

I could see she was uncertain. Family conformity versus independence and, I hoped, her own inclinations.

"I need someone to talk to," I added, "not a committee." I did my best to look like a fitting subject for the social services, needing help, just like Sally's old Mrs Thornton who she always visited on Thursday afternoons.

It worked. She was a little reluctant, but she came, and what was more it was the first time I had seen her got up for an evening's outing. She did not have much time to dress up but she made full use of such time as she did have: a lacey cream-coloured blouse, tailored to show off her figure, and a long grey skirt which covered her feet; a necklace of what looked to me like real pearls, and enough scent to allure without overpowering. I was allured.

The evening reinforced my opinion of her; and Nance's.

I had said I needed someone to talk to, so I had to talk. I went further than I had done before. I told her of my enquiries about the fishing tackle, and of how I had discovered that the Finn had bought it and the books, and of how it was designed to be used from a boat.

"So it looks as if the Finn was a friend of Dick's and was going to teach him to fish?" she commented, "that is, assuming he didn't know how to do it before. Did he, do you know?"

126

"I don't think so. I've never heard him talking about it, and apart from this fishing tackle and the book about fishing, which was new, there were no signs of it among his belongings. Besides, I remember a year or two ago I happened to see Dick not long after I had been down to Dorset and watched people fishing from the beach there. I was impressed by it, I remember, so I described it all to him. They were doing it from a pebbly bit of beach which shelved quickly into deeper water, and there were all these fishermen with great big fishing rods, and I watched them casting; the distance they could flick their lines out to sea was unbelievable, and some of them had buckets beside them overflowing with mackerel. Dick was interested enough to listen, but he knew no more about it than I did, I'm sure of it. Maybe I inspired him, though. Maybe that was one of the reasons he was taking up fishing here, now he had the opportunity."

Sally was not really listening to me, though.

"If the Finn was a friend of Dick's," she said, "it seems a funny kind of friendship, doesn't it? That he should attack his friend's brother as soon as his friend is dead, and then break up his caravan. It doesn't make sense."

It did not, and it was in order to make some sense out of it that I had been ransacking the Finn's caravan. But I had learned nothing.

"I could go and talk to him now," I said. "I could ask him if he'd like his fishing rod back again."

"You could, and his answer might tell you a good deal."

If he left me alive for long enough to listen, I added to myself. I had not told her enough for her to realise quite how scared I had been by the Finn, and by the way he had waited by my car.

"I'll do that," I said, without much conviction.

"And there's another thing you should do," Sally put in, "Go and tell the police."

It had to come sooner or later, I had realised that some time ago, and now seemed as good a moment as any to tell her.

"They wouldn't believe me."

"Of course they would. "Why ever not?"

"Because I lied to them once." I was watching her keenly to see her reaction.

"Lied?"

"Yes."

"Tell me, George,"

"It was about three years ago now. Do you remember I told you how I left a firm just as it became bankrupt?" She nodded. "Well, I left out a bit of the story when I told you before.

"You see, I saw they were in difficulties. I'd kept an eye on the contracts I knew about and some of them had gone wrong - one in particular had been losing money in quite a big way. Well, then I saw other signs that things were going wrong: they were slow paying their accounts, and they were put on the stop list by a few of their regular suppliers; and some of the cheques they sent out used to be unsigned - apparently by mistake, you understand - or post-dated; and when everyone else went home at the end of the day the lights in the offices of the general manager and the accountant were still on. Once when I went past much later in the evening, after ten o'clock it must have been, the general manager's light was still on. And they had a few mysterious visitors too, people who had never been near the place before, and whose presence was not explained, including the man who ran one of the biggest rival firms in the district; and people said he was behaving aggressively when our general manager showed him round, strutting about as if he owned the place. But if that was what he was after - buying it - he was too slow.

"Anyway, when I saw what was coming I took evasive action of my own: heaven helps those who help themselves. You see I'd been promised, when I joined the company, that I would have a substantial pay rise after my first 18 months. Probation for six months, they said, then a small increase, but a much bigger one a year after that. Well, I'd nearly finished my eighteen months, and I could see that if I waited the company might not last that long. I'd have some kind of redundancy money, but because of the way the rise was arranged it would be based on the low salary I'd started with instead of the increased one I was due. Either way the redundancy didn't add up to much, not after all the effort I'd put in, and it was the rise I'd been working for as hard as I knew how, not the pay I'd actually been getting, still less redundancy money based on it."

I paused as I thought sourly about what I was describing; just talking about it brought all my bitterness back to me. But Sally prompted me. "Go on," she said.

"So, as I could see they weren't going to give it to me, I took it."

"You stole it?"

"That's what they called it."

"How? They didn't leave the safe open for you to take it. How did you manage it?"

"Oh ... ways and means, you know. I just took every opportunity I could see..."

"Such as?" She was persistent when she wanted to find something out.

"Well, I diverted a new drawing board so that I got it rather than them.

"And I took some of the materials which had been bought for one of the jobs, the big one I was telling you about, which was going wrong."

"So you helped it go more wrong, is that it, George?" She did not mince her words, Sally.

"Not really. I may have helped it at the end, but it was already in a bad way. And when the company did go bust the receiver sold the rest of the materials on that job at a give-away price.

And I only took what was due to me - in return for 18 months sweated labour on false pretences."

I could see she was not impressed with my explanations. Perhaps I had misjudged her after all; perhaps the stodgy secure upbringing she had had was winning, when it came to the crunch, against the way I thought she had got over it - got over it because she, too, was disadvantaged; I had convinced myself that that was why she looked after her Mrs Thornton on Thursday afternoons, but I must have got it wrong after all.

Then I found her hand was on my knee, pressing it gently.

"Poor George," she said, "What happened? Did they prosecute?"

"Yes, they said they had to," 'had to' indeed - hypocrites! They found other people had been doing the same kind of thing, but some of them in a much bigger way. So they prosecuted the lot of us."

"And what happened?"

"The big ones were put inside."

"And you?"

"A suspended sentence."

"Poor George! Anyway it might have been worse, and I suppose you learnt a lesson."

Was that a question or a statement, I wondered. Her hand was still on my knee, and mine was covering it now.

"Anyway," I added, relaxing, "the suspense is over now, they'll have to give me a fresh sentence next time." A flicker crossed her face: she had not realised I was joking. "But you're right, I've learnt my lesson; there won't be another time." And I had better not mention the drawing board which I had nearly joked about, too. They had never caught up with that, and I had found it a godsend when I set up on my own. It was a first-class board, fully equipped.

The pub to which we had gone for dinner was exactly right. It was not big and pretentious, nor was it cheap and garish. We had

130

a table out of the way in an alcove. The food was good, the lights not too bright, the general feeling was friendly and intimate. We absorbed the general feeling and - at last - I had my kiss. It had been worth waiting for, too, soft and yielding, and she snuggled cosily into my arm when I put it round her.

As we left the dining room I helped her on with her coat, and then I slipped my anorak on, plunging my hands into the pockets. My left hand came up against a hard object and one of my fingernails caught on its rim; it was the bowl I had taken from the Finn's caravan, and it reminded me vividly of the events of the early evening, out on Sherningham beach. It also reminded me what the pieces of paper were which my right hand encountered: the papers which I had hurriedly swept off the shelf above the big window in the caravan and shovelled into my pocket, thinking as I did so that I would be able to look at them later at my leisure without fear of being caught in the act of burglary.

Immediately my curiosity became urgent. I must look at them there and then. The whole incident had produced nothing so far, but perhaps here, in my pocket, was the pay off which would make it all worthwhile.

"One minute," I said to Sally. "Let's have a drink before we go home." I indicated the lounge bar which opened off the hall of the pub in which we were standing.

She looked doubtful. We had had our outing and a cuddle and we were on our way home. It was scarcely the moment to start all over again.

"Please," I urged. "There's something I want to show you. I forgot about it until this moment."

She looked doubtful, but she came.

We found a table to ourselves in a corner of the bar with a light over it. When I came back with the drinks I placed them on beer mats on the table. Then I pulled from my pocket all the pieces of paper I had taken from the caravan. They looked a scruffy lot, and Sally said as much. "What are they?" she asked. "I'd forgotten about them until I put my coat on. They're things I took from the Finn's caravan down at the Beach. I didn't have time to look at them at the time and afterwards I forgot about. them. Let's see what they are, now."

A piece of pale blue paper was on top of the pile, folded, creased, and slightly rounded as if it had once been in a hip pocket. I opened it out. It was a receipt - for some fishing tackle and for two bob: "How to look at British Coastal Birds" and "Sea-fishing, a beginner's guide".

My frantic chase round the fishing shops of King's Lynn, Hunstanton, and Wisbech had been unnecessary. Here in front of me was the information I had been searching for. Now I had documentary evidence to confirm it.

"Funny," Sally muttered thoughtfully. "You'd have thought that if Dick had bought them he was the one who would have had the receipt." She was looking at the paper upside down. "What name is there at the top?"

"No name," I answered.

"Even if the Finn had bought them for Dick you'd have expected him to hand over the receipt as well as the goods. And they're worth a bit. Not the kind of thing a fairly new friend was likely to produce as a present."

"Maybe the receipt is one of the things which the Finn found in Dick's caravan, and took." But why should he bother, I added to myself, what use could he have had for it?

The rest of the scraps of paper were quite uninteresting by comparison, odd notes, printed instructions for use of a new camera (probably not so new now, judging by the frayed and grimy appearance of the paper), a bag containing a spare gas mantle and another from which the mantle had already been removed, and so on. But at the bottom of the pile was another folded piece of paper, white this time, again slightly rounded in shape, and as soon as I started to unfold it and glimpsed the writing inside I caught my breath.

The handwriting was Dick's.

I unfolded it and spread it out. It was a letter - to me.

"Dear George," it started. There was no address but there was a date: the day before he was picked out of the sea. "If you find this - and I really hope you don't because then my fears and suspicions will have proved groundless - but if you do find it what I have to say, and what is attached to it, may answer a few questions. I pinched it from Jason. It's only one of a number which he and Barry have dug up. To begin with I thought they were going to turn them in to the police, though now I am not so sure, but they ought to - they're treasure trove. They almost caught me red-handed when I took it, in fact for a moment I was positive they had seen me, and that they knew I had overheard them discussing how to get the things out of the country - through a friend, the master of a cargo vessel which calls regularly at Lynn. I don't know the name of the ship, but the friend they referred to as Jack - not a very helpful name for identification, I'm afraid. If they do catch me I'm not sure that I fancy my chances of survival very much - sounds melodramatic, that, doesn't it? but I don't think I'm exaggerating. If they don't, then I'll turn this over to the police - and maybe ask for protection! I'm pretty sure Eric is in with them too, though I couldn't prove it, and I get the feeling that they've been in touch with someone else, I've no idea who, for confirmation that what they've found is valuable, and that he or she will get some of it as a quid pro quo. I think it's some kind of mediaeval treasure, but where they've dug it up, goodness knows. I'll hide this in the hope that you'll find it if anything happens to me, and I'll leave you some kind of message to make you look. I think I'll be safer here for the night rather than creeping off to the police in a surreptitious way at this hour. If Jason & Co have any suspicions and see me creeping they'll jump - like a ton of bricks. Again, I hope you never have to read this. Dick."

"Phew!" Sally and I both said it, or words to that effect.

Suddenly the whole business had crossed a Rubicon. Previously I had been quietly mugged, caravans had been broken up and changed, but I seemed to be the only one involved. It had all seemed so pointless, and private, my affair and no one else's, but now there was a point all right, even though it made the immediate future no less certain.

"Poor Dick!" Sally murmured at last.

"Mm. It doesn't look as if it was an accident now, does it? Lug worming, indeed!"

"I wonder what could have happened to him."

I can guess, I thought, remembering the strength of the Finn's arms round me, and the sickening smell of the chloroform, and the nauseating feeling when I woke up. It looked as if Dick had been spared the last stage, at least.

"They must have come for him," Sally went on.

"Yes," I muttered grimly, and I thought of the vows I had made in the mortuary chapel while waiting for the cremation service to begin, talking to Dick as he lay in his coffin.

"What do you think they did?" Sally asked. She must have forgotten about my experiences at that moment.

"The same as they did to me," I answered, "and more! .... Chloroform ....and it was low tide later in the evening, and it all looked just like an accident."

"And the fishing tackle, and the books? Do you mean to say that they had them all ready, just in case?"

That did seem unlikely if they had only just discovered Dick knew all about them.

I turned back the other bits of paper until I came to the blue receipt from the fishing shop which had sold the stuff to the Finn - to Jason - we might as well use his name now that we knew it. I opened it up and looked for a date.

It was clearly written at the top: the same date as Dick's letter. "It looks as if they planned the whole thing immediately they knew Dick had found out," I said. "They must have sent Jason straight off to the shops before they shut, and when Dick wrote that letter he had already been condemned. He did not know it, but he suspected it."

"Yes," Sally added, "and if only he had chosen the other option he might still be alive, if he had tried to get to the police that evening he might have got away before they came for him."

"Might ... but I don't think so." I remembered the way Jason and Barry had been left to watch me in the caravan park, not just once, but twice.

Sally looked at me. "You sound very sure, George."

So this time I told her a good deal more about my games of Cowboys and Indians, and then we both sat in silence for a time, lost in our thoughts. Mine were plentiful, but utterly disorganised.

At last Sally picked up Dick's letter again.

"Well, there's no doubt now," she told me, "you're for the police."

"Yes," I answered vaguely, "yes,"

"Straight away, too."

"No," the vagueness was going. "I'll go, but in my own time; in a day or two."

"But you've a duty...." 'Duty'! As soon as she said the word I knew I was free to go about it in my own way. I had a duty to Dick, yes, but that was not the duty she meant, she meant my duty to the community, that precious thing which had shifted me and Dick from one foster home to another, which had left me without job or money when my firm had gone bankrupt, handing what was left on a plate to the bank and the receiver. I owed the community no duty. I would go to the police in my time, not theirs; my duty to Dick came first.

135

Sally was troubled. She bit her lip and looked as if she was going to argue. But then she thought better of it. "All right George," she said, "but only one day. And if you haven't been to them then, I'll go. I know enough about it now."

We sat in silence, not comfortably. Sally fingered the bits of paper. She read Dick's letter again, flicking its corner distractedly with her thumbnail. "It sounds as if something should have been attached to this letter," she said. "Was there anything?"

"No." I shook my head.

She turned it and folded it again. Then she turned the folded sheet over, and two marks became a visible. Why we had not noticed them before, I do not know, probably because we had been in such a hurry to unfold the letter and read it. In those two places, one on each side of the folded letter, the surface of the paper had been removed as if something had been stuck to it so securely that when it was torn away the surface layer of the paper itself had given rather than the adhesive.

"It was there," she said, "whatever 'it' may have been."

Chapter 10

Sally's parents were still up when we returned, we could hear their voices as we entered the front door.

Sally took my anorak when I had removed it.

"We'd better clean it up again," she said, going through into the brighter light of the kitchen to do so.

"What's this?" she exclaimed as her hand, passing down it with the clothes brush, came up against a hard object.

"I'd forgotten about that. It's an old tin bowl I picked up." I went over and pulled it out of the pocket.

Until then I had seen it only by torchlight, and hurriedly at that, in the caravan, so this was the first opportunity I had had to examine it by a good light. But it did not make any difference. It still looked to me like an old, battered, plate made of pewter or some alloy like that - probably not as good as pewter, when I came to think of it, much more likely to be something of the kind you buy in Woolworths. Sally took it from my hand.

She bent over it, examining it closely, "Something's knocked it at the rim," she said. "It looks very shiny just here, doesn't it?"

She put it down on the table and went to a drawer at one side of the kitchen. Out of it came a tin of metal polish and a duster. I watched as she started rubbing the polish on, and then cleaning it off.

Then we both stared in amazement.

She had only worked at a small area, a smoothish, convex surface on the underside of the bowl, and as she rubbed the polish off a white, bright surface came up.

"Phew," she exclaimed. "Do you know what I think it's made of?" She did not have to say any more. We chorused the word, "Silver!"

We both went on staring, and then she turned it over and round in her hands.

It was a good deal misshapen, as if someone had taken it in two hands, one at each side, and twisted, and then added a few dents and lines for good measure. And there was another curious thing about it which I had not noticed before: it had no hard rim round it at the bottom, of the kind you usually find in mass-produced kitchen wear; it was rounded underneath evenly enough, but not quite evenly - amateurishly, as if it had been made by someone who had not been going to evening classes long enough. Nor did it seem altogether uniform in thickness, as if the teacher at the evening classes had failed to get the fundamentals right in the first place.

Sally looked at me. "I think we'd better show it to Dad and see what he thinks of it. He'd be interested, and he might have some idea what it is." She paused, and then asked, "Where did you find it, George?"

"I picked it up in the Finn's caravan," I answered.

"Along with the bits of paper? But you didn't tell me, George."

"No, I'd forgotten it, and anyway I just thought it was any old bit of tin."

"Then why take it?" Sally could be persistent, and logical.

"I'd forgotten that, too. It was in the kitchen, stacked with all the plates and bowls and cutlery. But they were all clean, new, stuff. The bowl wasn't. It was the fish out of water. And besides, it caught my eye: I saw it glinting, like you did, at its edge."

Sally looked at it again, this time peering into the bowl, and then running her finger over two spots inside it, and then looking again, holding it to the light.

"There are two bumpy bits here," she said. "They're soft: I can push my fingernail into them."

I looked too. They were at each side of the bowl.

I put my hand into the anorak pocket again and pulled out Dick's letter.

We had flattened it as we read it, so I tried to restore its rounded shape, as it had been when I had first taken it from my pocket. Then I placed it in the bowl. It fitted, and the two rough places in the bowl corresponded with the patches on the outside of the letter where the surface of the paper had been torn by the glue Dick must have used to stick it to the bowl.

"They belong to each other," I said. "The bowl must be the evidence Dick left me, the thing Jason & Co had dug up. And they must have known he'd got it too. That's why they were so desperate to find it, why they went to all those lengths to swap the caravans over and why they pulled Dick's van to pieces." What is more, I added to myself, feeling the butterflies returning even as I thought about it, if I had found it first and they had known I had done so ... what would they have done to me to get it back?

It required no imagination to think of an answer to that one. After all, they had killed Dick because he had discovered their secret and taken the bowl as evidence, so the only thing I could not be certain of was the precise way in which they would have gone about killing me - scope for imagination there, certainly: a challenge to which they would have enjoyed rising! Perhaps they would have used the same method ... if I had been lucky. If not, other, more gruesome methods were available. I could think of a few mild and gentlemanly kinds of torture myself; they were not mild men though, nor gentle.

Sally was looking at me questioningly by now as I stood, plunged in gloomy speculation, so I pulled myself together with some relief; this was no time for planning assassinations, however speculative.

We went through into the drawing room.

The younger girl had gone to bed, so Mr and Mrs Anderson were the only ones there. They had probably been waiting up for us, I reflected, waiting to see if this stranger would really bring their daughter back without harm. I must be quite out of character with the kind of friends the family would normally bring in.

And as soon as we were in there, standing in front of the fire and talking to them, my awkwardness and inhibitions came back to me. Before we went in I was ready to explain the bowl and show it to them, but once inside, exchanging polite conversation about the evening - where we had been, whether the dinner had been good, whether the hotel had been crowded - once that started I became tongue-tied and all the explanations which had been on the tip of my tongue when we were in the kitchen evaporated.

I held the bowl out to Mr Anderson, but I said nothing.

"George has brought it in to ask if you can tell us anything about it," Sally explained for me. "We think it may be valuable."

Mr Anderson took it from my hand without a word. Suddenly he had changed - like me! A moment ago he had been the polite host; now he was the preoccupied professional, his expression still alert but also concentrated and neutral.

I had passed the bowl to him with its open side upwards, as if it contained something which must not be tipped out. Mr Anderson kept it at that angle for a moment, then he tilted it towards him, peering into the bowl, finding immediately the two raised marks of the adhesive, running his finger over them, pressing them at first gently, then more firmly, and finally prodding them with his fingernail as Sally had done and discovering, like her, that they were slightly soft. Then, still without a word, still expressionlessly, he turned the bowl over and examined its other side. His eye went straight to the patch which Sally had polished, revealing the white, shining metal, and he raised this and peered at it close to, pushing his spectacles up on to his forehead as he did so. Then he examined the remainder of it, finally turning it, cartwheel fashion, between his hands as he looked at the rim.

Even then he did not stop. He turned back and appeared to be looking at it all over again. But I was still watching him, and his eyes were not on it: they went straight past it, staring at the carpet beyond, and his brow was creased in a frown.

"Where does it come from?" he asked me, looking up at last.

I hesitated. It was one thing to tell Sally, who knew something of the background of my piece of private investigation in searching the Finn's caravan and the reasons for it; provocation and its justification by what I had found there. It was another to tell her father, respectable, upright, on the side of law and order.

Sally came to my rescue.

"It wasn't George who found it," she explained. "It was someone else who did so, and we don't know where." She paused; she must have been thinking along the same lines as me. "All we know is that it was dug up out of the ground, and we are pretty sure it was fairly local."

Bless her! I thought. Dear Sally! She had told her father enough for his purposes, all the information we possessed about the bowl including Dick's comments on it, but without saying a word of how I had come to have it in my possession.

But the information only seemed to have sent her father off into his brown study once again. Once more he appeared to be examining the bowl in his hands. Once more, though, I could see that his eyes were on the carpet, not the bowl, and that his thoughts, though concentrated no doubt on something connected with the bowl, were not actually on the bowl itself. What line of thought could he be following, I wondered? The only extra information Sally had given him was that it had been dug up, and dug up locally - not really a very surprising or thought-provoking revelation, I would have thought.

At last he spoke.

"A pity," he began. "I wish you could tell me where it had been dug up. That would be useful, and interesting. In the absence of that important information, any comments I make must be the subject of guesswork more than I like. I'm no expert on this kind of thing - I'm a historian, not an archaeologist - so anything I say

141

must be subject to correction, or confirmation, by the experts." He paused for some time, eyes fixed again on the carpet, and I was beginning to wonder if he would ever finish what he had apparently been going to say. Finally he went on: "I think it's silver," he said, "and I think it's mediaeval. If it's what I think it may be, it's a remarkable find. I think it's part of the furnishings of an early church." He appeared to be about to say something else, but then to hesitate and to think better of whatever it was he was about to say.

Instead he went on, looking up at me: "I do wish you would tell me where it was picked up. It could make all the difference."

"I'm sorry, I'm not trying to keep it secret, but I don't know myself."

"Can't you find out?"

"I doubt it," I answered. "Not easily, anyway." I smiled wryly to myself as I contemplated going up to the Finn and asking him where he had got it from. As clear an invitation to more chloroform - or worse - as I could think of.

Mr Anderson went back into his brown study, fingering the bowl, staring at the carpet. "No," he said finally. "If you can't tell me where it was found I can't tell you any more about it." He looked up, suddenly more brisk and decisive, as if this brief and negative pronouncement had taken a load off his mind.

"What about King John? What about his baggage train? Could this have been part of it?" It was Sally who made the suggestion.

Immediately the load was back on Mr Anderson's mind as he stared again at the carpet, apparently seeking inspiration from it. "I don't know," he answered rather mournfully, as if he disliked, even resented, being questioned about it now. "It's the kind of thing which might have existed in those days. But ... where was it found?" Full circle!

And then, suddenly, my brain was racing as inspiration crowded in - inspiration, or just idle speculation?

Here in front of me was the man who, only the day before, had delivered a first class lecture about King John, such a good lecture that even I, someone quite uninterested, had listened eagerly to much of it. And the moment when he had become most interesting, therefore most enthusiastic, was the moment when he was being questioned about the loss of King John's baggage train in The Wash, and speculating about where it might have been lost, and how. Now, only a day later, when faced with an object which might even have been part of that baggage train, all his inspiration, all his enthusiasm, was gone. Why? Why?

And the answer: Mr Anderson must be the person to whom Dick had referred in his letter, the expert to whom they had taken some of the objects they had salvaged and who had identified them as being valuable - the man who was to have a few of the pieces as his share of the proceeds, while the rest were taken abroad by the mysterious 'Jack', master of the cargo boat.

I was only guessing, but there could not be many people sufficiently expert in this kind of thing for Jason and his friends to have gone to, and Mr Anderson, well-known locally as a scholar with a great interest in King John and his baggage train, was an obvious person to start with.

It would account for so many things. It would account for his reluctance to offer an opinion, even when prompted by his own daughter, even on one of his favourite topics (had not Sally turned to me several times during the lecture to say how her father loved talking about it?), and it would account for his hesitation now, his long contemplation of the carpet while he tried to guess whether this bowl was part of the booty dug up by his confederates, and if so how it had come into my hands; it would account for his harping back perpetually to the question of where it was found; it would account for his lack of enthusiasm, and the time he needed to work out what and how much to say to us here and now; it would account for the way he had tried to discourage me from going to the lecture in the first place.

Pure guesswork, of course!

It might be someone else who was Jason's confederate. Mr Anderson's hesitation might be no more than a scholarly examination of the question in all its aspects, a right and proper reluctance to speculate.

Guesswork or not, though, it was a possibility, and one which at that moment I would have put my money on.

What was more, it was a possibility which I could not discuss with Sally. For if there were two things about her of which I was sure, one was her loyalty to her father, and the other was that she knew nothing about his involvement, if involvement it was, at the time we were talking things over in the pub and discussing Dick's letter. It had all been as much a surprise to her as it had to me, of that I was certain.

But my guessing game was brought to an abrupt halt, this time by Mrs Anderson who, until now, had remained silent.

"Don't you think, dear," she said softly, "that it would be a good idea to get a second opinion?"

"Eh?" Mr Anderson's mind was still elsewhere, apparently on the carpet.

"The bowl, dear. Don't you think it would be a good idea to get a second opinion about it? You'll be in King's Lynn in the morning. Why don't you take it round to Gerald Eke? This kind of thing is just up his street, isn't it?" To me she then added, in a voice which would have passed as a stage whisper: "Gerald's the archivist. He's very clever."

"Oh, I don't know...." Mr Anderson began. But at that moment Sally joined in as well, pressing him to take it with him. And so it was arranged before we all went up to bed: Mr Anderson would take it to Gerald Eke in the morning, and then Mrs Anderson and Sally would join him before going on to the Conservation Society's meeting which Mr Stevens had been talking about the day before. Marge had refused to go, but I seemed to have a kind of open invitation to join the party, at least an invitation from Sally if not from her father.

As I climbed the stairs a further thought occurred to me: Gerald Eke was another local expert who might have been consulted by Jason and the others. But I had never met Gerald Eke, and Mr Anderson's evasiveness and excessive thoughtfulness still left him as my favourite for gangster's accomplice. True, it seemed out of character with the family, but every family has a skeleton in its cupboard, and why should the Andersons not have one too? I had already seen that he had two faces to show the world: that of the polished, assured, man of substance, at home in his drawing room; and that of the thoughtful, impartial, scholar, working in his study. Why should he not have a third face which he kept hidden from the world? - that of the surreptitious conspirator?

Next day I had to recover my car.

Sally took me down to the Beach and I asked her to wait with her engine running while I got in and started. If Jason should reappear I wanted to have an escape route, and though he might have harmed me without a second thought if I had been on my own I did not think he would do anything in broad daylight if Sally was with me, sitting in a car, ready to drive off to fetch help. In the event, though, my precautions were unnecessary. The car started easily in spite of its damp night out and Jason was not about, or if he was he kept discreetly out of the way.

Then I told Sally that I had some things I had to do. She wanted to know what they were, but I would not tell her, not with my suspicions about her father. "But you'll come to the meeting this afternoon, won't you?"

I was not enthusiastic. The thought of listening to a self-important Mr Stevens with the stage to himself was not inviting.

"By then Dad will have seen Gerald Eke. He'll have Gerald's opinion as well."

145

Yes, I thought, I would like to hear that. I would rather have heard it from Gerald Eke himself, but I did not think Mr Anderson would distort it in any way; it would be against his nature as a scholar to distort the evidence and it would be too easy for Mr Eke to contradict him later.

"I'll be there," I told her.

***

I set off on what was becoming a well-worn trail, south along the road to King's Lynn, west at the big roundabout where the elevated section of the bypass took off, and then north west towards Sutton Bridge and Burbidge's depot.

I turned off towards the depot, but I was not going there.

When I reached the cluster of buildings where I had borrowed a spanner to change my wheel, I parked at the side of the road. I took a note from my wallet and approached the door of the workshop. Although I had thanked the farm hand for his help in lending me a spanner, I had not repaid him for it in any way. It was only reasonable that I should make good the deficiency.

I went through the same drill as before: I banged at the door of the workshop, waited a short time, and pulled it open.

No light, no man. But then it was lunch time, I had been careful to make sure of that.

There were no windows in the building so I turned on the light without hesitation, and made for the corner I was interested in, beside the door.

There were six mine detectors of four different makes. They were all in bits. But it did not look to me as if they were being repaired, no signs of soldering or replacement of broken or defective parts.

I wished I understood electrical gadgets better, I might be an electrical draughtsman, but all that meant was that I knew the symbols and some of the names. What the names did, why

146

the symbols were connected together in the way they were, and what the symbols looked like in real life were different matters of which I had only a smattering. Besides, this was electronics and I dealt in bigger stuff, old-fashioned electrics.

All the detectors seemed to have bits missing from them, so I started looking for the bits. Some were there, but not enough. Search as I would, I could find no sign of the missing parts.

Time was going on and the farm hand might be back from lunch at any moment.

I still had the bank note in my hands, but it would be a less convincing alibi presented to him from inside his workshop by someone kneeling in front of his equipment and examining it.

I stood up and cast round in case there was anything else to see. If there was I could not see it.

I pushed the door open and turned out the light, kicking a brown cardboard box as I did so. I thought I had damaged it because I trod heavily and it tilted towards me. It was so light it seemed empty, but something inside slithered across its bottom. By the light now coming through the door I saw that it was a brown cardboard carton, labelled 'English Apples', similar to the one I had found in Stevens' office in King's Lynn containing the King John pennies.

When I opened this one I found it contained a King John penny, too.

There was only one, and that was what had slid across its bottom when I kicked it; it must have been hidden under one of the flaps at the bottom, but my clumsiness had shaken it out of hiding. I picked it up, wrapped it in my handkerchief carefully, without wiping it, and put it in my pocket. If the owner did not know it was there he would not miss it and besides, I had a use for it.

I closed the door and returned to my car, driving on thoughtfully and keeping a lookout for a turning place. Then I drove back, equally thoughtfully, and saw that I had only just been in time. The farm hand's blue car was parked in the yard outside the workshop now.

The field beyond was being cultivated. A crawler tractor stood unattended about twenty yards from one of the corners by the road. I was scarcely moving by now and I stopped to look at it. One of the deepest furrows I have ever seen led up to the single furrow plough which the tractor was pulling; it was more like a trench than a furrow, and with a big crawler tractor pulling the single blade it was not so surprising. I had never seen a field ploughed as deeply as that. Curious, I left the car and started walking beside the furrow towards the tractor.

The ground was silty, but a fairly heavy silt, and the amount of moisture in it must have made it perfect for working.

Which is why I wondered why the bottom of the furrow was such a mess: not a clean, smooth cut but a messy, crumbly affair. When I reached the tractor I could see why.

The plough was not the deepest part of the implement. Beneath the plough, and set back behind it so that it plunged into the bottom of the trench, was a shaft, black even at its forward cutting edge: tough plastic of some kind, perhaps? How deep it was I could not tell because it was hidden in the ground. A sub-soil plough, I think a farmer would call it, but a sub-soil plough with a difference.

From its top came a thin electric cable. It was not something which had been dragged up by mistake and had then clung to the plough; it was fixed to the implement at intervals until it disappeared into the back of the driver's cab.

I moved round to the side of the tractor, the side away from the cluster of buildings, opened the door and peered in. It did not take long to identify the wire. It came through the cab at the back, was clipped to the side of the cab as it came forward to a ledge in front of the driver, and then disappeared inside a home-made looking box with a knob and dial on its side facing the driver. From another part of the box came another wire, this

148

time going to a set of headphones, an unremarkable thing for a tractor driver to be wearing so long as they were attached to a radio, not to a home-made device like this.

The knob was small and black. On, off, and volume? I could just reach it from the ground where I stood, beside the tractor and leaning in through its door, and I could just reach the headphones, and I was just reaching for them both when I heard a shout.

Rapidly I withdrew my hands from the instruments and my body from the cab doorway.

Making his way across the ploughed field from the group of buildings as fast as he could go was my friend, the farm hand. When he saw me move he ceased yelling, but he kept running.

I closed the door deliberately and unhurriedly and started walking down towards the road. Our paths should converge just about at the roadside, near my car, but whereas I had a relatively short and easy walk he was having a hard run, the mud of the ploughed field caking his feet. He would be panting and out of breath; I would be calm and collected. My hand grasped the note in my pocket again.

I hailed him when a few paces separated us.

"I was just passing, I explained airily, "so I called to give you this for your help the other day. Sorry I didn't give it to you at the time, but I had nothing on me." I held it out towards his hand as he stood there panting, almost forcing him to take it, not giving him a chance to get over his surprise and ask why I had gone to the tractor rather than to the shed to give it to him. But he took it. And as he stood there with the note in his hand, still recovering his breath, I stepped quickly into the car and was off. I could see his open mouth in the mirror as I drove away.

It had been a worthwhile visit, much more productive than I had thought it would be when I first squatted down and looked at these mine-detectors.

I wondered how deep the sub-soil plough went. Twelve inches, eighteen inches, two feet? I had no idea, but surely two feet was not impossible with a powerful tractor like that. Add the depth of the plough itself, and the tip of the gadget must be at least four feet deep, perhaps five. And how much further below that could a mine-detector detect? Again, I had no idea. One thing was certain, though: it must be much deeper than anyone could have looked before. How deep had Mr Anderson said the silt was here? Twenty feet, I remembered. But that could only be an estimate, based probably on one or two holes which someone had dug miles away. Supposing it was half the depth, here? The field itself looked as if it was two or three feet below the level of the road, and I had read somewhere that the ground level in the fens was slowly subsiding as the ground itself dried out and as dust was blown away, and perhaps it had subsided a bit before the road was made, as well as after it. If all these guesses were right then Mr Holden's little mine-detector might well penetrate right down to the bottom of the silt, right down to the stratum in which Mr Anderson would have expected to find King John's baggage train, and had he not said that the most likely place for it was on the direct route between Cross Keys and Sutton Bridge - on Mr Holden's farm.

And what a neat way of searching! No wonder Holden did not want snoopers round his farm. If no one came too close no one was to know that he was searching methodically. By combining the sub-soil plough with the detector he could carry out his cultivations - perhaps rather more elaborately than was strictly necessary, but no matter - and at the same time comb the depths with his detector as methodically and thoroughly as if he had planned the whole operation for that purpose and for that purpose alone. And all this in a way that nobody would notice, nobody would suspect.

And what had he found?

One King John penny, for sure. I had it in my pocket. And the other ones in Stevens' office: could they come from the same source rather than from Stevens' own cellar, as I had supposed? At least with a sample of each it should not be difficult for the police to confirm it. Or even for me.

But what else had he found?

The sky, or rather the depth, was the limit; and perhaps the limit included a small silver bowl; but if so the route which the bowl had taken from Holden's farm to Mr Anderson's and Gerald Eke's hands needed some explanation.

Chapter 11

I had plenty to think about as I drove slowly towards King's Lynn, but I drove slowly not only because I was thinking, but also because I had no wish to hurry the moment when I would be at the meeting listening to Stevens' self-important outpourings.

The roads to Lynn were empty, or empty compared with the hustle and bustle which I had found there before. Of course: it was early closing day. That was why Stevens was able to get away from his shop for the afternoon.

That was why his shop would now be empty.

That was why I would never have a better opportunity, knowing both that the shop would be closed and that Stevens would be busy elsewhere.

I parked in King Street, not opposite the shop because that would have been too obvious if anyone should notice my car, though who there was to notice was beyond my comprehension. Not for the first time I noted my own deviousness with wry amusement. It did not just have occasional fits now; it seemed to be permanently switched on.

I needed a tool. A simple jemmy was what I wanted, but it was not my habit to carry one, not yet anyway, so I opened the boot of my car to see what was on offer.

Not much. A broken and bent spanner for my wheel jack, but if that had bent when I merely tried to unscrew two tightened nuts it was not going to be strong enough to force a door, however flimsy the lock. The jack itself looked more likely. It looked strong enough and rigid enough to act as a lever, even if it was clumsier than I would have liked, and one end had a thin blade, designed with a hole in it to receive a lug on the spanner; with luck it would be thin enough to force between the door and frame, and strong enough not to bend. After that all I needed was a block of some kind to provide a fulcrum against which I could lever the door open; a salesman's sample of an insulating block would do for that so I slipped it from its box and pocketed it. Finally a torch; I always carried one in the car. I already had in my pocket the King John penny I had found in Stevens' workshop. It should not take me long to compare it with Stevens' pennies, and if I found the comparison more difficult than I expected I could always take a penny away with me: Stevens would not miss one among so many.

With my burglar's kit in my hands I closed the boot. I left all the doors of the car unlocked and the key in the dashboard. It was unlikely that anyone would try to steel it and it was, I feared, rather more likely that I should wish to make a quick get away, without fumbling for keys, locks, and keyholes.

It was only when my reasoning had reached that state that the butterflies started up in the pit of my stomach. They were as unpleasant as ever, but I must be getting hardened to them. They came to life much later than they used to, and although I enjoyed them as little as ever I found I had less difficulty in living with them.

And that was my loss.

I walked as nonchalantly as I could with my burglar's kit along the road.

It was almost deserted; just two people, away in front of me, looking in the opposite direction.

I turned down the alley which I had marked down when I visited Stevens' shop before.

I identified the ill-fitting side door without difficulty.

I jammed the end of the jack into the crack between door and frame. It would not go at the best place, opposite the lock itself, but I managed to insert it about six inches lower, twisting the door still further inwards.

The lock was stronger than I had been led to expect by the roughness of the door which held it, but my lever was effective and quite quickly the wood splintered and I was inside.

Quietly I marshalled the tools of my new trade. I set down the jack and block just inside the door, I took the torch from my pocket and turned it on, and I pulled the door softly behind me.

I remembered the little lobby from my last visit. The door on my right led into Stevens' office, and from there into the back of the shop. The door straight ahead led down the steps and into the cellar. But what I wanted had been in the office.

I pushed the door away from me and shone the torch through it. The door into the shop on the far side of the office was closed, leaving the office itself nearly in darkness; a little light, but not much, trickled round the door and through the half-obscured glass peep-hole which Stevens used for watching his customers as they walked round unattended. I passed silently, through the door towards Stevens' desk, covered with bric-a-brac and other clutter, which I saw now included the apple box.

As I reached it the lights went on.

The butterflies in my stomach went berserk. Dread and panic seized me as I started to turn round. All the symptoms were present: dry mouth, short breath, hammer blows in the chest.

"Well, well. Just look who's here," said Waters. "I warned you, George, now didn't I?" he went on in a fatherly way. "I just couldn't have made it clearer." He leant comfortably back against the wall behind the door through which I had just entered, and next to him stood Jason, and next to Jason stood Barry.

Well, I tried to tell myself nonchalantly, if I was caught in the act by one I might as well be caught in the act by all three, but the way my heart was behaving was anything but nonchalant.

"What are you doing here?" asked Jason.

"And what about you?" I answered. "What are you doing?" I must have recovered myself a little.

"Don't try to be funny," was Jason's response as he moved forward towards me, and I could see his point; he obviously had no sense of humour. "What are you doing here?" he repeated.

154

"That was my question...." I began, but I did not get to the end of the sentence because Jason's fist came out and pounded me in the wind. I doubled up, gasping and struggling for breath, groaning as it started to come back to me.

"Cut it out, Jason," said Waters. "This is no place for that kind of thing.

"We want him to walk out on two feet and we haven't time to deal with him here, anyway. Stevens may be back before long. We don't know how long his little meeting will last."

Jason looked undecided. He let me get up, but he stood threateningly near, and I did my best to cover all the most vulnerable parts of my body with my hands and arms. It was not easy: there was nothing which did not seem vulnerable with Jason so near.

Waters spoke again. "Jason, you keep an eye on him while Barry and I finish looking. All right? You could pass his torch, too, we need another."

"O.K."

Jason pushed me into a corner and made me turn round, facing it. As I moved I saw Waters and Barry start going round the room, each now with a torch, searching everywhere.

After a time I heard the door opening and footsteps going down into the cellar. I half turned to see, and was rewarded with a stinging slap to the face.

Now's my moment, I thought. Two of the villains are in the cellar leaving our hero to overpower the third and make his escape, report to the police, have the house surrounded, and receive the grateful thanks of the mayor. He'll be the toast of the town.

I felt Jason's breath on the back of my neck, and I stood just as still as I knew how.

Presently I heard the other two come up from the cellar.

"Finished?" Jason asked.

155

"Yeah. Nothing - except for these." I guessed Waters must be pointing at the apple box.

"Did you search the cellar properly, where old man Anderson said some of the stuff might be hidden?"

"Yeah. Nothing there at all."

"So what's he playing at?" It was Jason this time. "Where does he keep it?"

"Maybe there isn't any," answered Waters, "so he doesn't have to have anywhere to keep it."

"That's not the impression I had," Jason replied. "Nor you. D'you remember? - the very first time we came to see him he was suggesting he had a treasure house in his back garden. True, he only tried to sell us the silver pennies, but he hinted that there were other goodies to come."

"But he never actually offered to produce them."

"That came later. When we came back and made our proposition to him he was still making references to something better, wasn't he?"

"Sure. He's human, so he wanted to be one up. That was all he was after."

"But he tried again, didn't he? After he'd agreed to come in with us he said he had some stuff we'd like, didn't he?"

"Sure. He's a salesman, so he tried to sell us something. He'd try to sell you something on his death bed, even if it had to be his own corpse. But he never actually said what it was: all he did was to hint that he would have something; sometime, somewhere."

"So what was it? Where was he expecting to get it from?"

"It must have been in his imagination. By imagination and out of thin air, that was its pedigree."

Waters was finally succeeding in convincing Jason and at the same time he was opening up new lines of thought in me. What proposition could they have been putting to Stevens? If it was the proposition I was thinking of it threw light on Dick's letter to me, but if so it was one in the eye for my ideas about Sally's father helping them. I ought to have been glad that they were clearing away my suspicions about him, but I knew I was not; I resented it, and somewhere deep down inside me I knew why: Mr Anderson was too good to be true, that was what I resented. There must be a flaw in him somewhere even if it was not where I had been looking; he was too clever, too perfect, to be true. Still, after listening to that conversation I had to acknowledge that it was Stevens who must be the accomplice Dick referred to in his letter, not Mr Anderson after all.

Then we left.

They asked me where my car was and I saw no point in being obscure. If Jason could not pick it out blindfold in a snowstorm it was not for lack of looking at it. They sent Barry to move their car to the end of the alleyway and then to take mine away, and while he was gone Waters and Jason gathered up the box of pennies, closed the door into the alley, and marched me between them up to the open door of their car. Waters drove; Jason sat beside me in the back. I was beginning to know Jason's car as well as he knew mine.

We went in convoy back through Sherningham and down to the beach. I kept a despairing look-out for Sally when we reached Sherningham, but I knew she was at the meeting and that I would not see her. I could think of no other person who might conceivably be able to help, and any ideas of a heroic escape from my captors were stifled by the presence at my side of Jason.

At the caravan park Barry drove on towards the pitch of my own caravan, while Waters turned towards Jason's. I looked round as they hustled me from the car to the van, but not a soul was to be seen. There was no help about, so I either had to break and run for it, or submit. To break and run from Jason, let alone Waters, was out of the question. I submitted.

They sat me down on one of the bench seats. The table which had been between the two seats had been taken away. Waters and Jason were opposite but before they could say anything Barry reappeared. He carried Dick's pair of Wellingtons and he made me put them on. Then he turned to the others.

"It's all right," he told them. "I saw the old girl; told her our friend," he nodded towards me, "was back for the fishing, and she took it like a lamb.

"She even told me she had seen him at it when he first arrived. Says she saw him setting out across the beach, looking for lugworms, as soon as he arrived. Just like his brother." They all laughed, all mirthlessly. "Some people never learn, do they?" he added.

Before I sat down they had taken my anorak off, so that I would not be too hot. Kindness I thought, unwonted kindness. But then Jason started to go through the pockets and it was not long before he found the scraps of paper I had taken from the shelf above the window. Now they had come home he could put them back where they came from.

"So it was you!" His face had lost the dead-pan expression it had worn when he had spoken to me at the time we were, relatively at least, on good terms, though that seemed a long time ago now. His upper lip curved very slightly, his chin was thrust forward threateningly, and there was a hint of bared teeth. The whole thing reminded me of a dog owned by one of my foster parents: it used to look rather like that if you came near when it was eating, and I had imagined that if you went nearer still it would abandon its bowl of food for the moment and grab an extra course, but I had been careful never to give it the chance.

"You ...." Words did not come easily to Jason at that moment, though they were scarcely necessary. While he continued to growl and search for them Waters leant over and removed the scraps of paper he was holding. He unfolded them. He seemed particularly interested in two of them: Dick's letter to me, and the receipt for the fishing rod.

"I knew Dick had written to me," I remarked as casually as I could manage it, "so I guessed the postman must have delivered the letter to the wrong address.

"That's all I was after, Dick's letter. If only you had sent it round when you got it I need not have bothered you." I tried to look round innocently. I thought for a moment that I had overdone it, that I had moved too near the dog as it ate its dinner. Jason's jaws seemed to be working up for something.

"Oh, George," Waters said sadly. "You mustn't, really you mustn't. I've tried to help you, but you won't listen, will you? Anyway, it's just as well you kept these in your pocket, isn't it? Now we can destroy them, and no harm's done. Not, that is, if you don't talk about them."

"He won't." That was Jason, predictably.

"Those are only the originals," I answered, "but of course I had them copied as soon as I read them. You burn those if you like - but the copies will still be available, certified."

"Where?" asked Waters. I had shaken him and at that moment he believed me.

If they knew that copies existed, I reasoned, and that I was the only person who could safely dispose of them, there might be scope for a bargain: safe conduct in exchange for the copies. I was pleased with my presence of mind in thinking of it.

But I had not allowed for Jason. I suppose if you are sufficiently twisted yourself you can see through the little ploys of amateurs like me without any difficulty. "Don't give us that one." He turned to Waters. "If he'd had those copied he'd be carrying the copies and he'd have put the originals somewhere safe. He never even thought of it, not until now." He turned to me. "That's right, isn't it?"

"Clever boy!"

That was a mistake, too. He had just put himself in a good mood with his astuteness in seeing through me before Waters had done so, and with two careless words I had destroyed the benefit of his self-satisfaction.

Waters had recovered himself. "You're a prize pair of bone-heads, aren't you, you and your brother? First Dick has fantasies and writes a letter like this." He held it up, as if I had not already been familiar with it. "It's a string of lies from beginning to end; heaven knows how he dreamed it all up. Then he drowns himself in the sea, so you come along and start bumming around and taking it all seriously, as if it were God's own truth. I've no idea what we're to do with you, really I haven't."

I hoped he would not refer - or defer - to Jason, who obviously had plenty of ideas. But I was beginning to be puzzled. They were concentrating on Dick's letter, as if that was the only thing which mattered. But the receipt for the fishing tackle and the books, and the bowl I had taken from the kitchen, I would have thought they mattered too, particularly the bowl. Could they have just forgotten about it for the moment? If it were mine, and if it were as valuable as I believed it to be, I certainly would not forget it, not unless it was a very minor piece in my collection ...

But while I was still wondering I gave them fresh cause for thought. I blew my nose.

It was not the nose-blowing which did it, of course. When I pulled my handkerchief out something fell to the floor, and Jason was on it before I had even noticed.

"Where did you get this from?" he asked, holding the King John penny on the flat of his hand.

I did not answer. I had forgotten it, so I was just as surprised as everyone else.

"Let's have a look." Waters held out his hand and Jason passed it over.

Then Waters reminded me of the reason why I had been burgling Stevens' shop in the first place. He picked up the apple carton, which they had dropped on the floor when they came in, he took a penny out of that, and he laid the two of them side by side on his hand while we all stared.

They were not identical. I doubt if coins in those days ever were, even when they were fresh from the mint. But they were pretty similar and - the point I was looking for - they both had the same look about them, the same colour, the same freshness or lack of freshness, and the same tiny streaks of soil clinging to them where it had not yet been shaken off, where it was still held by a combination of caked mud and oxidisation.

If deposit from each coin were placed under a microscope and analysed in a laboratory I would lay a pound to a penny - not a King John penny - that the two samples would be identical. The source of each coin must be the same: Holden's farm.

That still left a few questions unanswered, of course.

Why were they in Stevens' shop? What was the connection between Stevens and Holden? And what, if it came to that, was the connection between those two and Waters and his gang?

"Well?" Waters looked at me questioningly, "where did it come from, George?"

"Out of my pocket, with my handkerchief." That gained me a little time, but I was not sure it was worth it. Waters' patience seemed to be just a little thinner, and Jason sensed it. It was as if he was starting to move in for the kill, as if the huntsman's restraining hand had been slightly loosened.

"Come on," Waters persisted. "We've had enough of that kind of thing. Jason here, is quite an expert in the means of persuasion. You learnt it all in Northern Ireland, didn't you Jason? Strong persuasion, no tell-tale marks." My heart missed a beat. Had they put Dick through it before administering the chloroform? - the chloroform and the final solution? And what were my chances? Until this moment the whole episode had seemed somehow unreal, so much so that there had been no place for fear, fear of what might happen to me, fear of pain, of death. But now I was reminded. I knew I was not a hero, and

161

anyway, what was the point? If I told them where I had found the penny what harm could it do? Holden was no friend of mine, nor was Stevens, and whatever those two were up to they were doing it in a secretive way. It was not my business to keep their secrets, still less at the cost of a lot of pain and suffering to me.

"I found it," I explained.

"You don't say!" It had not occurred to me that Jason was capable of irony.

"Where?" Waters was the more direct this time.

"In a field, out Sutton Bridge way."

"Whose field, George?"

"I think it was Holden's, but I can't be sure." Caution; cover yourself by vagueness so that you can alter your story later, the habit of a lifetime! But the game was quite different with these three.

They could not hold me to account for what I had said, not in the way a schoolteacher, or a boss at work, or client, or a law court can do. They had different rules and I was wasting my time.

"Holden!" Waters echoed. "I might have known it. I only said I'd keep my mouth shut if he told me when he found anything. The double-crossing bastard! And now when he discovers something we find he and Stevens are in it together...."

"Yeah," Jason broke in, a note of triumph in his voice. "That explains it."

That's Stevens' source; that's where the goodies were to come from, the ones he was offering us, not from the hiding place in his cellar which Anderson was talking about. We could have saved ourselves the bother of searching this afternoon. What's more, that's where his treasure house is; in Holden's workshop. And his treasure chests are a whole lot of apple boxes. Holden must have found a hoard of the stuff which he never even mentioned when we had a go at him. The crafty bastard! He told us so much, just to keep us quiet, so we'd believe him. But there was a hell of a lot more which he didn't tell us."

162

So Jason had had a go at Holden. A nasty thought, and my sympathies were with Holden. Obviously too, Holden had not found it very pleasant. He had given under the strain, that much was obvious, but how much had he given? At all events it looked as if he might have been cleverer, or luckier, or better situated, than I was. Whatever he had given had been enough; it had satisfied Jason and his friends; so he had been able to keep something back ...

But I was not like Holden. I had nothing to give, therefore nothing to keep.

Maybe, though, Holden was not out of the wood yet. I would not have liked to have been in his shoes, nor in Stevens', next time I met this gentle little trio. I longed for them to draw some of the antagonism away from me, but I had little faith in that. Jason, for a start, obviously had enough to go round us all, and to spare.

Waters stopped thinking of Holden and turned to me again. "Tell us George: how did you come to be looking there? How did you come to find it?"

"Pure accident," I answered. "I had a puncture as I went past his farm - as I was on my way to you - and the man there lent me a spanner and ... I keep my eyes open and ... I kind of tripped over the box it was in." It was so much easier telling the truth, and I think they believed me; at least, if they did not, they gave the impression they accepted what I had said. But I would have liked to have warned my helpful farm hand. If he was about when Waters and his friends called to see what they could find he could be in for a pretty unpleasant experience. Holden deserved it, perhaps, but not the man who had helped me.

While we talked I had continued to puzzle over the relationship between Holden and these three, but whichever way I turned it matters became no clearer.

Besides, I was increasingly distracted by something else which was of more immediate concern: what was to happen to me?

Waters, except at moments when he probably forgot himself, still talked as if we might have a continuing relationship. But not Jason. And although Barry said practically nothing it was he who had apparently fed to the caretaker the suggestion that I had come back for the fishing, and it was he who had made me put on Dick's wellingtons.

The sooner I could get away from them the better.

I considered shouting. The walls of the caravan were thin, and my voice would carry through them. But it would take three men only a moment to stifle my cries, and even the flimsy walls of the van would muffle the opening bars sufficiently to make them unremarkable, even if someone did hear. I would earn a few uncomfortable blows from Jason for my pains, gain nothing, and maybe even lose such opportunity as I might have for getting away from them.

But that was the point: what other opportunity would I have?

I could think only of one possibility, and on the face of it that seemed too puerile and hackneyed to stand a chance. It was the stratagem that every school child knows.

I grunted, so they all looked at me.

"The toilet..." I began.

"Too bad," was Jason's rejoinder.

Then they started talking, at least Waters and Jason started, but Barry continued to be strong and silent. I was becoming more and more convinced that he took third place in this trio. Waters was number one, there was no doubt about that, and he took note of what Jason said, and Jason was obviously a forceful character. But Barry did not enter into their strategic planning. Perhaps he was the new boy, and therefore although senior in age he was junior in authority to the other two, or perhaps his obvious physical strength was about all he had to contribute,

164

and he really had nothing up top. Yet I did not think so. Even in our short acquaintance there had been moments when he had not taken a back seat at all.

They were wondering what to do with me, but at the same time they did not want me to know what they were contemplating, so for me their conversation was not exactly informative nor, for them, constructive.

I grunted again, and Jason looked distastefully at me.

"Toilet..."

"It'll get rid of him for the moment," Waters said. He turned to Barry. "Take him away," he ordered, "but don't let him out of your sight for a minute. And keep near him. Get that?"

Barry nodded. He was used to receiving orders and carrying them out.

"Toilet paper," I said. The new abbreviated style I had stumbled on seemed to produce results, so I persisted with it.

Jason produced an impatient mutter, but Barry went into the kitchen. I heard him opening the door of a cupboard and while he did so I picked up my anorak from the seat beside Jason, and put it on. I was pretty sure there was still a pencil in one of the pockets. I might have a chance of writing ... of leaving a message somewhere ...

Barry returned from the kitchen with the toilet roll. I held out my hand for it and he passed it over. It would leave him with two hands free to deal with me, but I doubt if his reasoning went that far. Mine went in a different direction.

Before we left the van Barry made one of his rare contributions to the conversation.

"No funny stuff," he said, looking at me. At the same time he made a movement as if he was breaking a stick across his knee. The message was clear.

We set off, Barry slightly behind and to one side of me. The nearest toilet block was the one I was familiar with. Walking there gave me about three minutes more in which to work out my plan.

I had noticed when I first went into it that the door of the toilet block was held open by a hook; one end was screwed to the wall and the other engaged in an eye on the back of the door. The screws which held the hook had obviously been wrenched from the wall in the past by someone who had slammed it behind him without noticing what held it. They had therefore been wedged back again with slivers of wood. If someone else slammed it they would come out again; I knew that because I had nearly done it myself the first time I went there - and if I did the slamming and Barry was still inside as I did it he would need a moment to reopen the door. In that moment I could be up the bank which was immediately behind the toilet block. Beyond the bank there was no cover though, so Barry would be able to set off in pursuit. I might get away, but Barry was several sizes bigger than me and I did not fancy my chances much. Better: having crossed the bank I could immediately double back, recross it and hide in the undergrowth which had been allowed to grow up behind the toilet block, between it and the bank.

If I were to do that, though, I must get my timing right. If I were too quick I might be up and over the bank before Barry could see me, and in that case the first place he would look would probably be the undergrowth behind the block. No, I must make sure he had seen me set off so that, while he hunted for me vainly on the far side of the bank, I could either stay safely in my hiding place or be on my way to ... well ... safety, I hoped.

And I had already worked out how to make sure Barry would follow me. I would drop the toilet paper at the top of the bank, hold the loose end, and let the rest roll down. Even a half-wit on an off day could follow a trail like that surely?

We reached the toilet block without incident and, as I had asked for the toilet roll, I remembered to make for one of the cubicles. I pushed the door behind me, but before it had closed it was pushed back again.

No funny tricks," Barry told me. "Just you leave it alone."

He was taking Waters' instruction not to let me out of his sight too literally, I thought. We might both be men, but I did not feel comfortable, sitting there with Barry's beady eye on me. However there was nothing else for it, so I pretended to take no notice of the big man as he lolled against the wall opposite, watching as if I were a monkey in the zoo.

So much for my plans to write a note!

Then I became aware of a fresh sound, feet crunching on the stones outside, then softer, nearer footsteps as they came into the room. Barry looked to his left to see who had come, and at the same time I pushed the door of my cubicle, and locked it.

The feet came across the room and went into the cubicle next to mine. I caught a glimpse of a shoe under the partition, which extended from about six inches above the floor to about the same distance below the ceiling.

And then I really started thinking again.

With the new audience Barry had had to accept that my door was shut. Although it was shut, he was still there watching, but however hard he tried he could not see the top and the bottom of the partition beyond the door simultaneously.

That gave me a fifty per cent chance of passing something over or under without his noticing.

I decided that over was better. The something could be kept low, hugging the top of the partition, whereas anything passed under would probably drop on the floor.

Without wasting time I took the pencil from my pocket and started writing on the last sheet of toilet paper, using the roll to press against. What I wrote was just clear enough to read, but the pencil was a hard one and it was slow work and I did not know how long my neighbour in the next cubicle would wait for it.

167

"Help!" I started, in large letters to gain attention. Then I wondered what on earth I could ask him to do. Go to the police? But how was I to describe sufficiently concisely why I needed help and where they were to find me? I could think of no short and clear way to describe Jason's caravan. I did not know its number, and "the Finn's" or "Jason's" were scarcely useful directions for the police, who would probably treat the whole thing as a practical joke. Simply to write "Help, come and rescue me," left a lot of questions begging which I could answer only with a long essay, and at the rate at which I could write on the soft paper that was not practicable.

However there was an alternative: a note to Sally. She might be home again by now, knew enough of the background of it all to understand, and to know that urgency was called for. Indeed, was it not she who had urged me to go to the police? And I who had stubbornly refused to go? What was more, the police would take notice of her, more so than they would do of me.

"Help!" I wrote in the end. "Tell Sally Anderson, 5 New Road, Sheringham, that Jason & Co. have caught me and I can't get away."

At that moment there were stirrings from the next cubicle and I was afraid the occupant would leave before I had had time to give him the message. Hastily I finished the note: "George - urgent!"

I tore a dozen sheets of paper from the roll and, moving my feet as little as possible so that Barry would not realise what I was doing if he looked below the cubicles, I started feeding the sheets over the top. Luck was with me, for I found the partition between the cubicles was a fraction lower than the front, and as only the thickness of the paper rose higher than the top of the partition I was pretty sure Barry would not be able to see what was going on. I just hoped my neighbour would see what Barry could not, and that he would get the hang of my message without making some kind of exclamation which would give it all away.

If my stratagem succeeded there was a good chance that Barry would, for the first and last time, be my ally. His bulky threatening presence, still watching the door of my cubicle, must surely provide even the most unimaginative person with evidence, if it were needed, that my message was in earnest.

I felt rather than heard a pause in the movements from the next cubicle.

Then I felt a tug at the paper in my hand. I guided it to the top of the partition and let go. Then I glanced below to check that it had not arrived in a crumpled heap on the floor. With relief, I heard the cistern next door being flushed, the door opening, the same footsteps as before padding across the room, passing through the door, crunching on the stones, and fading into the distance. I prayed that whoever it was would take the message seriously and deliver it as soon as he could.

Then ...I nearly burst out laughing. Hardly appreciating what I was doing I had, for the first time for years, actually asked the police for help!

So far so good. Passing the message had been an unexpected bonus, no less welcome for that, but I remembered the plans I had been going over on my way from the caravan.

Barry was there to receive me as I emerged.

"You've taken your time," he greeted me. Then, keeping hold of me by a wrist, he went into the cubicle and looked round. Perhaps he was not as dim as he seemed; he had thought of my leaving a message there for the next person, just as I had done. It was as well that it had not been necessary.

Satisfied, he came out again, released my arm, and followed me towards the door.

He was closer than I liked. I would have to rely on surprise to get me through the door ahead of him. I rehearsed to myself again what I was going to do, and realised that when I had got

169

away I would have to make for Sherningham as quickly as I could, before my message reached Sally and she had time to involve the police.

When I was about three feet from the door I suddenly jumped forward and slammed it.

The hook came out of the wall easily enough as I had anticipated. The thing which went wrong with my plan, though, was Barry.

I did not hear or feel him move, but the door had only started to close when it came up abruptly against a door stop: Barry's toe. To have put it there in time he must have shot it out like lightning. He may have been big and not in his first youth but he was not cumbersome. After his foot came his arm.

It reached out and grabbed me by the scruff of my neck, lifting me from the ground like a small child. I wondered if he was going to knock my head against the wall, just to teach me a lesson, or worse, and I raised my arms defensively to protect myself when he did it.

But there was no need. He did not even shake me; he just put me down again. "That's enough," he told me. "Remember what I said? No funny stuff."

And with that we set off back to the caravan.

It was dark by now, really dark. As yet there was no moon. Even if it had risen it would have been hidden by the mist, which also blotted out the stars. There was no breeze, nothing to move the sea mist away. For the time of year it was mild. The noise which was missing, I realised, was the noise of the sea. It must be low tide, and the water a long way from the shore.

When we reached the caravan Jason and Waters were waiting for us, silent.

They must have finished their conference, so I supposed my fate had been decided.

Jason went into the kitchen, and I was told to sit down. When he came back he had a pad of cotton wool in his hands, and he put it over my face. With three of them holding me I had no chance.

Chapter 12

Coming round this time was a good deal worse than the last, and that had been bad enough.

Last time I had been lying on a bed, sheltered in a caravan, lit by electric light. True, there had been no heating, but it had been a good deal less cold than the outside air would have been.

This time the outside air was all round, chilling me to the marrow. I was not lying on a bed, but on a hard, knobbly surface. There was no light of any kind, but there was mist, and the sound of lapping water, and once more the throbbing, and the taste in the mouth, and the wish not to be alive.

I came round more quickly this time. I do not know why. It could hardly have been that I was acquiring an immunity; I do not suppose you can acquire an immunity to chloroform. Perhaps it was the cold, or the damp, or a subconscious sense of urgency, or more likely they had just given me a smaller dose than before. After all, their method of administering the dose was scarcely scientific.

When the water began lapping against me I started trying to get to my feet.

I rolled over, propping myself on my forearms, gradually straightening them and raising my body so that I was above the ground, and above the dribble of water which surged up and then filtered away, only to surge up again and filter away once more. Propped on elbows and knees I watched it for some time, filled with a sense of detachment, knowing what it was but unable to take action, as if all I wanted to do was to watch it, to admire its beauty or study its motion.

Then, laboriously, I started to stand up.

First I transferred my weight from elbows to hands. That must have raised my body by ... what? ... perhaps 15 or 18 inches. Not enough, I told myself authoritatively, not enough. You must not allow yourself to be deceived by that. The tide here would rise more than eighteen inches, so your head was not above high water mark yet. More action was required; you could not leave it at that.

The next stage was to draw a foot up under me, the first movement in standing up.

I drew it up. I found the foot was clad in a wellington, and the wellington was filled with water as well as with the foot. I must deal with that, but first I must stand up.

The water covered my hands and wrists, now, as it surged in and out. I thought with sudden irritation that my cuffs must be getting wet and it was really imperative that I should stand up and keep them dry. But I was too alert to deceive myself. Again, I was not caught out. I knew very well that my cuffs were already sodden.

Still, I must stand. The cuffs were beside the point. How else could I walk back?

So I stood. Not easily or quickly, quite the reverse. I stood, unsteadily, shivering in every limb, and looking down to where the water was surging in over my feet and out again. But I could not see it. Between me and my feet was a bank of mist and darkness. All round me was a bank of mist and darkness, I had water under my feet; I had water over my feet; but which way it was coming and which way it was going I had no way of telling.

I suppose now, that more time than I realised must have passed as I slowly stood up and ... I nearly said it ... got my bearings. But they were just what I did not get. However, what I did recover, to some extent at least, were my senses.

They reminded me of Dick, for one thing; they reminded me of how he had been drowned, and they made me realise that he had probably not had the luck (good or bad, I wondered?) to have recovered his senses before the water came over him and drowned him. At least I was conscious, and for that reason I had to cope with all the questions I had posed for him.

Which way to go? Uphill, or down? That was impossible: no hill. Which way was the land? - as if I could remember!

The only moving thing was the sea; and which way, I wondered, was it moving? I crouched down nearer to it, peering to judge which way it was going. But I could hardly see it, let alone judge where it was coming from.

I put my hands into it, like two sensitive paddles I hopefully thought, gauging the direction it was taking. One hand told me it was going from left to right, the other from front to back.

But then my feet started giving hints. Numb with cold they may be, but they told me that they were standing on firm sand, with ripples in it. The ripples would be shaped like tiny waves, a gradual slope one side, and a crest on the other, and one side would be towards the sea and the other towards the land, washed in that shape by the outgoing tide. I struggled to work out which way the ripples would lie, with the crest towards the land or the sea? The problem was too much for me, until I realised with relief, yes with relief, even though I had been certain a solution might have saved me, that by the time the ripples were beneath my feet the incoming tide would have obliterated their shape. No need for me to worry any further about ripples in the sand.

So I started moving, aimlessly. What else was there to do? I moved as fast as I could, convincing myself that the faster I moved the more likely was it that I could gauge whether the water was becoming deeper or shallower.

The going seemed to get harder, the water deeper. It lapped into my wellingtons now, reminding me that I had intended to empty the water from them. So I turned about and started in the opposite direction ... started, but having started it was less easy to go on. Was I moving straight, away from the spot where the water had been deeper? Or was I moving in a graceful semi-circle, or even a figure of eight, a U-bend, or a simple random wobbly line?

I realised that I had no idea; but I kept going. I had no alternative. If I stayed still, I would certainly drown. If I moved, I would drown almost as certainly, but at least it kept a chance open: that I would be there to take advantage of my luck, if there was any going.

It seemed to me that I had been wandering in the water for ages, cold and despairing, and as if the water had been getting steadily deeper, just as I would have expected it to do if I had stayed in the same spot, when my luck changed, for the worse.

The water had been knee deep; now it came up to my thighs. The ground on which I had been walking had been firm, but suddenly it was soft, and I was floundering in it, being sucked down.

Instinctively I twisted round and tried to move in the direction from which I had come, but my feet were too firmly caught by the sticky mud. The top half of my body left the bottom behind, and I fell. I arrested my fall with outstretched arms and the flat of my hands, and as I rested momentarily in that position I realised the odd thing about it. Where my feet were, the water level had been up to my thighs, but where my hands were it was only as deep as the length of my arms. Where my feet were it was soft mud, where my hands were it was ... well ... not quite firm ground, but a great deal firmer.

I struggled to my feet again, first pulling them towards my hands. And in a flash I realised where in that wide expanse of mud which I had surveyed through Dick's binoculars was the one place in which the level sloped perceptibly. It was in the channel of the stream which flowed out across the mud and in which were moored the two boats.

If I could do two things I might yet be safe. One of them was to follow the side of this depression, keeping close enough to it to identify it without actually falling into it and without getting stuck in its mud; and that pre-supposed that the mud kept to the channel itself, with a harder shoulder at its side, an unlikely enough chance in itself. The other necessity was that I should start in the right direction, towards the land rather than the sea.

I have no bump for direction at the best of times. The chances of knowing which way to go when I had started from unconsciousness and then stumbled round in I knew not how many circles in the mist and the dark and the water were nil. Yet I was as certain as could be that I should be going to the right, not the left. I had a very poor opinion of my certainty, but I had nothing else to go by, so I went by it.

Keeping to the channel was all but impossible. The ground did not slope quite steeply enough at its edge to feel it with my feet, even if I stood with them apart. So I tried to zig-zag from deep side to shallow side, and then from shallow to deep again, all the time trying to stop myself from falling into the sticky clutching mud, all the time remembering that unless I went as fast as the tide or faster it would overtake me, and that if only I could spurt now and get into shallower water I would find the going progressively easier.

I floundered on. I think the water really became shallower, but perhaps that was imagination, or wishful thinking. At least it did not seem to be getting much deeper, and that gave me hope. I was sure that I must have chosen the right direction, that I must be going towards the land, not straight out into the sea. If I had set out to sea surely I would be up to the armpits by now, getting ready to swim, or die?

Then I saw the oasis, or was it a mirage? Whatever it was, it was the thing I had been looking out for but which I had not dared to tell myself I had any hope of finding.

The first indication I had of it was a lapping sound, not the lapping of water on sand or mud, but the lapping of water against something hollow. I strained my eyes, ahead and to the right, but I could see nothing, even though the mist had begun to thin. Another zig-zag and I told myself I could see a dim shape. Yet another one and I was certain I could see it: the black outline of a boat. It was moored to my right, in the channel of the stream beside which I had been making my way. Even if the water there was not too deep it would be too muddy , so I would have to swim for it. As I stood, thinking, I realised that the bows of the boat must be towards me, that the incoming tide must have floated the boat up from the mud and in towards the land. If I started swimming from where I was, striking out into where I supposed the middle of the channel to be, the incoming tide should wash me with it towards the boat.

I did not believe what I told myself; it was much too theoretical, and the theory was all about a subject I did not understand. But, again, there was nothing else I could go by. And I let myself remember, for the first time, something which I had refused to contemplate when it seemed that it could only fill me with despair, and that was the sheer distance which I would have to travel if I were ever to reach the shore. By daylight, or with a compass and in a straight line, perhaps it was possible to cover a mile in icy water, knee deep, floundering in the mud from time to time, if I had been fit. But at night, in the mist, having just recovered from being gassed, and travelling in anything but a straight line, the chances of my actually making it to the shore were remote.

The boat must be the answer, and if my theories were wrong and the tide carried me past it the first time, I must just turn round and wade back and try again, and try quickly before the tide had advanced any further.

I waded out until I felt my feet sticking in the soft mud, and then I started swimming, if you could call it swimming. It was an apology for a breaststroke, designed more to keep me afloat than to make progress through the water.

Actually though, I did make progress, not by swimming, but because my toes caught the mud from time to time, and the tide propelled me.

And my calculations were just about right.

I found myself bearing down towards the black shape of salvation, finding it was much nearer than I had supposed, aiming straight for it, just flicking with a hand or a foot from time to time to give myself the impression that I was adjusting my course. But it did not need adjusting. My aim was perfect, and as the mooring chain came up beside me I felt the small buoy to which the painter was fixed, I passed myself along that, along the side of the boat to a point where the side seemed to be lowest, and with what I was convinced was the last of my strength I heaved myself over the side and fell, limp, inside.

I did not stir for some time, but then I made myself do so to keep warm or, rather, less cold. I looked round as well as I could do in the darkness and mist, feeling my way to supplement my sight.

The boat was half decked, and I had fallen into the open part of it towards the stern. It was a small, cramped space, bounded by wooden bench seats at each side, by a board which formed the stern on a third side, and by a slightly higher wooden wall on the fourth.

The wooden wall was the end of the cabin; in it there must be a door.

Feeling with my fingertips I located the edges of two doors, meeting in the middle, and a keyhole where they met. I felt no hinges at the sides, so they must open inwards. The doors fitted well, and when I knocked them with my knuckles they felt as firm as a rock. They could not have been a greater contrast to the flimsy side door to Stevens' shop; and this time I did not even have my amateur burglar's kit with me.

I looked and felt all round the cockpit, as I supposed the space I was in should be called. There was nothing, not even the whiff of a jemmy, though I acknowledged that that was scarcely surprising considering how exposed it all was, both to the sea and to lug-wormers wandering across the beach. So I did the only thing I could think of. I lay on my back at the bottom of the

178

cockpit, head towards the stern and feet towards the bows, and I started hammering with my feet.

After ten minutes or so I had achieved one thing: I was appreciably warmer.

After a further ten I achieved another: a slight cracking sound.

Then, it seemed to take no time at all. One of the doors gave, and swung inwards, and soon I had felt for the bolts holding the other, and that was open as well.

It was not until I was actually worming my way through the doors that I appreciated another thing: this was my second indictable offense within twenty-four hours. I had broken and entered a shop; now I was breaking and entering a boat. Perhaps, I comforted myself, my second crime was excusable on the grounds of self-defence, or maybe maritime law is different. At that moment I did not care much either way.

There was a glimmer of light about the mist by now. Daylight was not far away, but once inside the cabin there was no sign of it.

With my hands I felt a table in the middle of the room, and with my head I felt the low ceiling as I started to straighten up. I crouched, and sat on a bench seat on one side of the table. There was, I thought, an outside chance of there being an electric light, and if so the switch would be at one side of the door. It was, and it worked.

The cabin was tiny and bare. The table which blocked its centre could be folded away, so I folded it away. At the bows were a small cooker, a few cupboards, and a door which must lead into a space in the bow. At each side was a bench seat.

What I most wanted were some dry clothes. The chances of there being any there seemed slim, but it was worth looking. Even a dry sweater would make all the difference.

The bench seats were similar in principle to the seats in the caravan, though much more sturdily constructed. They were

179

hinged at the back and lifted to reveal lockers which held a variety of things: tins of food, oilskins, a fishing rod, a gas bottle for the cooker, a torch, and spare bits and pieces for the boat, but no soft clothing.

I tried the only other door big enough to hold out even the possibility of some clothing: the small door at the bow, into the forecastle. I was beginning to feel quite nautical, putting technical names to the various parts of the boat like this.

It did not look promising. A sheet of greenish canvas faced me when I opened it. I pulled the canvas towards me in the dim light and it proved to be a bag, empty. Beyond it the shadows were too black to see anything, so I took the torch from the locker and shone it into the hole.

At first glance there was nothing, at least nothing I could see. But then I distinguished dark shapes, so I leant in, clutched, and pulled. Another dark green canvas bag came out, this time full, and then another, and then a third.

Clearly they did not contain what I was looking for, there was nothing soft and yielding about them to indicate that they contained clothing. Instead they had hard shapes in them, jutting out and creating angles in the coarse surface of the canvas. The first bag was not very heavy, and when I shook it dull hollow sounds emerged, as if it contained a load of tin mugs.

There was nowhere else to look for clothes now, so instead of throwing the bags back I turned the first on its end and shook out its contents.

It was what I had guessed: old tin mugs, very old, many of them dented, and filthy dirty, almost black. As they poured out of the bag some fell to the floor, bouncing into the corners and getting in the way of my feet.

I threw the empty bag down and picked up one of the mugs.

When I looked closely I found it was not a mug, it was a narrow-necked pitcher with a handle each side. I held it up to the dim light and saw that the handles were fluted and decorated, and one of them curled up in an elegant loop at its bottom beyond the point where it was attached to the pitcher itself. There was something familiar about it: the colour and texture - it reminded me of the bowl I had found in the Finn's caravan which turned out to be silver and old .. and valuable ...

I picked up another one, this time a small jug, and I rubbed the two together. It was a crude method of polishing, but in both cases the result was the same, bright streaks of shiny metal. The streaks on the jug were slightly duller than on the pitcher and I held it higher, still nearer to the light. I could not be sure, but they looked to me slightly yellow, not dull - brass, perhaps, - or gold.

Hastily and with mounting excitement I put both down and picked up the second sack. I emptied its contents, and then I emptied the third.

By now I was standing ankle deep in assorted cups and flagons and other hardware, and both seats were piled high, but they were not all cups and flagons. I seized a long-shaped object with a cross-piece at the top. There was no doubt what it was: a sword, jammed securely in its scabbard which was studded with little knobs - jewels? Another object, too small for a sword but also with a cross-piece towards one end, could only be one thing when I lifted it to the light and examined it: a crucifix.

If all these things were made of silver and gold their value must be immense.

I stooped and picked up another object from the floor, larger and heavier than the others. It was a shapeless mass of metal, the size of a small football. I raised it too, to the light, but I could still not guess what it was, so I started pulling it about, bending the metal into different shapes, pulling it out so that instead of a smallish concentrated bundle of metal it became a larger, looser one. Some of the straps of which it was formed broke as I bent them, but enough held together to keep it in one piece and to make me realise what it was: a crown. I tried to put it on my head, but first it hit the ceiling, and when I bent my knees and placed it on my head it balanced precariously, the bent metal fitting my head nowhere.

By now I was feeling weak, with excitement as well as with exhaustion. I cleared a space on one of the seats and rested. Then I picked up the torch, went into the cockpit, and leant over the side of the boat. I shone the light at the hull. It was grey, just like one of the boats which I had seen tied to the wall of the reservoir when Waters had taken me, now understandably reluctantly, to look at the dredger.

I went inside again. It was not difficult to guess that the boat belonged to Jason, or at least was used by him when the weather was fine enough to go to work on the reservoirs. It would take a fraction of the time to cut across the sea from Sherningham that it would take to go all the way round King's Lynn by road, and if he did that he would still have had to go out by sea from Burbidge's depot to his place of work.

But it was more than a convenient means of transport. He had been using it as a hiding place, a risky one in some ways, but anything was risky, and the chances of someone with my knowledge finding the things they had hidden, and identifying them for what they were, were remote. If they had not been so careless as to put me in the way of the boat I would never have stumbled across them myself. I wondered what Holden thought of the way they looked after the stuff he had found with such methodical care and effort.

The windows had turned from black to grey, and some of the greyness had seeped into the cabin by now. Dawn was breaking, and with it a breeze had started to get up, not strong, but strong enough to blow the mist away. I went out into the cockpit to look round.

Behind the stern the coast was now visible, a horizontal line of deeper grey, the sky a clearer blue grey above. It seemed a long way off, further than I could have walked through the water, even in a straight line. Behind me, and to left and right, the greyness had not yet cleared sufficiently to reveal the shape of things beyond. A few gulls flew near me, but the seabirds' activity must be concentrated nearer the land. They would be too small to be visible at that distance, but what I could see were the figures of two men in a rubber dinghy, propelled towards me by an outboard motor. With a sinking feeling I realised they might be on their way to the boat in which I was calmly sitting, doing nothing.

I had not seen an engine when I inspected the cabin, but there must be one somewhere: the boat had no mast for a sail and no fixings for an outboard motor at the stern.

It was not difficult to find. The propeller must be under the stern, and there was only one space between that and the cabin, in which the engine could be.

I had failed to notice the brass rings and the flush hinges set in the floor of the cockpit when I had inspected it by night, but now they were obvious, and so were the controls, in a recess beside the cabin door and concealed by a cover which was released by a catch inside the cabin.

There was no time to lift the floor and check that there really was an engine and that it contained fuel. The controls seemed to be the same as those of a car: ignition switch - no key needed - starter button, throttle, and wheel. At the third try the engine spluttered and started, and I heard a yell.

Jason and Barry, I could recognise them now, were on their way as fast as their outboard motor would take them. When I turned to look at them Jason waved threateningly, then suddenly stopped waving and shouting. He had recognised me.

I laughed. That was the best joke of the night.

But simultaneously I realised that I could not just open the throttle and go because the boat was still secured at the bows.

I stopped laughing about as fast as I scrambled up on to the top of the cabin and forward to the bows. The fastening of the painter to the buoy looked a good deal easier to loosen than its fastening to the boat, so I took valuable time pulling the boat up to the buoy and untying.

As I tumbled back into the cockpit Jason and Barry were much too close, only about ten yards away. The tide, still coming in, was now carrying my drifting boat towards them, and I noticed with dismay that they both had weapons: each was wielding a paddle.

As fast as I could I reached the throttle and opened it fully. The engine coughed and for a horrified moment I was afraid I had choked it. It coughed, and coughed again, and then started to pick up, but after it had picked up the boat took time to gather way and in that time Jason and Barry were on me.

Jason grabbed the edge of my boat with one hand, locking it to their rubber dinghy by holding on to it with the other. In the meantime Barry was starting to clamber aboard. He had two hands on the stern, one still clutching his paddle as well, and he started to heave his great bulk over, relying on Jason to hold the two craft steady enough for him to do it.

I looked round desperately for a weapon, but I had found nothing in the evening when I had wanted to break down the cabin door, and I could see nothing now. This time, though, the cabin door was open, and in the nick of time I remembered seeing a short boat hook, secured in clips above the windows on one side of the cabin. I dived inside, stumbling through the cups and goblets on the floor, seized the boat hook, and dashed out again, clutching it with two hands at the ready.

By now my own boat had started to gather way, and with every moment it was going faster. It was pulling the rubber dinghy with it, locked to it by Jason, but even Jason was beginning to feel the strain. Although he held on as firmly as ever, a watery gap had opened between the two craft and, momentarily, it unsettled Barry.

In that moment I acted, at last.

I leaped towards Barry, wielding my boat hook like a club, striking him indiscriminately on whatever parts of his body happened to be at the receiving end of my wild, undisciplined, desperate blows.

Barry was a big target. Head, shoulders, arms, fingers: I must have hit them all, occasionally changing targets for a moment and taking a swipe at Jason as he clung determinedly to dinghy and boat.

Barry was the first to go. A harder, luckier blow from me caught him across the side of the head. It obviously hurt. More to the point, it made him lose his balance. He fell backwards into the water, but kept his hold for a moment on the stern of the boat. During that moment, though, I landed two blows hard on his fingers, and with an agonised yell he sank back into the sea, disappearing under the rubber dinghy, surfacing again beyond, wallowing, blowing, bellowing.

I nearly stopped my attack on Jason at that moment, fool that I was, I assumed he would relinquish his hold and go to the help of his friend. But I was being simple.

Far from leaving he started to clamber aboard, abandoning the dinghy.

Though I knew for a fact that he was stronger than me I had the wit to see that he was at a disadvantage.

There came a moment when he was half aboard, half at sea, when his weight was perfectly poised on the stern rail of the boat. At that moment I kicked.

His weight fell backwards. The sudden strain on the hand which still held the rail would not have been too great for him if I had not, immediately afterwards, fallen upon it, striking it with my boathook as fast as I could go. His fingers weakened. Instead of holding with a strong grip of the whole hand he held for a moment only with the last joints of his fingers, and in that moment I landed the hardest blow I had made squarely on those fingers.

They, and he, were gone.

I throttled down, grabbed the wheel, steered away from my opponents and from the land, and looked back.

Barry was clambering into the dinghy. Jason was swimming towards it.

In my ears I could still hear the only word he had uttered throughout the whole episode, a softly spoken "bastard" as my final blow had landed on his fingers.

At last I could take stock of what I was doing and where I was going.

Although the mist was still lifting with the aid of the breeze only one landmark was to be seen: the line of the shore from which I had come. To be sure there were buoys about, but buoys are not much use if you do not know what they are indicating.

The shore was astern. If I kept going as I was I would soon be out of sight of it, and just about as lost in the haze at sea as I had been in the dark on the beach only a few hours earlier.

I turned left, I set a course parallel with the coastline, keeping it on my left at what I hoped was a safe distance. As the tide was still coming in - I had recent evidence of that - even if I went aground I would be able to float off again quite quickly.

I pictured my map of The Wash. If I kept going like this I would run into the mouth of the river Ouse, and into King's Lynn.

And that is what I did.

I had calmed down by the time I reached it. I felt infinitely weary, and stiff, and although I was no longer as cold as I had been I longed to strip off my wet clothes and replace them with fresh, warm, dry ones. I felt exhilaration, too. Surely after everything I had been through, all would be well now?

I reached the docks and I went on past them. Three cargo boats were moored there: Annette of Boulogne was preparing to cast off, I presumed to go out on the high tide on which I was coming in; Royal George of King's Lynn was unloading timber;

and Candida, also of King's Lynn, was preparing to follow Annette.

I found some concrete steps leading up to a quay and a road when I reached the town. Beside the steps was a vertical iron rail, down which the painter would slip with the tide if a boat were moored there for any length of time.

With my cargo I had no intention of leaving it there for any length of time.

My knowledge of King's Lynn was limited, but I knew where the police station was and I started making for it. I did not like leaving my boat where it was, unattended with its valuable cargo, and besides, the wind was getting up in earnest now and I feared for its safety. However I saw no alternative.

It was still early and the streets were empty. I half ran, half walked. Reaction to my night out was setting in: my teeth chattered, I had uncontrollable fits of shivering, and from time to time I stumbled; I hardly noticed the occasional person I passed. My heart sank when I saw the policeman who greeted me. Even in the condition I was in, prejudice ran deep.

"Please," I began: "send a car. Stolen goods. Quick ... hurry." It was imperative to get back to the boat before anything could happen to it.

He was a young man. He did not exactly look disbelieving, but nor did he leap into action.

"Where?" he asked. "What kind of goods? Why the hurry?"

I was seized by a fit of shivering before I could reply. I could keep nothing still, hands knees, teeth. I must have looked quite a sight. The policeman waited while I got over it.

"Because they're not safe where they are. Please! It's urgent, really."

I suppose they must get used to cranks who come in with cock and bull stories, and mine must have sounded as unlikely as any.

187

The policeman picked up a pencil and was about to say "Name?" when I had another bout of shivering.

That must have convinced him, not necessarily of my sanity, but that I was not a mere practical joker. He left the counter at which he was standing, and I heard him talking in the next room while I got over my new attack.

Once they had decided to act they did not hang about. When the policeman came back he was accompanied by another, a sergeant, and at the same time a car drew up outside.
The sergeant and I got into the back.

Next problem: to direct them. I tried to make them take the road by which I had come, but we met one-way streets, and I had hazy recollections of walking along pedestrianised shopping malls.

"A quay, near a big square, I told them in desperation. The driver took over.

While we drove, the sergeant continued where the policeman at the station had stopped. He asked for my name, which I gave him, and my address, over which I hesitated and stuttered. No point in giving my home address, and I did not regard caravan number 133, Sherningham Beach, as my home.

"The Andersons," I said at last. "New Road, Sherningham. They'll know." Well Sally would.

I recognised the big square when we reached it, and the driver took us without hesitation beyond it and on to a quay, the right quay.

"Here," I gasped as I staggered from the car. I could feel another fit of shivering coming on. "Over here."

I led the way as fast as I could to the break in the low parapet wall through which the steps disappeared down and into the sea. The policemen walked on either side of me. The fastest pace I could manage now was no more than a stroll for them.

We reached the opening. "Down there," I told them. "Look." We looked.

188

No boat.

I could not believe it.

I was sure I had tied a strong enough knot. I had been so concerned about it that I had gone on tying knots until no slack was left in the painter.

I looked across the river, up the river, down the river. Still no boat.

The policemen glanced at each other and I could see them agreeing that I was off my head. Then they both looked at me. All I could do was stand there, feeling the next fit of shivering coming on.

I did not look at them. I turned round despairingly towards the car, and started for it. They came with me, resigned, one on either side.

"Steady, son," the sergeant said to me. "Not this way. Over here."

He took my arm and started to ease me gently in the right direction. But by then we were near the wrong car, the one I had been heading for, and I realised what I had been doing, so I tried to shake them off and keep going under my own steam.

They were gentle and good-humoured, but my bout of shivering intensified and they had to half lead, half carry, me back to their own vehicle.

I almost passed out this time, lying back in the soft comfortable seat.

They did not return to the police station. They had seen enough of me, and they took me to the hospital instead. I think my shivering must have been very like a fit, and it had scared them.

Through it all though, and through my subsequent delirium and semi-consciousness, I could remember the identity of the car I had been heading for.

It was Jason's.

Chapter 13

I was not aware of much for a day or two, and what knowledge I have came mainly from Sally when she visited me, and from the police when they questioned me.

She came that day, she told me afterwards, but I was not well enough to talk to and later, when the police had found out more, they told her they wanted to have first go at me.

It was the same sergeant as before, but the policeman who accompanied him to take notes was different.

"Feeling better?" he asked. At least he was trying to be friendly.

"Yes, thanks."

"Feeling up to a few questions?" He smiled as he asked, I'll allow him that.

I would have to answer them sooner or later, so it might as well be sooner.

"O.K."

"Well, we got your message, or rather your girlfriend got your message - the one you wrote on toilet paper and she passed it on to us."

I was relieved, even though it seemed to have served no useful purpose. "Good," I answered.

"Unfortunately we got it too late, not until after you had been to see us yourself."

All that effort and resourcefulness for nothing! I wondered what had delayed it so long.

"You'd better tell us what happened. Why did you ask for help?"

I would have thought it must be obvious to them by now. If three thugs attack you of course you need help.

"Because the three of them had caught me and would not let me go." I answered. Ask a silly question and you get a silly answer.

"Not so fast. Who were the three of them?"

So I told them, I could only put a surname to one, but Burbidge's ought to know all about Jason and Barry. After all Burbidge's employed them.

"And what did they do to you?"

"They gassed me, and left me on the beach at low tide near the water. Just as they did to Dick."

They ignored Dick. They made a note about him but they were more interested in how I got to King's Lynn and in the stolen goods. I described how I had floundered round in the water, how I had found the boat, how Jason and Barry had tried to stop me, and how I had reached King's Lynn by sea.

They sat there with poker faces, taking it all in, writing it down.

"So you left the boat where you landed and came straight to the police station?"

"Yes."

"Yet when we went back for it it had gone?" A hint of a smile hovered round the sergeant's mouth. Obviously he did not believe much of what I had been saying.

"Yes," I answered. "And now I know who took it."

"Now, but not then? Why didn't you tell us at the time?"

"I was too far gone," I answered. "You remember that car, the one on the quay I was trying to go to? Well, I made a mistake when I started towards it, but when we were near I recognised it. It belonged to Jason. He must have driven round from Sherningham when he saw the direction in which I set off. At that hour there was no traffic to delay him, so he probably reached King's Lynn before I did and was able to watch me coming up the river. I expect he watched me tie up and just stepped into the boat as soon as I was out of sight... I had had a day or so to work that out. "I wouldn't be surprised if all three of them were there; they seemed to stick together."

"All three are missing," the sergeant commented, more to himself than to me. "These stolen goods, what were they? You don't mean the boat itself?"

It was a temptation to say 'yes'. It might have finished the questioning sooner, and I was beginning to become tired of it.

"No," I answered. "The stolen goods were in the boat. I found them there. They were mediaeval bits of silver and gold, plates and bowls and pitchers, and things like that."

I had taken him aback. Obviously stolen goods do not often come in that shape.

"You sound pretty sure. How did you know what they were?"

"Oh, I know." I did not feel like launching into an explanation of how I knew at that moment. I was much too weary.

"You didn't perhaps find them somewhere else?" The policeman was smiling again. "You didn't take them from Mr Stevens' antique shop, for instance?"

I had forgotten all about Stevens' shop for the moment, and I must have looked pretty blank.

"You see," he went on, "we know you broke into his shop two days ago. Mr Stevens reported that he had been burgled, and you were careless enough to leave behind the tools which you used to gain entry. The jack was part of your car equipment, and the insulating block was yours, too wasn't it? We found the empty box which it came from in the boot of your car."

His half-smile hovered round his lips again. It seemed to me a smile of triumph, telling me to talk myself out of it if I could.

I sighed. Of course I could talk myself out of it, but I felt increasingly tired.

"O.K." I answered. "Yes, I did break in, but I did not intend to steal anything." The sergeant's smile broadened, and I could have hit him. It was just as well I had not the strength at that moment and that I was too far from him even to have a try. "I went there because I knew Stevens had some King John pennies and I wanted to compare his with one which I had picked up."

192

He did not believe me; that was obvious.

"You could have waited until the shop was open, until Mr Stevens was there, couldn't you?"

"Yes, but...."

"And although you say you did not intend to steal anything Mr Stevens has lost some King John pennies. He says they were stolen." No smile now; he was getting down to business.

"I did not steal them."

"Then perhaps you could tell me who did?" The smile was back again, oozing triumph.

"Certainly: Waters, Jason, and Barry."

The smile vanished and was replaced by impatience.

"They may or may not have been responsible for attacking you at Sherningham Beach," he said. "But just because you think you can hold them responsible for that you need not expect them to take the blame for your own crimes too."

"Take it or leave it," I answered. I was not going to argue. "What I am telling you is the truth. Waters and his friends were there when I arrived; that's where they caught me; and they took me back to Sherningham from there."

I flopped back on my pillow when I had said that and closed my eyes. To give him his due he took the hint.

"I may have to come back with some more questions," he said, "but that will do for now." The two of them got up, put their notebooks away, and made for the door. As he was about to go out through it the sergeant turned round to me.

"You may be interested to know that we found the boat." He paused for effect. I opened my eyes and looked at him. I tried not to look too alert, but there was no doubt he had rid me of my weariness for a moment.

"It was washed up on the beach near Hunstanton yesterday."

"And Waters, and Jason, and Barry?"

"No sign of them, but bodies often take longer than boats."

"And the stolen goods?"

193

"No sign of them either."

***

I slept after they had gone, and did not wake up again until Sally came in. She was tiptoeing across the floor, awkwardly, careful not to wake me. When I opened my eyes she came over and gave me a kiss on the forehead.

I grinned. "You're my favourite visitor," I told her.

"Better than the police, eh? Anyway, I'm glad you went to them in the end. Now you can tell me all about it." Then she paused, and looked concerned. "But only if you feel up to it George."

I felt up to it. I must have got in four hours sleep since the police had called. The police ...

"You know they want me for breaking and entering Stevens' shop, don't you?" I grinned at her. She did not believe me.

"And did you do it?"

"Yes." She looked disconcerted, but puzzled by my obvious cheerfulness in the face of the charge.

"I don't understand," she said. "You send me a mysterious note, you land up in hospital half dead, I'm told you were out in the sea most of the night before last, and all you can tell me is that you have broken and entered Stevens' shop.

"Mind you, I'm not sure he doesn't deserve it, but that's another matter. Odious little man?"

She sounded pretty vitriolic about him, a distinct change from her attitude when she had spoken to him politely enough at the History Society meeting. I was about to ask why when she prompted me to tell her about my own experience.

So I did, not many holds barred.

I left out some of the subtleties of the conversation between Waters and Jason in Stevens' shop, but that was partly because I found it too much of an effort to try to remember. When I came

194

to tell her of the things I had found in the boat she made me go through it in the greatest detail I could, and at the end she commented that I would have to repeat it all to her father when he came; he would be fascinated. And that made me remember something.

"What about that bowl?" I asked, "the one which your father was taking to the archivist, Gerald...." I could not remember the name.

"Eke," Sally came to my rescue. "Yes, he confirmed what Dad said; he thought it could be the same vintage as King John's treasure. And if that's the case," she went on, "it looks as if this stuff you found in the boat could be more of it." She paused, then she suddenly burst out: "Oh, I do hope it turns up again. Dad will be so excited, and ... oh, that kind of thing just shouldn't be lost. It's not right, and it's happened once already: it can't happen again."

I was not so sure. "Have you heard that they've recovered the boat?" I asked her. She had not, so I told her.

"And it was found up near Hunstanton," she repeated. "Where do you think they were making for?"

"Goodness knows." The question had occurred to me too, but not the answer. "What was the weather like Sally?" I went on. "The wind was getting up that morning when they went off in the boat. Did it rise anymore?"

"It did. It blew quite a gale during the day and by the evening it was even worse: a real storm, a big one even for February. There were pictures in the papers of waves breaking over quays and of fishing boats smashed against the sea walls at Hunstanton. In fact further round to the North, at Wells, a small coaster was washed right up on to the quay; it must have taken quite a wave to do that. And it was obviously worse in the open sea too. The lifeboats were out, and several ships were reported to be in difficulties, and one or two of them were lost."

"But that was later, the big storm. Earlier in the morning though, when Jason and the others set out, do you think the weather was bad enough to sink them?"

"It's difficult to say. I don't sail," she looked down at her club foot, "and I never saw the boat. But if it had a cabin, and an engine, and they did not run out of fuel, I'd have thought it stood a fair chance of survival - until the evening anyway."

"The fuel: that may be the answer. I never got round to checking it, but I must have used some, and if it was low to start with they could have run out.

Still, they knew the boat. You'd have thought they'd have checked, but they might have had too many other things to think of."

We lapsed into silence, both reflecting on what had been said, until I remembered another thing.

"That message I sent you," I asked her, "the police told me they didn't get it until after I'd been to see them myself, in Lynn. What happened to it? Why did it take so long?" There could only be three possible explanations. The man who took it had dawdled, or Sally had sat on it (but I did not believe that), or her father had put her off.

But there was another.

"It was the man's wife," Sally told me. "He was terribly apologetic, really embarrassed. But his wife poured scorn on it; told her husband you must be a practical joker or a crank; and then when he was about to set off that evening to see me she told him he couldn't go round accosting young girls so late, and he a grown man. So he put it off until the morning. In fact after he had been I was about to report it to the police when they rang me themselves to say they had found you and that you had given them our address." She looked down at me in a motherly, possessive way. "I'm glad you did that George," she squeezed my hand, "because as soon as you're well enough to come out of here you're coming home with us to convalesce."

196

I did not contradict her. At that moment I did not want to.

Her father came the next day. The whole family came. When they arrived Mr Anderson was the man of substance, all polish and assurance like the drawing room of his house. He asked how I was now, referred to the ordeal through which I had passed, made complimentary remarks about the hospital, and commented on the weather.

But then he changed. Suddenly he was a different man: he had become the thoughtful, impartial scholar of his study.

"Sally told you what Gerald Eke thought of that silver plate you brought in?" He looked at me inquiringly as he spoke, and I noticed he called it a plate, not a bowl. "He confirmed what I said; mediaeval, probably eleventh or twelfth century. It's an important find. And the first thing he did was to ask the same question as I had asked: where did you dig it up? But Sally's explained that now, and I can understand why you did not want to tell me at the time."

I looked across at Sally. "You don't mind, do you, George?" she asked as a slight frown of worry crossed her brow. But even if I had minded, it would have made no difference now: everything was coming out. Besides, what I had minded was telling Mr Anderson and explaining everything as if I were making excuses, and Sally had spared me that.

"But I gather that's not the only plate," Mr Anderson went on. "Far from it, Sally tells me there were lots of other things...."

"Three bags full."

"It's almost incredible, quite remarkable. And now ... we don't even know where it is." He sighed. "And it looks distressingly as if it is lost all over again, but this time in the open sea, so that it's even less likely to be found." He stopped to contemplate this horrible prospect. Then he came back to me.

"You realise what this may mean though, don't you, George?" It may mean that all this priceless treasure, priceless not just because of its intrinsic value, and heaven knows that is not to be

197

sneezed at, but also because of its immense historical interest, it may mean that all this treasure, which has been lost completely for more than seven hundred and fifty years, has been found, just for one brief part of one day, and has immediately been lost again. And during the brief time when it was found only a handful of people have seen it." He paused again, spellbound by the extraordinary nature of the event. "And those who saw it while it was found were three men who are now presumed dead - and you." He looked keenly at me.

"And the person who found it." I put in.

"Ah, that's the point. Who was it?"

"Surely there's no doubt about that: Holden."

"He denies it, and he's an honest man."

"But who else could it have been?" I asked.

"We just don't know. Holden's guess, and that's the only serious guess that has been made, is that perhaps Burbidge's men found it - using his, Holden's, machinery and on his land. He says they asked if they could use his machines one day, but told him they had found nothing."

"It would certainly have been a good haul for one day." I added.

"Precisely...." Mr Anderson fidgeted and seemed at a loss for words, something I had not witnessed before, "Precisely ... but there is another point, and I will put it to you bluntly. We have the word of only one person as to what was found and he, I am sure you will agree, did not have time to examine it carefully, and at the time he was not, shall we say, in the very best of health and in laboratory conditions for examining and recording the exhibits. He may have been mistaken, he may have exaggerated ... it has even been suggested, and I am sure you will accept from me that it is not my suggestion, that he may just have lied, lied for fun, perhaps, or lied to gain attention."

I was slow to grasp what Mr Anderson was getting at, but I got there in the end. The thought of my lying to gain attention made me laugh, and that made Mr Anderson, in his solemn way look at me as if I were lacking in respect, as if I were indulging in sacrilege. However, he went on:

"The police have therefore asked me to put a few questions to you about the nature of the objects which you found in the boat. They have appointed me to be, as it were, a temporary police auxiliary. They think my expert knowledge of the probable composition of King John's treasure will enable me to check your story and to confirm whether it is true or not." He paused and coughed, looking down to the floor and avoiding my eye in an uncharacteristic way. He seemed embarrassed by the role allocated to him. "Do you mind if I question you?"

"Fire away," I answered.

"In their presence?"

"If you wish."

Mr Anderson gave Marjorie a nod and she left the room, to return a moment later with the sergeant, who settled down with his notebook to listen.

Mr Anderson continued.

"We have what you may think is a surprisingly detailed knowledge of many of the objects which it is thought were in King John's baggage train. The knowledge is derived from Patent Rolls, contemporary records on which were recorded minute details of items which the king had received from various abbeys and other sources. Some of these I know about, others I can look up. What I want you to do, George, is to describe, in as great detail as you can, as many of the objects as you remember. I realise," he smiled, "and I'll say it again, that you have only seen these things briefly, in poor light, probably when they were dirty and encrusted with sediment, and that at the time you examined them you did not do it with a view to being subsequently cross-examined about what you had seen, nor to finding that you were the first and last person in over seven hundred and fifty years to set eyes on them. Nevertheless your testimony is the only evidence we have, the only evidence it looks likely we ever will have. Therefore it puts a grave responsibility on your shoulders. Now, would you like to begin? You must describe as much as you can of each object you can remember, keeping firmly to what you're certain of." At this point Mr Anderson also produced a notebook and pencil, and there I was, ringed with expectant faces. I have never had such an attentive audience in my life, and never will again.

"I wish now I had looked more carefully," I began, "but I'll do my best. The thing which impressed me most was, I'm pretty sure, a crown. When I first picked it up it was a jumbled mass of metal about this size," I demonstrated with my hands. "I had to open it up before I realised what it was.

"The thickest bit of metal was a hoop, the part which would go round the head, Above that was a superstructure of bands, interlaced with each other, and at the top was a cross."

"This cross, was it at the centre, or at the front?" Mr Anderson asked.

"I couldn't tell, it was too badly damaged, or perhaps I just didn't notice. But I did notice two other things about it: there were stones mounted in it, at least I think they must have been stones and not just metal studs, though they were so dirty it was not easy to tell the difference, and some of them were missing from their sockets; and there were some bigger, more elaborate, pieces of metalwork in a ring above the headband. I think they were in the form of flowers, but it was difficult to tell."

"How many?"

I laughed. "As if I had stopped to count them! I don't know," I answered. "Four ... five, at least. No more than ten, I would say - but I wasn't counting."

"Extraordinary!" Mr Anderson exclaimed. "I will tell you: if that crown is what I think it is there were seven; it is the crown which came from Germany and which was part of the coronation regalia which belonged to the 'Lady Empress'

Maud, King John's grandmother. It had been in the custody of the Knights Templars, and King John recovered it from them in May, 1215." Mr Anderson's words were greeted with a silence, as if of reverence for the crown. "Go on," he said to me.

"The only other thing I noticed in any detail," I said, "was a metal stick. It might have been gold or silver. It shone a bit when I rubbed something else against it. It was about a foot long, broken at one end, and on the other there was a bird."

"A bird," repeated Mr Anderson. "What kind of bird?"

Again I laughed. "Heaven knows," I answered. "I don't - but I am pretty sure it was a bird."

"A dove, perhaps?" Mr Anderson persisted.

"It could have been." It could have been a sparrow, too, for all I could tell"

"Remarkable, and logical. In all probability that was the golden wand which went with the crown you have already described. One would have expected to find them together. Go on."

They would be disappointed now. I simply had not noticed anything else in detail.

"I can't remember any other individual items, not well enough to describe them. There were two or three crosses, I think, and at least two swords. I tried to pull one out of its scabbard, but of course it wouldn't come. There were a few things which looked as if they might be buckles, big ones, and several belts, at least I think that is what they must have been. They had things attached to them, metal and stones. And apart from that, of course, there were these dozens and dozens and dozens of cups and bowls and dishes and jugs." There was a cough.

"You must not exaggerate," the sergeant interrupted. "Dozens and dozens."

"I'm not," I retorted. "There were literally dozens of them. I didn't count them, of course, I just stuffed them back into the sacks. But there were three sacks full of them and I'm not exaggerating."

The sergeant shrugged his shoulders and looked at Mr Anderson as if to say, 'I told you so'.

"It could be true," Mr Anderson said. "Immediately after Magna Carta King John wrote to fifteen or twenty religious houses telling them to send their valuables to him, and most of them obeyed; after all, they belonged to the king, and he wanted to make sure he had them with him so that his rebel barons could not lay their hands on them. There were more than one hundred and fifty cups and goblets of silver and gold at that time, and that was in 1215, a year before he died. And in the following year, as things became more difficult, he toured the kingdom, sacking and laying waste the estates of the rebels, and we can be sure that if there were any valuables in those houses he took them with him. And that was not everything. No," Mr Anderson looked at the sergeant, "there could easily have been dozens of them." He turned to me. "Is that all?" be asked.

"All! It's all I can remember seeing."

"No rings? No brooches? No small things? No robes and other clothes? - though I fear that in the sea they would have decayed long ago."

"I don't remember seeing any. No, I am sure there were none."

"Nothing else you can think of at all?"

"Nothing."

Mr Anderson turned to the sergeant.

"Well," he said to him, "I believe what George has just told us. To me it has the ring of truth, and such details as he has been able to give coincide with the knowledge we have from the records, and I do not see how he could have observed any more in the time and conditions which prevailed. It might be thought curious that none of the smaller things were there, but it could be that they were more difficult to recover from the silt than the larger items."

The sergeant was still busy. Now he was recording Mr Anderson's verdict.

I was relieved to see him doing that.

By now I was exhausted, and they could see it. It had been arranged that Sally should fetch me from hospital on the following afternoon if, as was expected, I was pronounced fit. They left me to make myself fit.

Before they departed though, 1 asked Sally to make some enquiries for me.

Lying in bed in hospital there was nothing I could do, but my mind had been active, and I was beginning to think there might be some things which everyone was overlooking, including the police.

***

I was up and ready to leave well before the time Sally was due to fetch me and when the door opened it occurred to me it was just as well I was in good time.

But it was not her. It was Holden.

He had dressed up for the occasion, as he had done for the History Society meeting. He carried his hat clutched to his chest, and I thought he looked a little embarrassed. But why? It was I who should have been embarrassed, I who had been caught red-handed examining his plough, I who had stolen his King John penny. I waited for him to start the conversation.

"They told me you were well enough to receive visitors," he began. "You don't mind one more?"

I was too surprised to see him to reply immediately, but I managed a kind of grunt, which must have sounded friendly, and Holden came forward. Suddenly he took his hat from his chest and uncovered a box of chocolates which he handed over. He did it as if he were a conjuror, and he looked all the more embarrassed. "I thought you might like...." he did not even finish the sentence.

But when he started to talk about the reason he had come his embarrassment receded.

"The police have been to see me," he explained, "and they told me a few of the things which have happened to you. Not very nice, I should say. If you ask me, you've done well to come out of it alive." He paused to collect his thoughts. "I met Eric," he went on, and again I heard that hard, left-behind, C at the end of the name. "I met Eric, and I met the fellow they called Jason, though I didn't know that was his name, but I never met the third of them." Holden had a curiously apologetic way of speaking, as if he were out of practice, which indeed he may have been if he spent too much time alone on his farm, dealing with tractors and tillage rather than people. "Not a pleasant fellow, Jason."

"No," I chimed in decisively. "I gather you had some trouble with him?" Holden's grin was lop-sided.

"Trouble? No, I don't think I'd call it trouble. The pair of them, Jason and Eric, came to see me one day. They'd noticed me at a public lecture about King John and that kind of thing - not the History Society meeting which you came to, nothing as interesting as that. I suppose that was what gave them the idea of coming to see me but I never did quite get the hang of what they came for. They started on about my land, how deep the soil was, and how the sea must have come up over it at one time, and of how the bit they were working on in The Wash might be just the same if it was drained instead of being dredged, and...." Mr Holden seemed to run out of steam.

"I gather you let them have a go at treasure hunting on your land," I put in to help him.

"Oh, you know about that, do you?" He looked surprised and sheepish.

"Yes, Mr Anderson mentioned it when he came to see me." There was no need to tell him I had known anyway. It looked as if his employee had kept that quiet, and I saw no reason to give him away.

"They were very pressing, Jason and Eric."

I wondered what form their pressure had taken. It was a good deal rougher than Holden was prepared to admit, I was sure. He obviously preferred to play things down rather than up, he was that kind of man.

"But that's just the point; that brings me to the reason I came to see you."

He stopped unhappily, but whether he was unhappy because of the reason, or at the prospect of telling me, I could not tell. Then it came, all in a rush:

"Jason insisted on trying out my tractor when he noticed what I was up to. You know about that?" I nodded. "But he didn't try for long, found it uncomfortable I reckon, not what he was used to. I left them to it - I'd had enough of them - but they couldn't possibly have found much in the time they had, and if they had found anything they'd have had to dig for it, and there was no sign of digging when they left off, and besides, they didn't have the equipment. It was in the workshop, right enough, but they weren't to know that, and even if they had known about it they'd have needed time to hitch it up. But...."

I had to prompt him. "Yes?"

"But the police, I don't think they believe me, and they are now coming to question me again this afternoon." At that moment he looked really wretched. I could sympathise with him too. I knew what it was like.

"What are they driving at?" I asked, but already I could guess.

"They think I'm lying," he answered miserably. "They think I've been digging up Treasure Trove and not turning it in. I suppose they think I must have dug up the stuff they told me you saw, and that I'm trying to get out of it by putting the blame on Jason and Eric."

"So what can I do for you?"

Either he had forgotten, or he was less certain now than he had been when he set out to visit me. "Well I thought ... I wanted

205

to make sure about the things you saw. All I have to go on is what the police told me, and they were not very exact, and I began to wonder if...."

"If they were making it all up? Just to catch you out?" He looked at me gratefully. He was a timid man and he did not like making accusations, or even appearing to make them, but he was cornered, and he had to do something. I could not help him though. "No," I told him. "They were not making it up. They were not even exaggerating. If anything they thought it was I who was exaggerating. There was lot of the stuff: three sacks full. It was not dug up in an afternoon."

Holden's face fell even further. I was beginning to think I might be able to help him, but I was not going to tell him, not yet anyway. Besides, I saw my opportunity of asking him a question.

"Did you never find anything?" I asked him. "Not even a bag of King John pennies?"

Expressions of surprise, guilt, and relief passed across his weather-beaten features.

"'You know about that, too, do you?" he said sheepishly. "Yes, but that was all I did find, just this bundle of coins. They came up when I was ploughing; I wasn't even looking for them. They were the reason I rigged up my treasure hunting device. It was Stevens who suggested it and who told me how to do it, and then told me to keep quiet about it. He warned me that if I said anything I'd have everyone in the country on my land, all with detectors, searching, and that I'd never have a moment's peace. And he was right about that, I'm sure.

"But if I hadn't kept it quiet the police wouldn't now be bothering me in the way they are. I'm just as sure of that too. They think I only found one coin, but they reckon that if I hid even that then I'm likely to have done it again."

"I can see their point," I said to him, and I racked my brains at the same time to think of any other questions I wanted to ask.

206

He was in a receptive, answering, frame of mind, and it was a pity to waste it.

"So Jason and Waters went away and told you to let them know if you found anything?"

Holden nodded unhappily.

"And I expect they told you what they'd do to you if you didn't let them know, and it wasn't very pleasant?" Again Holden nodded. "Physical violence, I should think, and a threat that they'd let the cat out of the bag so that your farm would be trampled to pieces?" I had it right. I was beginning to know how they went to work.

Holden could only nod once again in his wretchedness. He had been sitting on the front edge of a chair by the bed, still clutching his hat to him as if it contained further surprises and he was afraid of letting them out. Now he stood up, slowly like an old man, balancing carefully and waiting until he was upright before moving his feet.

"I'm glad you're getting on all right," he said to me, "and I'm sorry if I've tired you." He turned and started towards the door.

"One moment." I called him back. He was a bundle of misery, frightened of the police, frightened of what he had done, frightened that people and events were ganging up on him. I could sympathise - I knew what it was like to be frightened by the police - and I wanted to give him some kind of comfort. Not too much though; false hope is no good to anyone.

"Don't worry too much," I told him. "They're bastards, the police, and stupid. I reckon they have quite a few things wrong, and I've an idea where the treasure came from now. It's only an idea still, and I may be wrong. You stick to your guns with them. They'll have to believe you in the end."

Holden withdrew, still wretched, and I began putting what he had said into my nice little theory to test it.

It seemed to fit well enough.

Chapter 14

Sally arrived later than she intended, held up by temporary traffic lights which had sprung up on her way. She was apologetic. She had made the enquiries I had asked her to make, but the answers were not what I had hoped for.

While I was in hospital I had been looking forward to my convalescence in the Anderson's house, but as I crossed its threshold I felt less happy. Sally was fine; I could look forward to her; but my reservations about the rest of them welled up again inside me.

I had not been there long when the telephone rang and Mrs Anderson told me the police were on their way to see me. They had a statement for me to sign, and a few more questions to go with it.

We settled down in the lounge when they came, a repeat performance of the conference round my bed in hospital the day before. When they get you in their clutches they do not let go easily.

I signed their statement; it set out what I had said on the previous day in words I would never have used.

"We saw Mr Holden this afternoon," the sergeant began as he took possession of the piece of paper I had just signed.

"I know." He was not surprised. Holden must have told them he had visited me in hospital.

"Mr Holden said something which interested us. He said you knew where the treasure was dug up. Where? Why didn't you tell us?"

So that was it. Holden had been so desperate he had used me to get the police off his back. I did not blame him. I remembered the time when I would have done anything to be rid of them.

"You don't have it quite right," I answered. "I told Mr Holden I had an idea, no more than that. I didn't tell you because it's only an idea, I've not a shred of proof, and I was still trying to weigh

208

it all up when you came." I had had more time to work at it since then, and I had been able to add Holden's information to it. I might as well tell them now as later, and let them shoot it down. Mr Anderson was with us too, and I needed him.

"Well?"

I wondered where to begin. The deep end?

"I think Waters and Jason and Barry were the people who found those things." I paused.

They were not surprised, and they waited for me to go on.

"The place they found them was in the reservoir they were making."

There was more reaction this time, mainly from Mr Anderson. The others were merely interested: he was critical. He shook his head slowly from side to side, his lips framed the word 'no' and he leant over to a bookcase and removed a book, flipping through the pages until he came to a map. I waited for him.

"It's not possible," he said at last. "We can be certain that the crossing from Norfolk into Lincolnshire was roughly from Cross Keys to Long Sutton. There is plenty of evidence to support this: the old Roman embankment which bounded the estuary of the Wellstream, for instance, jutted forward at those two points as if to take a little more from the sea and make the crossing shorter; the main roads led to those two points; the villages and churches along the roads are ancient: the churches of Walpole St Peter and Terrington St Clement, for instance, have traces of Norman buildings under the present structures. So that must have been the accepted route and it must have been the route along which they set off. From Cross Keys to Sutton Bridge is a distance of two miles, and the river channel at that time was probably in the region of Sutton Bridge. Assuming that they started off in the right direction I think it is reasonable to assume that they came to the river more or less at Sutton Bridge before disaster overtook them. Are you suggesting that then, inexplicably, they turned ninety degrees and set off Northwards?"

"Yes."

He looked at me.

"But why?" He was beginning to sound impatient, I thought. "They had crossed the estuary in order to ford the river and reach Lincolnshire. Why turn North and head for the sea?"

It was my turn again.

"I'm not suggesting that they did it on purpose. It must have been a mistake. But then, the one thing everyone agrees is that they did not lose themselves on purpose - that was a mistake too."

I stopped and looked round. They were all listening hard, concentrating on every word I said. I went on: "You told us, didn't you, at your lecture, that this all happened in the autumn?"

"October 12th, 1216."

"And at that time of year there is often a sea mist?"

"Certainly."

"You also said that low water was at midday?"

"Yes."

"And that they were in such a hurry that they didn't bother with guides?"

"Roger of Wendover and Ralph of Coggeshall both suggest that, yes."

"And also that the baggage train would have been a long one, perhaps two miles long?"

"That was Major Anstruther-Grey's estimate."

"Well, my guess as to what happened is this:

"There was a mist that day: it started thin, but thickened after midday, so when they left King's Lynn it wasn't too bad, hazy at ground level, but clear above. They could not know it would become thicker, and as it was daylight they could see the ground on which they walked. By the time they reached Cross Keys though, it was probably a good deal worse, and perhaps

210

those who started last would never have set out if they had not been following others.

"I think they started later than they intended too, and pressed on when they reached Cross Keys, but then missed their way in the mist.

"It is difficult to go straight if you can't see, especially if you are hurrying, so their actual route may have been biased in one direction - to the North. If they had been tending northwards for a mile or so their route would have been longer and their arrival at the water's edge later, by which time the water would have been tidal, and it would have been difficult to tell which way it was flowing.

"Now, if I had been in front, searching for a shallow fresh-water river flowing from left to right, I would probably have concluded that I must be facing North and the open sea. So what could I do? I could turn left, following what I thought was the edge of the incoming sea until I reached the crossing place for the river, but by then it may have been too deep and difficult to recognise. Or I could turn back, brave the king's anger and the column I was leading, and try again at the next low tide. Or I could turn right and follow the edge of the incoming tide towards a part of the coast which must be nearer, not further away."

I had shot my bolt, and I stopped. Finally Mr Anderson spoke. "Interesting," he said, "But is it really conceivable that the ground on which they were walking would have been hard for three or four miles?"

"I don't see why not," I replied, "I did the same thing on Sherningham beach, on a smaller scale, admittedly, and although the bed of the watercourse was muddy, the shoulder was not. Anyway," I added, "we are talking about an unusual event, so surely the circumstances would have been unusual, too?"

Then I remembered two other points:

211

"Mr Anderson remarked that there were no small objects such as precious stones or rings: I think they would have gone straight through the sieve and back into the sea."

I paused for long enough for them to disagree, and when they did not do so I continued: "finally, the bowl, the only surviving object." I picked it up, turned it over, and could just see faint lines, very slight indentations, on a part of its convex surface.

"The dredger worked by sucking the sand and mud up through a big pipe, and then spewing it out into the sea," I said. "They had a cage over the inlet to stop foreign bodies entering and jamming it, and the cage consisted of a grid. These lines," I pointed to them "I think were made by that grid as the suction into the pipe brought the bowl hard up against the cage." I turned to the sergeant: "I'd have thought you can find the grids they were using and try them for size."

It was the bowl which convinced them in the end. Without it, and without those faint lines which the sergeant later confirmed did fit the mesh of the grid on the dredger hose, my suggestions would have been ignored. The police would not have bothered to contradict them; that would have been too much like an acknowledgement that I should be taken seriously and might have given me a chance to argue. Instead they would just have clapped me into gaol for shop-breaking.

However the bowl saved my bacon and Mr Anderson helped, to give him his due, by telling them that I could not have invented all I had said about the crown and about the golden wand with the dove on the end of it, no matter that it was he who had prompted me to identify the bird with such absurd accuracy.

But he never said he agreed with my idea about the route which King John's baggage train took, and how at least part of it had gone as far as the reservoir, though nor did he contradict it again. Maybe it was scholarly caution, just in case something else turned up to show that I had been wrong, maybe by then he half believed me but did not want to say so because he had

212

condemned the whole idea so strongly to begin with. Whatever it was I did not mind; it was enough that he no longer contradicted it.

Stevens' name was so detested in the Anderson's house that it was some time before I found out what had happened at the meeting which took place while I was doing my shop breaking.

Sally told me:

"He had it all worked out," she said gloomily. "He put up a proposal that all the little local societies which come and go, and thrive at times when they have good vigorous people running them, and then go into the doldrums for a few years when there's no one like that about - he wanted them all in what he called an 'umbrella organisation', which of course meant his beastly Conservation Society. And he'd done his canvassing so well, and he's such an oily, persuasive, speaker that he got away with it. There were representatives of all these little societies there who fell for his smooth talk and voted for it. So now Stevens is strutting round like a peacock talking about 'his' societies as if he owns them, and how it's all part of a national movement with strength to its elbow and the ability to lobby parliament, and all the rest of it."

"So the History Society doesn't exist anymore?"

"Now it's the Historical Division of the Conservation Society, and it's run by a sub-committee of the Council of the Society, not by its own little committee any more, and the main Conservation Society Council has a right to nominate a member to the sub-committee - so, as like as not, we shall find Stevens himself bobbing up and running the Historical Division too, telling Dad to give lectures here, there, and everywhere. In fact that's one of the things he mentioned. 'Cross-pollination' he called it, the contribution which the King's Lynn sub-committees could make to the sub-committees of sister Divisions in affiliated societies. I expect he'll be telling Dad to go off and give a lecture to a Divisional flower-arranging sub-committee in Darlington or

Hemel Hempstead before we know where we are, and drawing up standard rules of procedure, and co-ordinating meetings, and ... oh, it'll just kill everything. It's not so much that I'm fond of the History Society for its own sake, but Dad'll hate seeing it go downhill, and he's worked so hard ..."

"Perhaps he'll be able to start up another rival society?" I suggested.

"Not a hope. He's not like that. He's not a fighter: he's a worker, Dad is. And I'm afraid that therefore he'll put all he's got into this new set up, but as Stevens' interest in it is only in the power it gives him, all the enthusiasm will be driven away and it'll just die - either that, or it'll change so much that it will lose its enjoyment, its real interest in history, and the only things that'll matter will be membership numbers and resolutions."

I could see it all too. Stevens was one of those people who come out on top, and who have the luck. He had come out on top at the meeting itself, and his luck was in at his own shop while the meeting was going on, although he did not realise it until later.

Waters and Jason and Barry had been breaking and entering Stevens' shop that afternoon, as well as me. I had not gone there to steal, just to compare pennies. But they had gone to steal, and they had stolen the King John pennies to add to the booty they had planned to make off with. Stevens' first reaction was to report the theft, but he soon changed his tune. He could not say, suddenly, that it had not happened after all, so instead he told the police that he had made a mistake when he had reported the theft, that he had forgotten, he had sold the pennies some time before, and that when he looked up his records he found there were not as many as he had first told them. It was a thin story, but the police had to accept it because they had no proof to contradict it, just the word of an unreliable witness: me.

And that had saved Stevens - and Holden - from getting into real trouble about not declaring what they had found. If there

214

was no one to produce the pennies, or even to describe them, there was no one to make a fuss, was there?

The bodies of Waters and his friends never turned up. For a time that seemed to be the biggest puzzle of all, for surely out of three bodies you would have expected at least one to be washed ashore somewhere? But Sally opened my eyes to the reason.

The information I had asked her to find, while I lay in hospital, was the names of the masters of all the ships in King's Lynn docks on the day when the boat had been wrecked I had told her I expected the Christian name of one of them to be Jack - that was the name Dick had given. But she told me none of them was called Jack, nor even John.

And then, when I was convalescing in their house, she produced her notes and read out the names of the ships and their masters, as much to pass the time as anything else.

"The Royal George," she began, "Martin Williams."

"Not much Jack about that," I commented, "but I suppose he could have had another name."

"He had another initial, E, but how do you turn that into Jack?"

"I can't."

She went on. "Candida Harry Percival, and his other initial is M."

"That's no good, either."

"Annette - Jacques Martel."

"Jack," I said, "precisely!"

For a moment she looked at me blankly, but then she realised what she had said and how she had been misled by the spelling. It was obvious. I had listened to the name, not just read it as she had done.

But by now Annette would be miles away, as well as her cargo, human and freight.

"You must tell the police," Sally said immediately. But I had had enough.

215

"You can if you want," I told her, "but count me out. And if you try to drag me in I'll deny it. I can't stand any more, and they'll never recover the stuff now, and you can't say the police have exactly encouraged me to help them, can you?"

I expected her to argue when I said that. I was lying on my back on the settee in their drawing room, eyes on the ceiling above me, perfectly relaxed and more at peace with the world than I had been since my fateful visit to Norfolk had begun. Now I closed my eyes, confident that Sally would argue, confident that I could parry her arguments without difficulty.

But no argument came.

I opened my eyes again. Sally was sitting in her chair, the notes she had been using still spread on her knee, but her attention was not on them. She was staring, unseeing, through the window, as beautiful now in the calmness of concentration as I already knew her to be attractive when lit by the animation of her conversation.

Slowly she turned back until she faced me, her lips just parted, her brow puckered slightly with the effort of remembering. "Annette," she spoke slowly and thoughtfully, "Annette was one of the ships which was lost in the storm I can remember now. The Cromer lifeboat went out to look for her, but she was too late. All they found was debris, timber I think, which the ship had been carrying. All the crew were lost, I'm sure - all Frenchmen. They never mentioned any passengers."

"They wouldn't," I answered, "not illegal, non-paying passengers like that. No one but the crew knew they were there. No one but the crew knew they brought extra cargo on board with them."

We both remained silent, thinking of the storm, of Annette foundering, and of the life-boat's arrival on the scene to find nothing but wreckage, tossed by the waves.

"There's one thing," I said to Sally at last. "King John's treasure may have been lost again, but it's better off in Annette than

216

dropped overboard by Jason and Co. from their boat. In fact it's probaby better off there than it was where it was sunk in the mud in The Wash. At least people know how to find wrecks and salvage them nowadays. One day somebody will find it again."

But Sally was not convinced.

***

My convalescence came to an end and I went home. The Andersons were sorry to see me go, at least that is what they said, and Sally kissed me goodbye in front of the rest of her family. It really made me feel good, and when she made me promise to come back and see them I was not slow to say I would.

Back at home I found I was immediately pitched into some hard work. I had to get on with it or I would have lost the business. Sue, or painted nails to Sally, had done well. She had put people off and persuaded most of them that I really could not help being away, but that I would be back soon. She does a lot for me, Sue, more than I had let on to Sally; she had kept my house straight and had it warm and aired when I returned, with my bed made and food in the fridge.

I had to deal with Dick's affairs too, which were more complicated than I had expected. He had left no will and when the solicitors asked me if I was his only living relative I told them I was. I remembered what Nance had said about his father visiting her, but I still could not quite accept it, and if he had kept away for all those years he could keep away a bit longer as far as I was concerned: no one was to know that Nance had told me of his visit.

Dick's estate was worth more than I had expected because he was covered by a life insurance policy. It came from Burbidge's, who I discovered provided life cover for all their staff employees, and it amounted to quite a useful sum. So I wrote to Nance saying that I would be sending her a cheque - I felt she deserved it and Dick would have liked it - and I planned to pay off part of the mortgage on my house with the rest.

I dropped back into my old routine with relief. It was reassuring to be doing work with which I was familiar once again, to be living in my own house once again, to be able to keep myself to myself once again. The events of the days I had spent in Norfolk seemed far away, and I shuddered when I remembered the way they had bruised and battered me, mentally and physically. A s soon as I found I was thinking of them I would shut them away because I knew that remembering would only upset me.

Then came Sally's letter: I had not kept in touch, I had not kept my promise, and when was I coming to see them? It was a warm, inviting, letter, and it ended in love and kisses, and it reminded me ... and a spark flared up inside me.

But then it died, for I knew it was no good. As soon as I had stepped into my own home once again I had known it was no good.

I put the letter on my desk in the lounge, together with a newspaper cutting enclosed with it showing pictures of the men from Burbidge's who had been 'lost at sea'.

I meant to reply straight away. I could not go of course, but I had become fond of Sally, and I wanted to explain why. When I settled down to write though, I remembered her family with whom I would have been expected to stay if I had visited them. Even the thought of them made my heart sink and, more important, the words which I had ready to put down escaped from me.

So the letter was not written then, nor the next day, nor the next.

Sue had seen Sally's letter, I was sure. She always has a good look round. She did not say anything, but she was very meticulous about looking after me.

It was shortly after Sally's second letter arrived, less assured, more appealing, that someone knocked at the door on a Saturday afternoon.

It was Nance.

She had been in the district, and now that she knew my address she thought she'd call on me.

She swept past and into the lounge, and it was not long before her eye fell on Sally's newspaper cutting.

"Well, I'll be ..." she started as she fell on it. "Just look at that!"

"They were at Dick's funeral," I said. "You remember them?"

"I remember those two," she answered, pointing to Waters' and Jason's photographs. "They were at the funeral. And I remember him." she jabbed at Barry's picture, "he wasn't there, but I remember him all right!"

I had forgotten that Barry had not gone to the funeral.

"Phew! The cheek of it!" She was getting quite worked up, but I was blessed if I could see why.

"You know who that is?" she demanded.

"Yes," I answered. "Barry; he worked for Burbidge's, and he was one of the three thugs who tried to do for me."

"Barry, indeed! His name was Larry, not Barry - Larry Smith, Dick's father. He's the man who came round to see me at about the time Dick died. You remember, I told you about it?"

Until that moment I had forgotten.

My first thought was that he would have been entitled to Dick's money.

My second was that he would not have got it, not if I could have helped it.

My third was the same as Nance's: to wonder again why he had called on her.

And my fourth was the answer.

"Burbidge's life cover," I said softly, but Nance looked puzzled.

"Burbidge's provided life cover for their staff employees," I explained, "Dick was covered. His estate will get several thousand pounds. Who should know that better than another employee of Burbidge's? That's why he called on you and left his address: he wanted the insurance money."

It took a bit of time for Nance to grasp it. "So he got what he deserved," she said finally, looking at the paper again, "and none of Dick's money."

She's a simple soul, Nance. She would never have understood it all if I had told her quite what Dick's father had nearly got away with, and perhaps she would have tried to propel me towards the police, just like Sally. So I left it at that.

But Sally ...

Nance grabbed her letters and read them.

"When are you going?" she asked me.

"I'm not," I explained. "I haven't answered."

A cross between a gasp and a hiss escaped from her. "You remember what I told you," she said. "I told you to keep on to her - and all you do is leave her letters around, unanswered. You need your brains tested, really you do."

She is a woman of action, Nance; instant, impulsive, action. Before I knew where I was she had me in my car setting off for King's Lynn, a telephone call having announced my impending arrival. I left her in possession of my own doorstep saying that she would lock up and tell Sue where I had gone.

Once on the road I found I had more time to think.

I felt sorry and a little guilty about Sue, but there was nothing I could do about it now.

Sally's family, and in particular her father, kept looming at the back of my mind. At first I shied away whenever he loomed, but after a time I stopped doing so. Why should I shy away, I asked myself, now that I had begun to know him a little better? Was it not I who had thrown doubt on his views about the fate of King John's baggage train? The police had ended by accepting what I said, and although Mr Anderson had not agreed the very fact that he had not contradicted me showed that I had shaken his confidence. And Sally herself had remarked that he was no fighter, that he would knuckle under to Stevens, and who in their senses would knuckle under to a man like Stevens? No, he was still not my scene, but I had seen chinks in his armour now; for me he no longer belonged to such a completely impossible and incompatible other world.

Further on, as I passed King's Lynn and went on towards Sherningham, I found I was driving into butterfly country again. This time though, I realised they were not fluttering with fear, they were fluttering with excitement.

a condition. And ... she herself had remarked that he would
dispiriting that few who found an order in Sloane... and with the
... force of one ... ordre ... to transcribe... strong... too, he
was still not my scene, until I had stepped quietly in less than now...
put me to no longer bothered to ... a complicated supposition
and reconstitute other soul ...

Further on, we passed ... [...] that went on towards
Shoreham and, I found I was driving on himself... century again...
this time though, I realised they were contributing with ...
they were little-or... reflection.

222

Author Biography

Christopher Pearson was born in Zomba in Nyasaland (Malawi) and came to England by sea on his 5th Birthday. He was educated at Shrewsbury School and is a graduate of Lincoln College, Oxford.

Having trained as a Chartered Surveyor he set up a property development firm - Winchester Homes – to focus on small developments of traditional quality homes in Suffolk. The firm is now in the hands of his son Oliver.

It All Came Out in The Wash is his first novel written one summer in the 1980s.

BV - #0030 - 160124 - C0 - 210/148/13 - PB - 9781804674987 - Matt Lamination